Building a new city on Ierilia, Bernie as chosen ruler, is facing a difficult task…

Starting anew on an alien planet is no mean task—especially if that planet is rife with magic, shapeshifters, dragons, and a villainous sorcerer, not to mention a fallen evil god.

Now that the king and queen have granted the people from Earth their own realm, Bernie Henderson has been elected to rule it and oversee the building of their new city.

Zohmes and Odoxon have not given up. Bernie finds himself immersed in the trials and tribulations of Ierilia. How will this affect his budding interest in Julia, the mother of Satan's son?

Initiation Genesis
Crimson Realm Chronicles Book 7
Copyright © 2019 Taryn Jameson and Gabriella Bradley
ISBN: 978-1-4874-2464-0
Cover art by Angela Waters

Published by eXtasy Books Inc or
Devine Destinies, an imprint of eXtasy Books Inc
Look for us online at:
www.eXtasybooks.com or www.devinedestinies.com

INITIATION GENESIS

CRIMSON REALM
CHRONICLES BOOK 7

BY

TARYN JAMESON

AND

GABRIELLA BRADLEY

DEDICATION

Taryn Jameson -

For my son, JT. You were and will always be the brightest star, and I will forever love and miss you.

Gabriella Bradley –

To JT, a beautiful young man who left for the realm of dreams much too early.

CHAPTER ONE

Captain Bernie Henderson stood on his balcony and gazed at the building site and the construction in progress. He was still in awe at the beauty of the realm the king and queen had awarded them. The location they had chosen for their first town was close to the ocean, so close, he could see the beach and water from his house. Inhaling the briny scent carried on the breeze, he concentrated on the verdant valley and the green hills flanking it on both sides. Like on Earth during that time of year, spring flowers bloomed in a colorful assortment. They had tried to save as many of them as they could while excavating.

Several of their people were farmers. They had already picked out where they'd like to farm, but their homes had to wait. Foremost, they had to get the temporary accommodations built. Those houses would converted into inns and taverns later as people slowly began to build a new life and their own places. And who knew how many would fall in love with an Ierilian man or woman and move away. Down the road, there would be no lack of lodging for travelers, farmers, and traders passing through their capital.

1

The snow had not delayed the construction of their town on Initiation Genesis. There was an ocean inlet, and they had voted and chosen to situate their main city, that was to be the capital, closer to the sea. So far, it had no name because not everyone was present to vote. Some of their people had joined King Biryn's troops and were off to fight in the war, but many of the Ierilians had donated their time and labor, and King Biryn had provided them with all the needed materials.

The landscaping of the grounds had not yet begun, and there were no fences or gates, so he could see what was going on easily from where he stood. He shivered and rubbed his hands together. Though it was spring, the mornings were still quite cool. Everything was moving along as planned and on schedule, much to his surprise. Erica was supposed to oversee all this with him, but she was a captain in the king's army and was off to fight against the invaders. He felt lonely in his task.

He had been voted in as ruler of Initiation Genesis by an almost unanimous vote. He had no idea who had nominated him, but deep down he wished he could just be one of the engineers. *If only Yolanda were with me.* He squashed the thought. Thinking about his wife and little boy was too much to bear. They had succumbed to the virus that had hit and killed so many of Earth's people. It was after he had become a widower and felt so very much alone that he had applied for the space relocation program, and after rigorous testing, they had accepted him. It would never have happened if Yolanda and their baby had lived. Mark and Amanda were the only married couple accepted into the program, and when she became pregnant a few months before take-off, they had kept her pregnancy a secret or they would have been disqualified. After they had accepted Mark and Amanda, for whatever reason, they ruled that only singles could apply.

From what he knew, Amanda had only been three months

along when their ship had crashed on Ierilia and taken Amanda's life.

And now, here they were. Not on unpopulated Thauro, the planet where they were supposed to land and build a settlement, but on a different planet that was populated. And not just populated. Its inhabitants were like characters from some kind of science fiction or fantasy movie. He knew everything that had happened, and was happening, was real, but he had a difficult time wrapping his head around it all. In many ways, this planet was so medieval, yet so much more advanced than Earth in its space and futuristic technology. It was all too strange.

Everything was so otherworldly on Ierilia. Sorcerers, dragons, lion shifters, gods, and goddesses. Then there was that evil god, Zohmes, and his sorcerer sidekick. He heaved a big sigh. As long as all the craziness stayed away from their new home. After all, neither Zohmes nor Odoxon had grievances against the people from Earth—though three of the crews had been captured by the twisted bastards when their ships had crashed on Ierilia. But that was mainly to thwart the king. How could they have a grievance at total strangers from another planet?

He strode off the balcony and entered his new house. At Biryn's insistence, his was the first house that had been built. The king told him a lord needed to live in a suitable home and have his own estate. Lord? He would remain just simply captain. It was a lifetime job, he was told, and the title would pass on to his heirs. There were no reelections every four years, like back in the US. Once a ruler, always a ruler. And if that ruler passed to the realm of dreams too early, and an heir was too young, a temporary ruler was designated by the king until the heir or heiress was of age.

The house was fantastic, a home he could only have

dreamed about on Earth. He had designed it himself and had combined the classic Ierilian culture with modern Ierilian technology and some Earth concepts, like a rain shower and wall jets in the bathroom. Though he liked having a bath, a shower was often faster and more convenient. He had created a home that was almost surreal. The king and queen had donated all the furniture, paintings, vases, statues, and whatever else he needed from the overflow of gifts they had received when they got married. *I feel so blessed and rich. If only I could share it all with someone.*

For a moment an image of Julia danced through his mind. He'd felt more than attracted to her from the moment they'd met on Earth during their two years of training, but she came with so much baggage now. First John, whom she had dated back on Earth for a short while before their departure, and their relationship had continued on Ierilia. He'd known he didn't stand a chance anyway. But John had died. He'd realized then he had to bide his time and give her time to grieve. Then to give her even more space when her son, Jonathan, had mysteriously appeared from the future. To lose one's lover, to find out she was carrying his baby, then suddenly she was not, and to have a grown-up son appear out of nowhere? Poor Julia was confused as hell, and he couldn't blame her. But even though his interest in her hadn't waned, she was even more difficult to approach now. Sometimes, during the moments when he felt utterly lonely, he wondered if he shouldn't look elsewhere for a partner or at least a very close female friend. Then again, he hadn't been interested in beginning a relationship with anyone. Not until he'd laid eyes on Julia. From the first moment he'd seen her, met her gaze, he'd felt a connection, a pulling at his heartstrings and soul.

A shout from outside broke his thoughts. "Captain, we're having a problem with the foundation for the community hall. The soil keeps sliding. We can't pour the concrete."

He and Jim called it concrete. The Ierilians had a different name for it—ground compound. It was something like concrete but consisted of different components. He knew one of them was iron shavings from the mines in Xynnar. It made super hard cement. He walked back onto the balcony and looked down at Jim Forest, his foreman. "I'll be there shortly."

Main street, yet unnamed, was a flurry of activity. Several stores were already finished, and the clinic and other shops were nearing completion. He had not forgotten a stable. It was located just outside of town. There were two more streets, one on each side of the main. Both roads had five large houses in the last building stages, with ten bedrooms in each home, a kitchen, living room, dining room, an entrance big enough for a reception desk, and a large recreation room that was designated to be a dining area and bar later on. Every bedroom had its own bathroom with a tub and a shower. It was a similar concept to the compounds, except homier, cozier and a mix of Ierilian and Earth architecture. For now, they would have to share at least two to a room, but it wouldn't be long before everyone could begin moving in.

The church was in its beginning stages, the foundation poured, and the carpenters had started framing that morning. He had designated another area, not far from the church, for their community hall. This was the first problem he'd encountered since they had begun excavation.

He arrived at the site he'd chosen for the hall and studied the mess. It almost looked like a mudslide, except the ground was dry. "Jim, we may have to find a better location for the hall."

Jim nodded. "Yes. This is hopeless. I don't know what's with this soil, but it's not solid enough for us to build here."

"Leave it with me. How about if you start on the roads?

Our people are anxious to move in."

"Too fucking anxious. We're already working at warp speed. They're forgetting we're building a whole goddamn town, for crying out loud. We're not fucking magicians like some of the people on this planet."

"I know. And not just magicians. If it weren't for Ierilian technology keeping the ground free of snow and ice during winter, we wouldn't be this far."

"Yeah. On Earth, everything would have come to a standstill, except for internal work."

"Exactly. I'll go and find another location for the hall." Bernie hurried to the toolshed to fetch his surveying equipment. He was not just an engineer, but also an architect and surveyor. He had tested the soil for the hall. How could he have missed that the ground wasn't stable in that area? He also needed to test the plot designated for the church. It was close to the hall and could be unstable as well. If so, they'd have to halt that project, too. Maybe he should halt it anyway, at least until he'd finished his testing.

He sighed at the unexpected delay. It meant creating new plans, excavating again, plumbing drawn to the new sites, and new framing for the foundation. Then again, housing was the most important item on the list right now. If they needed to have a meeting, the weather was nice enough to hold it outdoors.

He finally found a suitable area close to where their park was going to be. He closed his eyes and envisioned it. Trees, lots of flowers, a pond with ducks and swans, people going for a morning jog, women pushing strollers, children playing... Well, future children. Eventually, people would find a life partner, marry, and have kids. Swans and ducks? He was sure there were similar waterfowl on Ierilia. He made a mental note to do some research.

He'd finished surveying the land and walked to where Jim was overseeing the laying of stone pavers. "Jim, I found the new spot for the hall. I've stopped construction on the church. I need to do further testing of that section. While I was walking around, I also found the right area for the market."

"Great. Are we going to use the same plan for the hall?"

"After I make some adjustments. I'll head home and do that now."

Just as he was about to go up the steps to his front door, he heard the sound of a flyer landing. The landing pad they had created for flyers and hovercrafts was not far from his home. He turned. They didn't expect any deliveries that day.

The flyer sported the royal emblem. Couldn't be Biryn. He was with his troops. Several women came down the steps and began walking toward his home. He took his hard hat off, ran his hand through his hair, and waited. The queen, accompanied by Hirsuta and Julia, approached, followed closely by Dunmore. Cylena looked heavily pregnant. According to Ierilian calculations, she shouldn't be more than about four months, but she looked ready to deliver. Not surprising since the calendar on Ierilia was so different. What was four months on Ierilia was actually nine or more on Earth.

Bernie bowed. "Your Highness. What an unexpected, pleasant surprise."

"Lord Henderson, I hope we are not imposing. Julia expressed the wish to see your new town. You have met my mother?"

"Yes, I have had that pleasure. Hirsuta, Julia, welcome. Come in. Let me offer you refreshments."

His heart finally calmed a bit. It had gone into overdrive when Julia approached the house. Was it a coincidence that just that morning his mind had dwelled on her? "Dunmore, would you like to come in for tea or juice?"

The guard declined. "Thank you. I will stand guard here."

"Bernie, your house is gorgeous. And that's an understatement," Julia told him, eagerly advancing inside and exploring. "Oooh, I love the kitchen!"

She appeared so much calmer and happier than the last time he'd seen her. "Glad you like it. Go ahead and look at the rest of the house."

He listened to her squeals of delight as the women explored his home. For some reason, it was important to him that Julia liked it. When they returned to the living room, he had fruit juice ready and a platter of cookies that he'd baked the night before to alleviate his boredom. He'd always enjoyed cooking on Earth and had often surprised Yolanda with what he could concoct from their meager rations. Now, with so much abundance available, he liked baking and cooking even more.

Julia nibbled on a cookie and took a sip of her drink. "It's a big house just for one person."

Bernie offered the cookies to Hirsuta and Cylena. "I hope not always to be alone, Julia."

She tucked a stray blonde strand of hair behind her ear. "Oh, there's romance in the air?"

"Not yet. But I can hope." Was it his imagination, or was there a glimmer of interest in her pansy-blue eyes?

"Anyone we know?"

Oh, this was dangerous territory. How to answer that? It was safer to avoid the question. "I see you've finished your drinks. Would you like to see how far we have progressed? It's quite a long walk, Your Highness. Would you like to wait here for us?"

Cylena laughed. "I am with child. I am not sick or feeble."

"Oh. Sorry. I apologize."

"No need. You were just being thoughtful."

"You've built quite a few stores, Bernie. What is all going in them?" Julia asked as they walked along the main street, followed closely by Dunmore, forever keeping an eye on the queen.

"The large one over there will be the general store. Olivia is going to have a clothing store. We'll have a market like all other towns on Ierilia. What the other stores will sell, I don't know yet. Maybe a bakery?"

"How about a fast-food place? I'd give anything for a good burger and fries."

"What is that?" Hirsuta questioned.

"It's a food we eat on Earth. Don't forget, Julia, once everyone moves into houses of their own, the communal houses will become inns and taverns. They'll probably serve bar food," Bernie reminded her.

"That could take quite a while. I don't see everyone getting married in a hurry. Meanwhile, a fast-food place would be nice. Ice cream, milkshakes, burgers, fries, chicken wraps, and chicken nuggets. And they have to sell coffee."

Bernie grinned. "And you're going to run it and do the cooking? Don't forget, on Earth most of the fast-food places had their supplies delivered ready-made. That's if one could afford to go to one. When we left, there weren't that many left and only the rich could afford it."

"True. I only had a burger and fries twice. I lucked out winning a free meal both times. Laura and I shared. And both came with a real milkshake and a few chicken nuggets. It was heavenly!"

"How are Laura, Erica, and Jonathan? Have you had any news? And the rest of the royal team?"

Cylena answered him. "All are fine, but the war still rages. Sadly, some of our soldiers have lost their lives. We will all be thankful when it's over."

"Will Zohmes ever be defeated?"

Hirsuta, who had been very quiet, spoke. "Most of his army will be, but I think the battle against Zohmes and Odoxon will continue for many years."

"Not for too many years, I hope. That sorcerer is pure evil and Zohmes the devil himself. They come up with some really nasty stuff."

"What is that on top of the mountain, Bernie?" Julia asked, shading her eyes with her hand and gazing at the structure in progress.

"That's the observatory science center. Dr. Reed and Dr. Brooks are overseeing the building of it. Ierilian scientists are in collaboration with them. The plan is to also build a Hubble Space Telescope, the same as the one they launched from Earth. Most of the components for it that were on the cargo ship were salvaged. With the help of the Ierilian scientists, Dr. Reed and Brooks are hoping to optimize the telescope even further by adding Ierilian technology."

"Wow. Big plans."

"It will take quite a while to build it all. Much longer than our town."

"We should head back to the palace, Julia. Hirsuta, are you ready?" Cylena asked.

They said their goodbyes. Bernie held Julia's hand and squeezed it. "Julia, you're welcome to visit any time you feel like it. Contact me, and I'll arrange to have you picked up."

Bernie watched her face. Had he gone too far, too quickly? But she smiled, her blue eyes reflecting her pleasure at his invitation.

"I'd like that, Bernie."

"How about dinner? I'm not a half-bad cook. Then I can finally test out my new kitchen. I don't cook much for just me."

"That's a date. I'll contact you soon to set up a day and time."

He watched them walk back to the landing pad, the flyer taking off. He whistled a tune as he went back into the house. A shower first. He took off his clothes and stood before the mirror for a moment. Hell, if he'd known she was coming, he would have shaved that morning. How could she be interested in such a scruffy-looking guy? His brown hair was sweaty and straggly from the hard hat. Should he cut it? Nah, most of them had let theirs grow. The men on Ierilia all had long hair. He would stand out like a sore thumb with it short or shaved. He rubbed his brown eyes, then examined his body. He'd been into bodybuilding on Earth, so except for his height, he could compete with the handsome Ierilian men. He was sure he'd seen a glimmer of interest in Julia's eyes. Dare he hope?

He stepped into his shower and turned on the jets, allowing them to massage his aching muscles. Picturing Julia, how delectable she'd looked in her Ierilian blue gown, her blonde hair braided, he felt his cock jump to attention. Lord, how long had it been? After his wife's death, his libido had come to a standstill, but it seemed Julia had awakened it in full.

CHAPTER TWO

"Don't you think Bernie is hot?" Julia asked Cylena and Hirsuta as they walked up the steps to the palace.

"Hot? He didn't look overheated," Cylena questioned.

"Handsome, desirable, nice looking."

Hirsuta pulled a face. "Your Earth language continues to confuse us."

"Fifty years from now, I bet many of the Ierilians will be using our words and expressions," Julia said, then grinned. "That always happens when cultures mix."

"No one is more desirable to me than my king. But as men go, I suppose Bernie is pleasant to look at. Let us go to the royal quarters. Would you like to join us for dinner, Julia?" Cylena asked.

"I'd love that. Thank you."

"I am anxious for news from Biryn. He has been quiet for a few days. I hope to receive communication today." Cylena frowned worriedly.

"Yes. I'm worried about Jonathan. I haven't heard anything either."

"It must be strange for you to have a grown son," Hirsuta said.

"It is, and it isn't. Since Rania granted me the images in my mind of when I gave birth, and his growing years, I feel so close to him now. The weirdest part is that he's only a couple of years younger than me. And he's been gone for months now. I argued against him joining the team, but he wouldn't listen to me."

Cylena rubbed her growing belly. "Do children ever listen to their parents? I know I did, but I had little choice, seeing the circumstances I was in."

Julia nodded. "Being invisible must have been hell."

"It was not pleasant. I could have no friends, could not participate in anything, could not go to school. My adoptive parents were ridiculed by their family because they didn't believe that I existed. Otherwise, I had a good upbringing. My foster parents were sweet, loving, educated me at home, and I could not have wished for better. Sorry, Mother. I am sure you would have given me just as great an upbringing. Alas, Zohmes and Odoxon interfered with that."

Hirsuta wiped a tear off her cheek. "Yes. Many years were stolen from us. And now Cewrick is off fighting alongside the team. We have hardly had time to reconnect and be the family we are supposed to be."

"Wait, I have word from Biryn!" Cylena picked up her tablet and scanned the message. "Zohmes and Odoxon have retreated. The enemy has mostly been defeated. Zohmes and Odoxon have gone for now, and whatever is left of his army is on the run. Victory for us. Our men and the team are on their way home! I am so happy. Biryn will be here in time for the birthing."

"Will it stop here?" Julia wondered.

"Not as long as Odoxon and Zohmes are in league with one another. Let us pray to the gods and goddesses that they are quiet for a while. They need time to regroup after their defeat.

I hope it will not take our men long to return," Hirsuta said.

Julia admired the woman silently. She had recovered so fast from her ordeal and had gained the weight she needed. Beautiful, curvy now, with long, blonde, wavy hair cascading down her back, and a face that was close to perfection, she could have graced the cover of many a magazine on Earth. Cylena looked so much like her, yet different, with her gray eyes and black hair. Hirsuta's natural platinum locks added to her beauty. "How long before they are back? Any idea?"

Cylena shook her head. "No. But now that it is spring, traveling should be easier. The final battle took place in the Xavena Realm. It is far, much farther than the Dreaded Peaks. And since they are traveling on horseback and the warriors on foot, it will take time."

"I'm sad about the warriors that gave their lives. I grieve for their families." Julia wiped her eyes with a tissue.

"Yes, we all are. Their families will be cared for. Biryn and I will make sure of that. But such is the cost of war. Men that enlist know the dangers they could face."

"I am so thankful that Jonathan is okay. I haven't been able to sleep thinking about him and the hazards he faced every day."

"Your Jonathan is a force on his own. He is Zohmes' son. He has great powers."

"That scares me even more. What if he takes after his father?" Julia frowned.

Hirsuta placed her hand on Julia's arm. "Fear not. Jonathan has all of your goodness in him. He abhors even the thought of being Zohmes' son."

"It is so strange. I didn't raise him, yet it feels like I did. I love him so much."

"You were granted limited memories of carrying him, giving birth, glimpses of you and he together during his

growing years. That instilled the love within you. Cherish it."
Hirsuta smiled and patted Julia's hand.

When they entered the royal quarters, dinner was all ready
and set on the table.

Julia paced her room. The weeks had dragged by slowly
since they had received word that the war was over. Even
with the technology they had, messages were few and far
between. She received word from Jonathan or Laura every
couple of days that they were safe and had set a fast pace to
return to Cront. At least they were traveling in spring and
would not have the snow and ice to hinder their homecoming.

She walked to the bed and flopped down on the soft
downy comforter. Since her kidnapping by Zohmes and
Odoxon, she had been living in the palace. Cylena and
Hirsuta insisted she remain with them, warning her that it
would not be safe to let her return to the compound or join
the crews in their new realm. If she left the palace, she had to
have a guard, even when Bernie sent a flyer for her to visit
Initiation Genesis. She'd had dinner with him three times now
and really liked the man—so much, she looked eagerly
forward to his next invitation. Having the guards follow her
everywhere drove her insane, but she understood the need.
She may no longer carry Zohmes' child, but she could still be
used as a pawn in the games Zohmes and Odoxon played. It
was the sick bastard's fault that her son had been ripped from
his life and shoved back in time—a tactic used by the gods to
keep her and her son safe from Zohmes' clutches.

She took a deep breath and let it out slowly. God, she was
about to go stir-crazy. The wait for Jonathan and Laura's
return was killing her. If it were up to her, she would have
been fighting beside them. What Zohmes had done to her was
unspeakable, and she deserved the opportunity to pay the

bastard back, not only for Jonathan but for what he had done to John.

She sighed. John had been taken much too young. Their brief relationship had hardly had a chance to blossom. A few months on Earth, then a few months on Ierilia. She lay back on the pillows, pushing the sad memories from her mind, and thought about Bernie instead. He was a good man. Not only that, but he was hot, as she'd told Cylena. Was it possible that she was developing more than just friendship for him?

It was still very early morning, so she decided to stay in bed for a while. Still thinking about Bernie, she had almost drifted back off to sleep when a knock broke the silence in her room. It was too early for someone to be knocking on her door. *Cylena... The baby.* Could it be time? The Ierilian calendar was weird, and the queen looked ready to pop. She shifted off the bed quickly and donned her robe, then opened the door.

"Mother!" Jonathan engulfed her in a tight hug.

Holding him at arm's length, she inspected him from head to toe. He appeared to be all in one piece. She gazed up at his handsome face and smiled. He had her father's strong chin, beautiful blue eyes, and looked mainly like her side of the family. Except for that red hair. Not that she hated it, but it was a constant reminder of Zohmes. "You could have warned me!"

Jonathan chuckled. "And spoil the surprise? Come to the dining room in Biryn's quarters. A well-deserved home-cooked breakfast is waiting for us. After living on rations for so long, and if we were lucky, roasted korobeast, I'm so looking forward to a hearty eggs and whatever else meal."

"Wait, I'll get dressed."

"No need. The queen and Hirsuta are in their robes, too. Come on, Mother." Jonathan grabbed her hand and pulled her into the hallway, then ushered her to Biryn's rooms.

"When did you get back? During the night?"

"Close to midnight. We didn't want to wake anyone, and we were so exhausted all we could think of was a hot bath and bed."

She hugged his arm as they sat at the table. To her surprise, a young woman sat beside Taylith, Laura on his other side. She glanced from the young woman to Ciara and back again. She looked just like Ciara, with her raven hair and violet eyes. They could practically be twins. "Who is this?"

"I am Liana, Taylith's sister," Liana introduced herself. "This is your mother, Jonathan?"

"Yes, this is Julia. I told you our story during our journey back."

"You have a very brave son, Julia, and his magick is powerful." Liana sent her a smile.

"Not as powerful as yours. You're the one who managed to banish Odoxon back to his cave on Wuits Peak," Jonathan responded. "And at this point, I don't know what the hell I'm doing. It just happens."

"Laura, I'm so happy you're home in one piece, too. I bet you all have tons of stories to tell us." Julia looked at them all questioningly.

Biryn had his arm around Cylena. "First, has everything been quiet while we were gone?"

Hirsuta nodded. "Yes. Zohmes and Odoxon were far too busy plotting war against you and your army."

Taylith entered the conversation. "After we eat, Brenn, Ciara, Laura, Liana, and I, need to leave to go and see our parents. The rest of you can talk all morning telling our stories."

"I am more than curious, how is it that you have a sister so suddenly?" Cylena commented, her eyebrows raised. "I clearly see the resemblance, but it is quite astonishing."

"The others will tell you everything. Please, Liana is anxious to go and see our parents."

"Yes, of course," Cylena told him.

"Thank you."

Julia, Cylena, and Hirsuta were still in their robes when lunch was served.

"My heart is heavy for the families of the men who lost their lives," Cylena said as she helped herself to some bread and cheese. "It feels wrong for us to be so happy to be reunited while others are grieving."

"Has Catrice given any indication when we can expect our little prince?" Biryn asked Cylena, changing the subject.

She smiled. "Any time. Now that we have heard all the stories of your journey and the war, I think I would like to bathe and get dressed."

"You have hardly eaten, Cylena." Biryn stood and held her arm as she got up off her chair.

Julia noticed Cylena grimace, pull a face, and clutch her back. "She's going into labor!"

Before Biryn had a chance to lead her to the bedroom, Cylena crumpled to the floor. "Call Catrice!" he shouted.

A sickly green mist appeared, enveloping Cylena. Biryn cradled her head in his lap. Astiana, Icaras, Cewrick, and Hirsuta rushed to the queen, Cewrick chanting a spell, but it did not remove the green fog.

Julia's heart thudded against her ribs. "My God. Jonathan, can you do something?"

Catrice came rushing in, followed by Jason carrying a stretcher. "What the hell is all this green stuff? Incense? Get rid of it! Place her on the stretcher. We need to take her to the infirmary."

They ran through the hallways, the green mist swirling around the gurney. Once in the clinic, Catrice and Jason shifted Cylena to a bed. Julia watched from the door as Catrice took out her stethoscope and listened to Cylena's heart. Then, placing it on her belly, she listened for the infant's heartbeat. Lifting Cylena's eyelids, she shone a small flashlight at the pupils. Tears soaked her cheeks as she stepped back and shook her head. "Too late. They're both gone." Placing her hand on Biryn's back, she said softly, "Biryn, I am so sorry. There is nothing we can do."

Biryn roared. He gathered Cylena into his arms and sobbed. "Nooooo! This cannot be happening."

Julia had not even noticed Taylith and the others had returned and joined them. Laura pushed her way through and rushed to Cylena's side. Julia watched in awe as her sister placed her hand on the still woman's heart and her other hand on her distended belly. Her hands glowed bright enough to light up the small room. Even Laura's body began to glow, the light cutting right through the green mist.

Cylena suddenly took a deep breath and another. Catrice placed the stethoscope on her chest and nodded. "I have a heartbeat." Then she listened for the baby's and nodded again. "The infant's heart is beating strongly."

"But she is not waking." Biryn's voice was hoarse with emotion.

"Biryn, I don't know, but it almost appears as if Cylena is in hibernation, in stasis," Catrice told him.

Julia grasped Jonathan's hand. "Zohmes."

"Can you wake her from it?" Biryn wrung his hands.

"I've got no idea what this green mist is. Honestly, I don't know if our medicine can fix this." Catrice looked mortified as she talked to the king.

"I need to consult with Rania," Ciara said from somewhere

behind them.

"Let's leave them alone," Julia suggested. "Cylena is in good hands."

CHAPTER THREE

Julia quickly went to her room and got dressed before returning to the king's dining room. The mood was somber around the table. Biryn was still with Cylena, and so were Cewrick, Hirsuta, and Icaras.

"I could do with a glass of wine," Jonathan said. "Anyone else?"

Brenn nodded. "Yes, pour us all one. Or maybe some eldalas spirit. This is the ultimate shock. To be so happy about our victory, and now this."

Ciara joined them and sat beside Brenn. She gratefully accepted the glass of wine from Jonathan. "I spoke briefly with Rania. Zohmes has managed to release Odoxon once again from Wuits Peak. Our reprieve from the two of them did not last long. The curse placed on Cylena is called the spell of eternal rest — a spell forbidden by the gods in the early days of Ierilia. Rania could not remember the last time it had been used on anyone. The spell causes all bodily functions to slow to such a degree that it simulates death. In the old days when the spell was used, many were sent to the realm of dreams, the family not realizing their loved one was in reality still alive. Laura was able to restore Cylena's internal functions. But that particular spell will cause a person to be in a deep sleep forever. There is only one cure for it, a counter-spell and a black gem, of which there is only one on Ierilia. It must be placed on her forehead when the spell is applied. None of our magick will help in this instance. Only the most powerful of sorcerers or sorceresses can counter the spell."

"So who can administer this spell? Where is the gem?" Jonathan asked. "Will any of it harm the baby?"

"No. The infant is in stasis, too. But we must go and find the book. Centuries before Odoxon, the grimoire was taken by I Am and placed where no one could ever find it. That Odoxon and Zohmes were able to get their hands on it or were able to read the spell is a mystery for now. What is a concern, we need the four swords for this mission. How are we going to tear Biryn away from Cylena's side?" Ciara worriedly said.

"Can anyone else use Biryn's sword?" Jonathan asked.

"No. Only the owner of the sword can ignite its magick and wield it. If the owner travels to the realm of dreams, the sword can be gifted to someone who deserves it, like Erica's sword. It once belonged to General Heshir, gifted to him by the king's father, King Razota. Zohmes possessed the general who assassinated Razota and attempted to kill Biryn. Aldis saved our king, but when offered the sword, he did not want it and the danger associated with it. That sword was gifted to Erica by Biryn, but Biryn is very much alive." Ciara sighed, obviously frustrated.

"I am assuming Biryn kept the sword safe for many years, but how did Taylith and Brenn get their swords? Both of their fathers are alive and well." Julia took a sip from her wineglass.

Brenn leaned back in his chair and crossed his arms. "The sword was bequeathed to me by my grandfather, who received it for bravery when he fought by the king's side. My father has worked in the mines all his life and had no use for the sword. When I became the king's general, my grandfather decided I should have it."

"My story is much the same. My grandfather fought for the then king, who gifted him the sword. My father did not want it. The sword was hidden within the vault of his castle on the Tideless Abyss during the time I was cursed as a black dragon," Taylith said. "After the curse was lifted, my uncle gave me my sword."

Julia looked at Laura. Her head rested on Taylith's shoulder, and she appeared to be drained after she had applied her healing magic to the queen.

"Catrice will have Cylena on intravenous now to keep her electrolytes stable. Ciara, maybe you can go and talk to Biryn?" Laura suggested.

"And Cewrick. All of the team will need to go."

"You haven't told us where," Julia pointed out.

"Rania has not told me yet. I will speak with her again, but for now, she is at Cylena's bedside."

"Why was the grimoire not destroyed?" Erica asked. "And if the gods hid it, how did Zohmes and Odoxon get the spell? It's all too puzzling."

"So many questions, many of which I cannot answer at this time. You saw for yourself how many ancient books were in that cave on Wuits Peak." Ciara sipped from her wine.

"Yes, I remember you taking one particular very old book. Could that be the one?" Icaras wondered.

"No. That book is also filled with dangerous spells and curses. It has already been restored and preserved and placed in the museum in an airtight glass container." Ciara held her empty glass up for more wine.

"Why even keep these books? Like Erica asked, why not destroy dangerous books?" Julia questioned again.

"They are part of history. The book is safe now in the museum." Ciara stood. "I am going to check on Cylena."

"I am going with you." Laura joined Ciara.

"What do we do now?" Julia wondered.

"I'm having another glass of wine," Jonathan said and poured some into his glass. "Anyone else?" He was pouring Taylith another when suddenly Taylith dropped his glass and grasped his head.

"Taylith, what's wrong?" Julia yelled.

"I think he's having another of his visions," Laura said, her voice laced with worry. "I'll come and see Cylena later. I'm worried about Taylith," she told Ciara.

"Well, he scared the shit out of me. Look how pale he is."

Taylith snapped out of it, and Julia noticed the bewildered expression on his face.

Taylith rubbed his face with his hands and grimaced. "Why does I Am choose me for these visions?"

Jonathan handed him another glass of wine. "Here, drink up. You look very pale. Then tell us what you saw."

Taylith drank deeply from his glass, then set it on the table and began. "I saw war. Terrible war. Sorcerers and sorceresses, many of them, hurling their magick at each other. I think I Am showed me a piece of history. I remember learning about the ancient wars. Then I saw high marble walls. Within stood a white temple surrounded by some smaller buildings. I Am said it was the temple of the god and goddess of fertility. Their names are Evena and — "

"Olion," Ivran interrupted.

"Yes. I Am, and all the gods and goddesses were furious at the killing, havoc, and disorder on Ierilia. They rained thunder and lightning down. It caused many soil shifts, and the temple was completely buried. I Am said we will find what we need in that temple and its underground passages."

"What about the god and goddess?" Julia asked.

"They are with all the others in the realm of the gods."

"Did I Am give any indication where this temple is buried?" Laro asked.

"No. But he did say he will assist us."

Taylith had no sooner finished telling them his vision when Brenn's communicator sounded. "It's Bernie." He turned the speaker on.

"Brenn? I've been trying to get in touch with the king, but no response."

"We are dealing with an emergency here. Can I help you?"

"There is an emergency here, too. My men were laying pavers on the main road. When they got to the cross-section of the two side streets, there was a sudden bolt of lightning from a clear blue sky. Next, the whole middle section began to cave in. Some of the workers fell in and are trapped down there. It's a huge hole and very deep."

"Did you contact the emergency hotline?" Aldis asked.

"Yes. They're on their way. But soil keeps pouring from the sides. It's not safe until we can fortify the walls somehow. I've lowered a light, and I can see part of some kind of structure, like a building or a house, that got buried here a long time ago. I thought the king should know what happened."

"A sinkhole?" Laura asked.

Bernie answered her. "No, Laura. This is no ordinary sinkhole. That at least I would have an explanation for. Bolts of lightning from a clear blue sky striking the ground? Producing a huge hole? I think there is magic involved in this."

Brenn took over the conversation again. "You could be right. Let me talk to the king and the team. I hope you can get the workers safely to the surface."

Ciara returned, followed by Icaras. "How is Cylena?" Julia asked.

"She is resting peacefully, but she's still in her deep

slumber. The infant sleeps in her womb. The green fog has dissipated."

"Let us tell you what we just learned. Taylith, tell them of your vision first?"

Taylith sighed audibly, then repeated his tale. "Now you can tell them what Bernie communicated to you right after I told you of my vision, Brenn."

When Brenn finished, Ciara stood and looked thoughtful. "I Am said we will find what we need in that buried temple. The god helped us by opening up the hole and exposing the temple, or at least some of it. Rania already told me we need the four swords. I will try and speak to Biryn now. Icaras, you need to stay with Cewrick and Hirsuta and help to guard the queen. Cylena had obviously begun labor before the attack. She will deliver the prince not long after she wakes. Zohmes and Odoxon will stop at nothing now to prevent us from breaking the spell."

Somehow, Julia had to talk him and the others into letting her come with them. She had friends that were working to build Initiation Genesis' town. They could be trapped below the ground. During the months the team had been gone to war, she had become very close to Cylena and Hirsuta. They treated her as if she were family but were also over-protective of her.

Since her pregnancy and kidnapping—and now Jonathan—the team handled her as if she were a fragile flower. She was far from it. When her parents died in an accident when she was seventeen, she fought tooth and nail to keep her then eleven-year-old sister. It was hard, and for the first several months they moved from shelter to shelter until she could finally afford to get them a room in a boarding house. She had landed a job as a data processor for NASA thanks to one of their counselors. When Julia had found out about the early stages and planning of the space relocation program, that same counselor helped her get Laura into an accelerated botany program. Because of that and their ages, they were able to sign up to test for the program when applications opened and were lucky to get accepted.

Julia looked at Brenn. "I am going with you."

Laura placed her hand on Julia's arm and squeezed. "Jules, hold —"

She shook Laura's hand off her arm and pinned her with a stare. "Don't even start it, Laura. I'm not a creampuff and can bloody well handle myself. You forget who raised you."

"Mom… These missions aren't safe. You could get injured or killed." Jonathan's face was full of concern.

"Jonathan, I can handle myself. I have the same training as Erica and Laura." Julia planted her hands on her hips. "Besides, I'll be surrounded by a bunch of magic users, and my own son is the spawn of a damn god. I highly doubt anything will happen to me."

Taylith shook his head and chuckled. "I see where Laura gets her temperament and stubbornness from."

"What would it hurt to let her come with us?" Liana brushed her hair from her face.

Julia smiled at her. Finally, someone on her side. "Thank you, Liana. It is possible that some of my friends are trapped in that sinkhole. I can't sit here idle when their lives are at stake."

Brenn took a deep breath, then nodded. "Fine, you can go. This mission cannot be as dangerous as the previous ones. It is only a temple we have to navigate."

Julia glanced at the door as Ciara and Biryn entered the chambers. They seated themselves at the table. Biryn's face was pale, his expression pained. Brenn handed him a glass of eldalas spirit.

Biryn took a sip from the glass and set it back on the table. "Ciara explained I must accompany you on this mission. I do not want to leave Cylena's side."

Brenn clapped him on the shoulder. "We cannot complete this mission without you, Biryn. There is no other that can wield the magick of your sword."

Biryn nodded. "I will do whatever it takes to save Cylena. Icaras, Cewrick, Hirsuta, and Rania will watch over her."

Brenn looked at the team. "Get changed into your gear quickly. We leave for Initiation Genesis in fifteen minutes. Bernie is waiting for us."

CHAPTER FOUR

Bernie took off his hard hat and brushed the sweat from his eyes. With one crazy lightning strike, everything had gone to hell in a handbasket. From the headcount he finally received, they had fifteen people trapped underground, and two of those were seriously injured. He sure as hell hoped Brenn and his team made it to the site soon. If they didn't get something figured out, they would lose the two injured men.

He heaved a sigh of relief when the royal flyer landed. When he'd communicated with Brenn, he had mentioned an emergency at the palace. He wondered vaguely what it was when shouts interrupted his thoughts.

He rushed to the side of the huge hole and peered down. They had hung lights inside the crater, so they could see through the dust and darkness. One of the walls began to crumble. He was at his wit's end at what to do. They'd had to reinforce the walls to rescue the men they could see. The two injured workers were still partially buried by large rocks.

Brenn came up behind him. "Bernie, we're here. What is happening?"

"The walls are still collapsing. We need a helicopter, but

you guys don't have those."

"What is that?" Laro asked.

"Sort of a flyer. On Earth, we use rescue copters. They lower a basket for the injured and a harness to pull up survivors. That way it wouldn't involve disturbing this cave any more than necessary."

Aldis answered him. "We have something similar. I will call—"

"Not necessary." Liana stepped forward. "Hello, Bernie. My name is Liana. I can fortify the walls, and there will be no more collapse."

Bernie looked at Liana, then at Ciara and felt confused. At first, he thought he was seeing double. But there was no time for questions or explanations.

A hand touched his shoulder. He looked up to see Julia standing beside him.

"Don't worry, Bernie. Everything will be fine now."

He placed his hand over hers and squeezed. "Thanks for coming."

He noticed her son, Jonathan, standing beside Liana. They held hands and began to chant. The magic on this planet never ceased to amaze him.

Jonathan and Liana stepped back. "It is done. There will be no more collapse."

"So we can descend into the hole safely now?" Bernie asked.

"Yes. But allow us to go down first. We will remove the debris from the injured men and bring them to the surface safely," Ciara told him. "After all the men are safe, you can begin to fortify the walls with wooden beams and commence to unearth this temple."

"Unearth it? A temple? Oh, you mean dig it out. That's going to be a hell of a task." Bernie rubbed his chin.

"I will call on our reserve soldiers to come and help with the unearthing," Biryn told him.

"Thank you. That will be a huge help." Bernie saluted the king.

"Laura, you need to come with us," Ciara called out.

"Are you sure it is safe?" Taylith wanted to know.

"Taylith. You doubt the holding spell Liana and Jonathan created?"

"Sorry. I worry for my mate."

"And right you are. I worry about her, too," Julia said.

Ciara, Biryn, Icaras, Laura, Liana, and Astiana linked hands. They chanted, and Bernie saw them disappear.

When he looked over the edge again, the bottom of the hole was lit up brightly by their glimmer sticks. The thirteen survivors huddled together in the center. The two seriously injured men were near the wall, half buried. The sound of chanting drifted to his ears. The rocks burying the men disintegrated into small rubble. He watched as they carefully dug the men out from it. One had a broken leg. Even from a distance, he could see that it was a compound fracture. Both were unconscious. Laura kneeled next to the men. An eye-blinding white light lit up the hole, and for moments Bernie couldn't see anything.

Through a haze, he saw the two injured, and the other survivors appear on the surface. What in hell had he just witnessed?

He stood and unthinkingly grasped Julia's hand. "Is any of this real? Am I hallucinating?"

Julia chuckled. "You haven't seen anything. It's amazing what they can accomplish with their magic."

Still holding Julia's hand and pulling her along, Bernie rushed to the two men lying on the ground. "Keith, Peter, how are you feeling?"

The man with the broken leg managed a weak grin. "Like a mountain just fell on me."

Bernie kneeled and looked at the broken leg. There was no evidence of the compound fracture, no bone protruding from the skin, but the wound was still bleeding and raw. He was sure he'd seen the bone sticking out. He shook his head. Again, hallucinations, or maybe the lights had played tricks on his eyes.

"Bernie, now that the men are safe and can be transported to the hospital, we would like you to come with us?" Aldis asked him.

"Go with you? Where?"

"We need to clear the entrance to the temple. You are a qualified engineer, and your expertise will be needed on this mission," Brenn added.

Bernie felt more confused than ever. Go on a mission with the king and his team? He glanced at Biryn. The king looked pale and seemed agitated. Again, he wondered about the emergency at the palace.

"I'm going, too, Bernie," Julia said, threading her arm through his.

"Do you all realize how perilous it will be even to attempt to begin exposing the entrance? Never mind what we find beyond that. This building could have been buried for centuries and be extremely unstable. It is dangerous to just begin digging." Bernie frowned, looking from one to the other.

Brenn stood close to Bernie and spoke quietly. "The queen has been attacked. Her life hangs in the balance. What we need to restore her, and the unborn infant, lies within that temple. We have no choice. The gods and goddesses would not send us here if it is unstable. They watch over us."

Bernie's frown deepened. "And you know this how?"

"They communicate with the gods and goddesses, Bernie. There is much you don't know. Much of what happens, and their abilities, is kept under wraps and must remain so. You are privileged they have asked for your help," Julia said softly.

"And you're definitely going on this expedition?"

"Yes, I am."

"Okay, I guess. What else can I say? If you're brave enough, then who am I. I will not let you go alone. All this has addled my mind. Didn't they just return from the war?"

"Yes. But that god Zohmes and his accomplice Odoxon will not rest. This was a desperate attack on the crown to prevent the birth of the heir to the throne."

Bernie let go of her arm and looked at Ciara. "The walls are stable enough to lower rope ladders?"

"We do not need —"

He held up his hand. "Do we really want the gathered crowd to witness more magic?"

Biryn clapped him on the shoulder. "You are right. We shall descend the hard way."

Bernie approached the crowd of spectators. "Everyone, go back to work now. Everybody is okay. The injured are on their way to the hospital. This area is off limits." He turned to his foreman. "Jim, please barricade this whole area?"

"Aye, Captain."

Biryn frowned. "Captain? They should be calling you Lord Henderson now."

Bernie laughed. "I'll be captain to them for many years. It's okay. I don't feel like a lord."

The onlookers had dispersed and gone back to work, and Jim was already coordinating barriers to be set up. Bernie noticed Biryn and his team standing at the edge, waiting for ladders.

Brenn took a coiled rope from his backpack. "This is taking too long. Time is of the essence. We will use ropes."

"What about the women?" Bernie asked.

Julia nudged him. "We can handle the ropes just as well as the men."

"Okay. I guess. I'll get some picks and shovels. I don't see any of you carrying those."

He quickly fetched shovels and picks and threw them down into the hole. He was hardly prepared for an expedition. No backpack, no supplies. And how long was this all going to take? He had no food either.

"We will share," Astiana told him.

Mm, can they read our minds, too? He thought about the shifting soil where they'd planned to build the hall. *Maybe that's why we couldn't pour the foundation for it. It was too close to the temple. Their gods and goddesses prevented us.*

They slid down the ropes and stood at the bottom of the hole. Brenn handed him a glimmer stick. He watched how they ignited it and lit his. An untarnished bronze or golden entrance was partially visible. Bernie picked up one of the shovels and began to clear the rubble away while the other men, using their picks, chipped carefully at the caked-on dirt and stones around the top and sides. It didn't take long before they cleared the entrance.

Bernie stood back. "How do we open it? I don't see a keyhole or knob or anything."

"The four swords," Erica muttered.

Taylith, Erica, Brenn, and Biryn drew their golden swords and moved to stand in front of the ornate entrance. Bernie watched, awed, as the tips of the swords touched and rested against the door. The swords glowed a bright amber. Sparks seemed to crawl up and down the blades. The entrance creaked, groaned, then slowly opened inward.

"Great galloping galaxies!" Bernie followed the others into

the temple.

They held their glimmer sticks high, lighting up the interior. Sconces hung on marble walls. Brenn and Aldis hurried to light the torches in them.

CHAPTER FIVE

They grouped together in the middle of a large room. It looked like the entrance lobby. Though everything was coated with a fine film of dust, this part of the temple was intact.

Bernie gazed around the room. It had a very high arched ceiling that reminded him of the elegant cathedral styles he remembered from pictures of the larger churches on Earth. An extravagant, massive golden chandelier hung from the center. The floor was marble tile, veined with gold. In the center of it, beneath the chandelier, was a marble-tiled mosaic. Though the lighting was rather dim, Bernie could still see the depiction of a verdant valley, teeming with lions, and a blue sky dotted with jewel dragons. Stairs flanked both sides of the room, leading to a second level. Beside the stairs and directly across from the entry were three doorways.

"Bernie, can you examine the structure?" Biryn asked.

Bernie walked around. Damn, he had no instruments and would have to rely on his hands and senses. "I don't feel or see any cracks or damage. These walls appear to be stable." He shone his glimmer stick toward the ceiling. "No cracks in the ceiling either. The place must have been built like a fortress. How old is this place? Do any of you know?"

"This was Olion and Evina's temple. The god and goddess lived here many centuries ago. It was buried when Ierilia was still in much turmoil. The gods sent a ground shake, and it caused a mountain to cave in and bury the temple," Brenn told him.

"Damn. What about the god and goddess? Did they die?"

Astiana smiled. "We cannot die. They live with all the other gods and goddesses now and have for centuries, ever since it was buried."

"This was a very large temple. We need to continue," Aldis said.

"A floorplan of the place would be nice to have," Bernie muttered. "What is it exactly we're looking for?" He had no sooner spoken when a shaft of light appeared out of nowhere. The thin stream almost resembled a pencil. He jumped back. It moved rapidly over the floor. When it faded, he held his glimmer stick up. "A floor plan. Your gods heard me."

Kneeling, he examined it. "There appear to be two levels to this temple. This room here looks like a place of worship. There are seats and an altar." He pointed to a room drawn on the plan.

Astiana knelt beside him. "There is also a door at the back of the temple."

Julia leaned over his shoulder and pointed to the center of the diagram. "Is that some kind of arena or theater?"

"We are wasting time trying to decipher this. We need to move forward," Biryn said impatiently.

"I will take a holographic image of it." Aldis stepped to the floor plan and recorded it with his datapad.

Bernie had to take a second look. After Aldis finished recording the floor plan, it completely faded away. He stood and shoved his hands in his pockets and looked at the others. "So where do we start? Do you know what we are searching for?"

Julia placed her hand on his arm. "We are looking for an ancient book and a large black gem. There is only one of its kind."

Bernie glanced down at Julia and smiled. After their three dinner dates, she seemed to feel more relaxed around him. "An ancient book in a centuries-old temple? I would check the altar first."

"We wouldn't need the team if it were that easy, Bernie," Erica remarked.

"The altar is as good a starting point as any." Brenn shifted his pack on his shoulder. "Follow me. Bernie, you come with me to check the doorway."

Brenn led them to the door on the right. The frame was ornately carved with strange symbols. The door itself was made of a solid sheet of marble, its face carved with scrolling flowers and ferns. On each side of the door stood a pillar high enough to reach a man's waist. On one pillar was a small statue of a magnificent lion, on the other a regal dragon. Both appeared to be made of gold.

Bernie couldn't believe how much the design looked like pictures he had seen of ancient Rome and Greece on Earth. Yet it was so much different, otherworldly. It was incredibly beautiful, even if everything was covered in dust.

Bernie shook his head. "It is amazing how well this building has stood up to being buried under tons of rock and dirt. I don't see any cracks in the door or frame at all."

Brenn ran his hand along the door. "There is no way to open the door. I don't see a handle or knob."

Astiana came forward to stand beside Brenn, then started touching a sequence of symbols. The doorframe glowed lightly, and after a moment, the door slid open. "It is the language of the gods. The door is bespelled to open with the proper symbol sequence."

Bernie followed Astiana and Brenn into the hallway, the others filing in behind them. The hall was dark, so they used their glimmer sticks. Before long, the hallway came to an abrupt end, opening up into a large fan-shaped room. There were several sections of seats placed in rows, much like a movie theater. Opposite the sections of ornate, red silk-covered gilded chairs was a large altar. Like the pillars of the entryway, the altar base had a depiction of a lion on one side and a dragon on the other. Between them, the verdant valley was pictured in colored mosaic.

All the walls were covered in murals of what looked like the Clyss or another valley similar to it.

"Hey, look! Is that our Astiana?" Jonathan called out and pointed to a picture of a woman dressed in a flowing gossamer gown, sitting by the bank of a basin.

Liana held her glimmer stick close to the image. "I think it is."

"Oh my God! The man standing next to her could be my twin!" Jonathan peered closer at the image.

Astiana nodded. "That is Zohmes before he changed into the creature he is now."

Jonathan grunted. "Hard to believe it is the same man. All I've seen of him was monstrous."

Bernie finished examining the altar. "I've gone over every inch of this altar and can't find the book. Unless there is a hidden compartment, I don't think we'll find it here."

"The gods will have hidden it in a place where one would be least likely to look," Ciara said.

"The proverbial needle in a haystack," Erica muttered. "This place is huge. Where could it be?"

Biryn paced impatiently. "We need to continue. You can all admire the beauty of the temple later after it has been unearthed and cleaned."

"Why don't we break up into pairs. That way we can search faster," Brenn suggested.

"If you find the book, do not touch it. Contact the rest of the team. We cannot be sure what protective spells may have been placed on the grimoire," Astiana warned.

"I'll go with you, Bernie," Julia said, standing close to him.

They split up, each team moving in different directions, choosing a room to inspect.

Bernie followed Julia through the door closest to them. The bed was still covered in bedding, and the dressers and closet were filled with clothing. It was as if the person that had occupied the room had just vanished.

"I can't believe how well preserved everything is. Nothing has deteriorated, except some plants." Bernie stroked the silk bedding on the large bed in the center of the room, creating a cloud of dust.

Julia shook her head after inspecting the closet. "Nothing here. The clothes are all still intact, too, and the dresses are dusty but gorgeous. Shouldn't they fall apart after being buried for so long?"

Bernie closed the drawer he was searching. "Lack of oxygen has preserved it all, or maybe the magic of the gods. I haven't found anything either. Let's move on to the next room."

They searched through room after room but came out empty-handed, and again, in each room, the occupants had left behind their belongings.

They came to a large room with several huge marble tables and benches. A long buffet table ran the length of one of the walls. Across from it was a double door.

"Seems everything here has been built from marble." Bernie lovingly stroked a wall. "Gorgeous workmanship."

"The gods probably built it. That must be why it's all so solid and undamaged." Julia opened the double doors and peeked inside. "There is nothing here. Let's search the kitchen."

Bernie was surprised at how modern the ancient kitchen was. There was a row of coolers along one wall, several ovens along another. A large cooktop took up half of a counter, and next to it were two doors that Bernie guessed led to a pantry and storage.

They started at the coolers, checking each one for any sign of the book or gem, then moved to the ovens. Bernie opened one of the large oven doors. The interior of the oven was made of a strange metal material. It was highly polished to a mirror finish with a silvery-blue tinge. It appeared to be glowing faintly. *Strange.* He'd never seen anything like it.

"I think I found the book!" Julia sounded excited.

Bernie peered into the oven she had opened beside him. An old book sat in the middle of it. He couldn't see it in detail because of the size of the oven bay unless he climbed in to grab it. Remembering Astiana's warning, he took his communicator out of his pocket. "I'll contact the team."

Once Bernie had messaged the team, it didn't take them long to find the kitchens. Astiana approached the oven Julia indicated. When she reached inside to take the grimoire from the oven, her hands began to glow. She pulled the ancient book from its hiding place, blew the dust off it, and turned to face everyone.

"I have placed a protective spell around the grimoire." Astiana pulled her backpack from her shoulders and placed the book inside.

"The grimoire appeared untouched. So how were Zohmes and Doxie able to put the spell on Cylena?" Laura wondered.

Astiana smiled wryly. "Odoxon is very, very old. He has

lived for so many centuries. He could have remembered the spell from the olden days, when Ierilia was a planet rife with war and magick, before he was sent to Wuits Peak."

"Did anyone find the black gem? If it hasn't been found yet, we must split up and continue our search." Biryn fidgeted with his pack.

Bernie could see the worry on the king's face. When Bernie had lost his wife and son, it had almost destroyed him. And from what he had seen of the wedding ceremonies, the Ierilians were not just bound by a mere promise. On Earth, wedding vows were *'til death do you part.* And even those words on Earth meant nothing. Too many people broke that promise and ended up in divorce court. The vows on Ierilia spoke in terms of an eternal bonding and joining of souls. Their gods and goddesses performed the ceremonies and used magic. Could it be possible that the Ierilians took the term soulmate to a whole new level? If that was the case, losing Cylena and their child would more than destroy the king. It might just kill him.

"We have searched everywhere, Biryn. I don't think the gem is in the temple." Aldis patted Biryn's arm.

Ciara gasped and looked at the team. "The gem is not in the temple. Rania has told me that we must leave the temple to find the black gem."

Julia cocked her head at Ciara. "Leave the temple? Your gods showed the temple to Taylith in a vision. They uncovered it, for God's sake. Wouldn't the gem be here, too?"

Erica chuckled and shook her head. "Nothing is ever that easy, Julia."

"Hush now. Let me finish," Ciara admonished them. "There is a series of tunnels behind the temple. We can access them by exiting the rear door."

Bernie shook his head. That was it? That was all the

goddess had told Ciara? "Wouldn't it be easier if the gods just tell you where this gem is?"

"Oh! I can answer this. The gods and goddesses are only allowed to help us to a point. They can't just hand everything over to us on a silver platter," Erica told him.

"We should continue our search for the gem." Brenn shifted the straps of his backpack and started for the door.

The cavern at the rear of the temple was pitch-black. The cave in caused by the lightning hadn't affected the network of caverns and tunnels behind the temple. It had to be still covered in a thick layer. His crews would have a lot of work ahead of them to excavate the building and whatever lay around it and beyond.

Each of the team held a glimmer stick to cut through the darkness surrounding them. Bernie was surprised at how much of an area they illuminated, but it still wasn't enough for him to see if it was all structurally sound. If a cave in were to happen within the tunnels, the whole team would be covered in a ton of dirt and rock.

Bernie held his glimmer stick out and scanned the walls of the cavern to see if he could find an exit tunnel. "We need to find a way out of this cavern. Does anyone see an exit?"

"I can't see anything." Julia stood beside him, shining her glimmer stick toward the wall. "Oh yuk. Are those huge spiderwebs?"

"They are kurakelda webs, but it looks as though the creatures died out a long time ago. The webs are old," Taylith commented.

"Fan out. We need to find a tunnel out of here," Brenn ordered.

The team spread out and moved forward, almost as a unit. It reminded Bernie of a FOD walk on the flight line when they had trained at NASA. One small object left on a runway could be sucked into the intake of an aircraft's engine and destroy it. Groups were sent out several times a day to scan the ground for foreign objects.

They had made their way halfway through the cavern when Bernie's foot hit a soft spot on the cavern floor.

"My foot is stuck," Julia grunted.

He could hear her shifting and moving as she tried to free her foot from whatever had trapped it. He carefully walked toward her. The floor of the cavern was no longer hard rock.

"Stay still, Julia! The ground isn't stable." Before he could reach her, the soil shifted, and a chasm formed beneath her feet. Her scream echoed back up to him as he kneeled beside the hole and shone his glimmer stick as far as he could.

The others were beside him in seconds. "What happened?" Brenn asked.

"The ground gave way beneath Julia's feet. She fell down this hole." Bernie leaned forward and shouted down the hole. "Julia? Can you hear me?"

"I don't hear anything," Liana said.

"Oh my God. If anything has happened to her..." Bernie took the rope from Brenn's hands and fastened it to the bolt anchor Brenn had pounded into the ground. He wound the rope around his waist, then lowered himself into the hole. "Stay here until I get to the bottom," he told the team.

"I hope the rope is long enough," Ivran muttered. "Who knows how deep it is."

Bernie held the glimmer stick between his teeth as he descended. He was surprised that the walls of the downward tunnel were so firm. Whenever he placed his feet against the walls, all he felt was rock face.

It seemed to take forever, though he was going down quite fast. Finally, his feet encountered solid ground. He quickly turned and shone his glimmer stick. Julia lay on the ground. She appeared to be okay but lay very still. He hurried to her and knelt by her side. "Julia, honey…"

After he called her name several times and stroked her forehead, she opened her eyes. "Bernie? What happened?"

"You fell down some kind of tunnel. Are you hurting anywhere?"

"I don…don…don't know." She began to sit up, then yelped. "My leg. I think I've broken it. I can't move it, and it hurts like bloody hell!"

Bernie shone the glimmer stick over her legs and saw the odd angle of her right limb. "Yes. Stay very still." He tapped his communicator. "Julia is okay, but I think she's broken a leg."

"Is it safe for us to come down?" Brenn asked.

"Yes. From what I can see, this appears to be the entrance to a mine. There are several tunnels leading from it."

"We will join you shortly."

Bernie was glad when the team was all there. Ciara and Laura immediately tended to Julia. "We will need to get her back to the surface and to the hospital," he told them.

"No need, Bernie. There is nothing wrong with Julia," Laura told him calmly.

He could hardly believe his eyes when he saw Julia stand between the two women. "How is this possible? I know her leg was broken."

Ciara chuckled. "Bernie, you will have to learn when you are with the team, everything and anything is possible. Julia has been healed. She is fine, except for some shock from the fall."

Biryn interceded. "This might be a good time for a break. I do not want to waste time as Cylena's and my son's lives are in danger, but we do need to regroup."

CHAPTER SIX

After they had a snack and drank some water, Brenn addressed them. "It appears we need to search for the gem in these passages. They look like mine tunnels. How stable everything is, who knows. That is why Bernie is with us. The main problem is, there is more than one tunnel. Which one do we explore, Ciara?"

"Biryn, Jonathan, you need to concentrate. Taylith, you, too," Ciara told the three men.

"Why would there be a mine directly behind and below a temple?" Julia questioned.

"I don't know, but I suggest we watch out for creepy critters," Erica said.

"We need to investigate the third entrance," Jonathan told them.

"Yes, I agree," Biryn said.

Bernie took Julia's arm. "How do you feel? Are you sure you don't want to go back? I'll take you. It's not like you're quitting, you know."

"Hell, Bernie, I'm fine. Ciara and Laura healed my broken leg. I can walk again like the rest of you. Stop fussing over me," she retorted.

Though their glimmer sticks gave off a lot of light, it was

hardly enough to illuminate the pitch-black tunnel. They saw abandoned equipment, helmets, pickaxes, shovels, and knew that the workers of the mine had vanished as fast as everyone else.

"What kind of mine is this, Bernie?" Julia asked.

"From what I can see, it's a diamond mine. There is still a load of unmined wealth here."

"So, it's a diamond we're looking for?"

"Julia, you know how rare a black diamond is?"

"Yes. I do know a bit about that kind of stuff."

They meandered on along the tunnel, shining their glimmer sticks everywhere, on the floor, the ceiling, the walls, but they had no idea where they would find the black gem required to heal Cylena. They finally came to a fairly large area. Equipment stood in the center, carts resting on tracks to transport soil and findings.

"So far, nothing. Have a drink, and we shall continue," Aldis called out.

They had no sooner sat down and taken out their waterskins when some falling rock disturbed their rest. Laro yelled, "Duragons! Get ready!"

Astonished, Bernie saw Laro convulse, bones causing the skin to protrude, and in seconds, a huge lion faced the creatures. He shook his head. Had he really just seen that? A moment ago there was Laro, and now, in his stead, stood a lion larger than he'd ever seen on Earth!

Ciara and Taylith jumped to their feet. "We are the only ones that can destroy these creatures. They are Zohmes' minions."

"What about me?" Liana asked.

"Yes, you can, too. Only our dragon fire can kill them," Ciara answered.

Instantly, the lion turned back into Laro. Whatever in the

hell a duragon was, they were huge. They reminded Bernie of a scorpion with their long, segmented tail and stinger, but they had more legs and eyes like a spider. Their claws were enormous. He imagined they could cut a man clean in two with one snap.

"Am I going nuts, or did I just watch you change into a lion?" he asked Laro.

Laro nodded. "Ivran, Brenn, and I are lion shifters. Go and hide. Ciara said their dragons will take care of the duragons."

Bernie turned to Julia. "You go and hide. Please?"

"Are you kidding me?"

"Julia, I'll be right there with you. You and I don't have magic to defeat these creatures. You really want to get eaten alive? Now come with me?"

He was glad when she took his hand and allowed him to lead her to a crevice. Holding on to her tightly, he watched as the huge scorpion-like monsters attacked and the dragons annihilated them. "Did you see that, honey?"

"Yes. I did. Eh...honey?"

"Sorry. I feel very protective of you."

"Thanks. But I'm not a fragile little thing, you know." Julia squirmed out of his arms.

Bernie sighed. He never knew when to say the right thing. "I know you're strong. I admire you for it. But I do worry about you."

To his surprise, she relaxed against him. "Sorry I snapped at you. Though I wanted to be a part of this adventure, it's all overwhelming. You know?"

"I understand. But I'm by your side at all times. Just know that. You and I don't have their magic and powers, so we kind of have to stand back."

"I just don't get it. Erica and Laura are from Earth, but now they have powers? How is that possible? It addles my mind."

He stroked her hair. "I know. I wonder myself."

They watched the fight between the duragons and the dragons. It took a little while before the creatures were all defeated and slain.

"Is everyone all right?" Aldis called out.

They all affirmed. Bernie nudged Julia. "We had better join them. Who knows what we will meet up with next."

They seated themselves beside Laura and Taylith. The dragons didn't look winded even with the exertion of battling the scorpion creatures.

After everyone had rested a moment and refreshed themselves with a drink of water, Brenn stood and motioned for them to continue.

Bernie and Julia moved to follow the others as Brenn led them to the opening of an access tunnel. It was such a tight space that they had to walk single file.

"Julia, you and Bernie go ahead. Taylith, Liana, and I will take the rear." Laura patted Julia on the shoulder.

"You first, Julia." Bernie ushered Julia into the narrow opening. After witnessing them defeat the duragons, Bernie had no issue letting the dragons cover their backs.

The tunnel was long. They seemed to have walked for a couple of hours. Luckily it had widened gradually as they moved forward. There was enough room now for them to walk in pairs.

"The tunnel branches off," Brenn yelled out.

Up ahead Bernie could see that the tunnel widened considerably into a small cavern. Across from them were three access tunnels. The group stopped when they reached the cavern.

"We will rest and eat," Aldis said.

They seated themselves on the rock floor and started rummaging through their packs. Julia dug in her pack and pulled out two packets of rations, then handed one to Bernie.

He grinned at her. "Thank you."

His breath caught when she smiled back. She was so incredibly beautiful, even with the dirt smudges on her face. It had been so long since he had seen her truly smile. All he wanted to do was lean down and kiss those beautiful lips. He shook himself back to reality and took a bite of the dried meat from his ration pack.

"Eat quickly. We don't know how long it will take us to find the gem," Brenn commented.

After they ate and packed up their things, Bernie turned his gaze to the cavern and tunnels. The area had to be very rich in whatever ore or gem was mined so long ago. He spotted veins of the substance as it glittered in the light of their glimmer sticks.

"Does anyone have an idea of which way we should go?" Bernie brushed his hair from his face.

Astiana stepped forward and pointed at the tunnel to their left. "We must go this way."

Bernie examined the tunnel she had gestured to. "How do you know? We could very easily get lost and not find a way out."

Astiana skimmed her hand across the rock surrounding the tunnel. To Bernie's shock, the entry began to glow. Strange symbols appeared in the rock face surrounding it. When she did the same to the other tunnels, nothing happened.

Erica chuckled. "Never question the gods or goddesses, Bernie."

Brenn took the lead and they followed in the order they had been previously, with Taylith, Laura, and Liana taking the rear. The tunnel was much wider than the one they had traversed before. They were able to walk in groups of three.

"Hey, check this out. It looks like the stuff the ovens were made of in the temple." Julia ran her finger along a vein of ore that ran along the wall.

It was a thin line, but the slight glow was unmistakable. Taylith, Laura, and Liana stopped behind them and peered at the glowing metal.

Taylith pulled a datapad out of his pocket and took a picture of the ore, then put it away. "We need to catch up with the others."

"You don't think the team should see it? Could it be magical?" Julia asked.

Laura pulled her sister's arm. "Jules, hon, finding the gem to save the queen is more important right now."

Julia turned, a pained expression crossing her features. "Yes, you are right."

Bernie took her hand in his, hoping to comfort her. He knew the queen and Julia had become close while she stayed at the palace. They hurried to catch up with the other members of the team.

They had walked for quite a while when Bernie noticed that the tunnel had taken an incline.

Bernie looked at Julia. "We seem to be going up. Are they sure we are going the right way?"

Julia squeezed his hand. "If Astiana said we should go this way, then we need to listen to her. There must be a reason she chose this tunnel. You saw the inscriptions at the entrance. The gods placed them there."

"Stairs ahead," Aldis yelled out.

A little further ahead the floor of the tunnel changed shape. Stairs were carved into the rock. They now had a steeper upward climb. When they came to the end of the staircase, the tunnel opened to a large cavern. Tables stood along one of the walls. Mining tools, helmets, and other equipment was thrown upon them. There were several large rolling carts.

Some of them were empty, but others were filled with gems and the glowing metal ore they had seen embedded in the tunnel walls. Across from them was a huge metal door with carvings on it. They were some of the same symbols Bernie had seen at the temple.

Brenn and Aldis tried to push the door open.

Aldis shook his head. "It won't budge. I think it may be covered on the other side by dirt and rock."

Bernie studied the frame of the door, looking for any sign of light shining through the cracks. Though he didn't know what good that would do since it could very well be nightfall on the other side of the door — or it could just lead to another cavern.

"I can't see any type of light coming through."

Ciara moved to the door along with Astiana. She turned to Taylith and Liana. "If it is a door leading out of the mine, it could be blocked by rocks and dirt. If that is the case, we can shift it out of the way."

Bernie watched in amazement as the group began to chant, their bodies taking on an otherworldly glow. They pointed their hands to the door. A stream of shimmering light issued from their fingertips, engulfing the door in its radiance. It creaked and groaned, then gently pushed open. Whatever had been blocking it had disappeared.

"Holy hell!" Bernie rubbed his eyes, not believing what he had just seen. Then again, everything he had witnessed so far made him feel as if he were an actor in a movie.

Ivran peered out of the doorway. "Why would the gods and goddesses send us to the mines near Xynnar?"

"That's a million-dollar question," Erica murmured.

The door was high above the Xynnar mines. Bernie looked down and saw miners moving around. It appeared they were finished for the day and going home. One man stopped and suddenly gazed up at them. He took his hard hat off, shaded his eyes, then began up the side of the mountain toward them.

"By the gods, that's my brother, Tanoth. He is a mineral and gem geologist and works in the mine. He is often called upon to travel to other mines to give his advice and to test soil samples in various areas." Ivran stepped forward. "Tanoth! Brother!"

"That's why the gods and goddesses told us to take this tunnel even if it was not the right one to find the black gem. Tanoth must go with us," Ciara said.

"Your deities are wise," Bernie muttered. "We sure as hell can use him. I'm a surveyor and engineer. I'm not that familiar with gems and minerals. Especially alien stuff."

Tanoth had reached them. He embraced Ivran, then bowed before the king and greeted the others. "Brenn, good to see you, too. Now tell me, what brings you all here? And how did you find this old mine?" he asked, looking at the pile of soil and rocks that had been dislodged when the door was uncovered.

Brenn answered him. "Long story. Since it is almost nightfall, I suggest we break for the night."

Bernie agreed. "Yes, let's find a spot to camp."

"Not necessary. Xynnar is not far from here. Our parents have rebuilt, and our house has enough space for you all to bed down for the night. I am sure a warm meal will be welcome?" Tanoth suggested.

"Mother will never forgive you for bringing home so many guests without notice," Ivran warned Tanoth.

Tanoth smiled. "Nonsense. She will be more than happy. Especially you, brother. It has been a long time since your last visit. How are Reana and the little one?"

They chatted on their way down to the village and filled Tanoth in about their mission, Tanoth, and Ivran leading the way.

"Look at that! Our village is almost back to what it was, except better. I am happy to see new technology used for many of the houses," Ivran said.

Tanoth stopped in front of their new home. "You go in first, Ivran. Surprise Mother."

Bernie smiled as a squeal of delight came from inside. They followed Tanoth into the house.

"Mother, we have unexpected guests for the night."

Bernie saw the astonished expression on Ivran's mother's face and felt bad. So, apparently, did Brenn and Laro.

"We should go and see my parents while we are here. Ciara and I can stay with them for the night," Brenn told her.

"Erica and I will do the same. I know my parents will be quite surprised," Laro said.

"Oh, Brenn, Laro, your parents will be so happy! We often complain that we do not see enough of our boys."

"By the gods! The king? Your Majesty!" She bowed.

"Please relax? Tonight, I am merely Biryn."

Bernie threw a warning glance at Tanoth and the others. "Thank you for your hospitality. We are on a field trip with the king, and then Tanoth saw us and invited us to sleep here instead of in the forest."

It was good they had caught his warning. Tanoth told his mother, "The king has invited me to accompany them for the rest of the field trip."

They talked of normal everyday things while their hostess busied herself cooking a meal for them all.

The door opened. "Son, how good to see you." Ivran's father walked inside and grasped his son's hand. "I ran into Brenn and Laro on my way home from work. They told me you were here. And who are… By the gods, the king in my humble house? They did not warn me. Your Majesty, good evening." He took his hard hat off and bowed.

"Like I told your mate, relax. Tonight, I am just plain Biryn."

The meal consisted of a hearty stew and freshly baked bread. Bernie thought it sure as hell beat chewing on dried stuff.

Brenn returned, accompanied by Laro. "We can split up. My parents' house has three empty bedrooms. Just in case of future grandchildren wanting to visit." He grinned broadly.

"We have some extra rooms at my parents' home as well. Some of you can stay there," Laro offered.

They divided into three groups. "We need to get up at first light, so should not stay up late," Aldis warned.

"Tell us what this field trip is all about?" Ivran's father asked.

"We are just exploring, Father. The king needed a break from his royal duties," Ivran said.

"If the others in Xynnar knew the king was here, they would be lining up at the door. Good thing you are leaving at first light. Is it not almost time for the heir to the throne to come into this world?"

Bernie hastily answered that question. "Yes, but we are not going too far. The king is in constant contact with the palace. If need be, they will send a flyer to take him back."

"Yes, I do not want to miss the birthing of my son," Biryn said softly.

Bernie noticed the pained expression on the king's face and quickly changed the subject to mining and the Koriam crystals. "I am fascinated by it all. I'd love to talk more with you on this subject. Maybe you can both visit my house at Initiation Genesis in the near future?" he invited.

"Does your town not have a name yet?" Biryn asked.

"No. We are waiting for the last votes to come in. It will

have a name soon. I hope. And then comes the naming of the streets."

"You name your roads?" Ivran asked.

"On Earth we do. Maybe it won't be necessary here. Not unless we multiply fast, which I doubt will happen any time soon. That makes me ask another question. How have you kept your population down? Many of you have lived for centuries. Ierilia is much older than Earth, yet no realm is overpopulated. A huge part of Earth's problems was not only caused by pollution, but also by the worldwide population explosion. China, one of the realms on Earth, had over two and a half billion people when we left. China made it law that people could only have one child. India followed close behind, and our realm, the United States, was heavily overpopulated in many areas."

Astiana answered him. "During the early years of Ierilia, the planet had far too many people. Millions died during the endless battles. Our population dwindled almost to the point of extinction. After the wars ended, that all changed. I Am stepped in and limited the amount of offspring many of our species can have. I Am controls it all."

"So not everyone lives for centuries?" Bernie asked.

"No. Ierilian humans have a longer lifespan than your Earth humans, though your physiology will adjust to this planet. Deities, sorcerers, and shifters, unless they are killed, are given the choice of when they want to enter the realm of dreams."

Bernie shook his head, trying to digest all this information and wondered what the lifespan for him and his fellow travelers was going to be on this planet.

"I suggest we stop talking and get some rest," Aldis said.

Bernie, Julia, Astiana, Aldis, and Ivran were staying there. They had to share two rooms, but it was much more comfortable than sleeping in a bedroll on the ground.

Bernie woke to the aroma of what promised to be a great breakfast. The only thing he wished for was coffee. He was the first one up and quickly bathed and got dressed. He wished he had clean clothing, but his dusty clothes from the day before would have to do.

He went downstairs and found Ivran's mother busy setting the table. "Let me help you with that."

"Thank you, but I am almost finished. Are you hungry?" she asked.

"Yes, my stomach woke me." He smiled at her. She was a pleasant little woman. Little? Compared to women from Earth, she was quite tall, but not next to their men. They would dwarf her. He could tell where Ivran had inherited his good nature. He looked a lot like his mother. Were they lion shifters, too? Of course, they had to be. Why would only one member of the family be a shifter? "Breakfast smells fantastic."

"What do you eat for breakfast on your planet?"

"Eggs, bacon, which is a type of smoked meat, sausages maybe, hash browns. I don't know how to explain those. Toast or bread. Toast is bread that is browned on both sides. And then there are pancakes."

"What are those?"

"Small flat round cakes fried in a pan, slathered in butter and syrup. Mm...when we have finished building our new city, maybe we should open a pancake house. There's an idea."

The rest of the team began to appear. He smiled at Julia. "Morning, Julia. How is the leg?"

"It's as fine as it was before I fell. Thanks for asking."

"How did you sleep?"

"Surprisingly, like a log. I'm looking forward to today. I hope Tanoth can help us find what we're looking for."

Bernie placed a finger on his lips. "I'm sure Tanoth will be an excellent guide to help us explore new territories and find the herbs the queen asked for."

CHAPTER SEVEN

Tanoth looked at Ivran, Laro, and Brenn. "We should have told our fathers of this mine. It could be important."

"It could be, but for now we need to keep everything secret. Imagine if the people heard. There would be widespread panic. And even after the mission, the general public can never know about any of the details. We must find the black gem. We need to move fast to save the queen and the little prince. I'm glad you caught my warning last night," Bernie said.

"Yes. I apologize, but you should have warned me ahead of time that it be kept secret."

"Yes, my bad." Bernie opened the metal door that they had closed before heading down the mountain. "I hope no one from below sees the door."

"Unless you really look up, which most of us do not after a hard day of work, I think it will be safe until the existence of the mine is made public." Tanoth followed them into the mine tunnel.

"We can use a spell and make the door invisible for now," Astiana suggested.

"Good plan. Go for it," Bernie said.

After the door was closed and Astiana had placed a spell on it, they ignited their glimmer sticks.

"We need to head back to the cavern. I hope the gods and goddesses will show us the correct tunnel this time," Aldis said.

"We took the correct tunnel. The gods showed us that Tanoth is needed on our quest," Astiana said.

Bernie nodded. "It makes sense. He is a mineralogist and gemologist."

They walked for quite a while until they came to the narrow tunnel. Now and then Tanoth stopped to examine the ore glittering from the walls.

"What do you think it is, Tanoth?" Brenn asked.

"I hesitate to speculate, but I think it is the ore that helped to create the four swords. The mine that produced the most powerful ore disappeared a long time ago. The ore we mine now has magickal qualities, but nothing like the original metal. I will need to test some of it. If it is truly what I think it is, we have found the ingredient to give all our warriors weapons that cannot be broken or defeated, weapons that will slay almost anything."

"Holy shit. That means a whole army can have magic swords like us?" Erica asked.

Bernie shook his head. "Erica, I don't know what powers the four swords. Their gods may not allow thousands of warriors to have weapons just like yours. It will need to be investigated."

"That is my task, to investigate." Tanoth stroked the wall next to him.

Astiana had heard their conversation. "The four swords were made from this ore, but they were also infused with special powers and magick by the gods and goddesses. That is why they are unique."

"That clarifies it. Thank you," Tanoth said.

They squeezed through the last of the tunnel and stood in the cavern again. "Okay, which one of the two tunnels?" Bernie asked, looking at the other two entrances. He felt Julia's hand seek his. He clasped it and squeezed, grateful that she sought his company all the time now.

"Rania told me we need to take the tunnel on the right," Ciara said.

"I hope this is where we find the black gem," Bernie muttered.

"I just hope we don't run into more creepy critters." Julia pulled a face, and he felt her shudder.

The tunnel was narrow, just like the first one. They had to walk in single file. "Walk behind me," Bernie told her.

"I don't think I want to go on any more missions. I can't imagine going to the bowels of Ierilia, or Yanata," she told him. "And from the stories I've heard, it was horrible."

"No. It's not for me either. I'll stick to my regular jobs. Unless the king specifically needs me. Then I have no choice."

The tunnel widened. Bernie heard Tanoth exclaim.

"Look at all the ore. This is unbelievable. I am sure now that this is the lost mine my grandfather often talked about."

Eventually, the tunnel became even wider, then opened into a fairly large cavern. Carts filled with ore stood against a wall, and crude mining tools were lined up neatly.

"This mine was abandoned centuries ago, just like the temple." Bernie scratched his head.

"Look at the far wall. What are those things?" Laura pointed at long metal tubes that resembled coffins.

Bernie walked toward them, wiped the dust off one of the caskets, then turned around. "They have a Russian flag painted on them."

"Russian?" Brenn inquired.

"It's another country on Earth. Another realm. We are all from America. Our ships were launched from Florida, a state in America," Bernie explained.

"That doesn't make sense. Can you explain better?" Laro asked.

"Earth has different countries, or realms. Each realm is divided into smaller realms. They're called states or provinces."

"Very confusing," Biryn mumbled. "So this Russia, you know that realm?"

"I've never been to Russia. What is curious, how would these tubes get here, and how is it they were buried along with the temple and the mine?" He counted the tubes. "There are eight."

"I wonder what is in them?" Julia said.

"I guess we won't know unless we dust them off and open one of them. How the hell they got in here, so far below the surface, is beyond me." He used his sleeve to wipe off some more of the dust. "Holy shit. There's an astronaut in it!"

"That's even more unbelievable. The USA was first to initiate a relocation mission. Is he or she alive? Are these stasis units?" Erica rushed to join Bernie.

"No. They're more like hibernation pods. It wouldn't surprise me if we open one, the person inside will crumble into dust," Bernie said. "Now, I do know that much research was being done into hibernation. They actually tested it in China on humans and kept them in hibernation for two weeks. I know Russia was experimenting as well. It appears they actually launched a ship with these eight people in hibernation aboard. But they wouldn't have tried to send the ship much farther than Mars. The ship these chambers were on must have gone off its course, traveled through a black hole or something, then crashed on Ierilia. How could the pods have ended up in this mine?" Bernie peered closer at the person inside the chamber.

"Bernie, there is a date below the flag." Erica rubbed more dust away to display the black lettering. "It says July fifteenth, two thousand and forty-five."

"That's more than a hundred years before our ships were launched. There's nothing in the books about this one. I'd know. I studied the development of space travel of all the various countries that were experimenting with it," Julia said.

Bernie grunted. "It was obviously a secret failed mission. If the Russians had been successful, they'd have made it known worldwide. They're not going to boast a failure."

"Well, whatever happened, we will never know. If the people from Xynnar are going to work the mine again, these chambers will need to be removed and the remains disposed of," Brenn told Erica and Bernie.

"Brenn, once we open them, they will crumble to dust. There won't be anything left. The chambers are too heavy to transport and the tunnel too narrow. I'm not sure what we can do." Bernie scratched his head.

"How did they get down here in the first place? There are no tunnels leading from this cavern that I can see. No door leading to the outside." Erica rubbed her chin.

"We'll have to take the chambers apart. That's the only solution," Laura said.

Bernie nodded. "Yes. It still doesn't explain how they got to be in this cavern in the first place."

The rest of the team had been quietly observing and listening. "We do not have time for that now," Biryn said.

Jonathan spoke up. "I can help. I can disintegrate the chambers. That way no one will ever see them or know they were here."

"You can do that?" Bernie asked, shaking his head at the magic.

"Yes. It just came to me how to do it."

Erica looked shocked. "You can't just get rid of them with the people in it. It's indecent."

Bernie cleared his throat. "Erica, they're dead. They won't feel anything, and there is no family to account to."

"Nevertheless, let's at least open them and allow their bodies to crumble to dust. We can gather their ashes and have some sort of burial ceremony for the unfortunate souls," Erica suggested.

"There is a small panel just below the transparent dome. I doubt any of it will work, but here we go." Bernie pushed some buttons. The lettering and symbols were foreign to him, so he pushed the buttons randomly. Suddenly, the dome opened. He waited for the body to turn to dust, but nothing happened.

The woman didn't appear to be dead. She looked as though she were in a deep sleep or her body had been perfectly preserved—as if she had died only moments ago. Bernie placed his fingers on the side of her neck and checked for a heartbeat. He shook his head.

"There is no heartbeat, and I don't see any chest movement. She isn't breathing. She is dead, but her body has been fully preserved."

Laura stepped up beside the tube. Her hand began to glow brightly when she touched the woman's arm. She pulled her hand back quickly, and the glow subsided. "She is alive. I can feel her spirit."

Astiana spoke behind them. "It is the forever-rest spell. The gods rescued these people after their ship crashed and placed them within this cavern. They have kept them alive until today. It must be written in the book of knowledge that we would find them. You must open the other chambers. We have to break the spell."

"God, that's all we need. Eight foreign astronauts to take care of. As if we don't have enough on our hands trying to find the black gem," Erica muttered. "These people will be disoriented and confused. Someone needs to take them to the surface and to the hospital."

"We will transport them to the hospital after we wake them. Brenn, can you communicate to Catrice and Jason that there will be a group of foreigners arriving at the hospital? Have them meet them there," Astiana told them.

"I hope they speak and understand English," Bernie said as he opened the last pod. He had a strong feeling that their gods were guiding his fingers because he was just randomly pushing numbers on the pads. There were three women and five men. All appeared to be approximately between twenty-five and below forty years old.

Astiana took the grimoire from her backpack. The book was ancient from what Bernie could see of it. It had strange symbols carved into it that had an ethereal glow. Astiana opened the book and flipped through the pages, then stopped almost to the center of the book.

"Jonathan, Biryn, Ciara, Taylith, and Liana. You must work the spell with me. There are too many for just one of us to break the spell."

Bernie gave Astiana a puzzled look. "Don't you need the gem to break the spell?"

Astiana smiled patiently. "No. On the queen, Zohmes and Odoxon used the spell with malicious intent. We need the gem to focus and strengthen the magick to release Cylena."

"The gods placed these people under the spell to keep them safe. As Astiana suspected, it was written that we would find them and release them using the spell. Rania just told me,"

Ciara commented.

The magick users joined Astiana and clasped hands. Astiana read the lengthy spell first. When she finished reading it aloud and began to chant, the others chanted along with her, their bodies illuminating brightly, until the intense light encompassed all eight tubes. When the incantation ended, the light turned into a cloud of shimmering mist, then slowly faded.

Suddenly, one of the astronauts, in this case, a woman, opened her eyes. Her lips parted, and she took a deep breath.

Bernie stepped back. "This is fucking unbelievable. Am I the only one seeing this? It's impossible they can be alive without being hooked up to computers and some sort of life support. I'm hallucinating."

"You're not hallucinating, Bernie." Julia stood beside him. "I see her breathing, too, and looking at us. She's scared."

Julia helped the first woman out of her chamber. "Can you speak English?"

The young woman stared at her for a moment, mumbled something in Russian, then nodded. "Yes. Where are we?"

They helped the others out of the chambers. The eight grouped together, looking at the team uncertainly. Bernie approached the man who seemed to be the oldest. "Do you speak English?" The man nodded.

"Where we are? How we are in cave?"

Bernie was glad their English was fairly fluent. "You are on an alien planet in another universe far from Earth. Your ship must have crashed."

"What year this is?"

"I don't know. Some of us here are from Earth. Our ships crashed on this planet, too. The people here are very friendly and hospitable. Before we answer more of your questions, we need to get you to the hospital and get you all checked out."

He turned and looked at Astiana, who nodded.

"My name Andrei Kuznetsov. I am captain."

"Pleased to meet you. Please stand close together so we can transport you?"

Astiana, Biryn, Liana, Ciara, Jonathan, and Taylith linked hands and stood around the small group. They chanted, the eight astronauts looking completely bewildered now.

Even Bernie was astounded when he saw a shower of sparkles descend on the foreigners, then watched as they faded and disappeared. "Between seeing a man shift into a lion, breaking that spell, and this, I think I've seen everything now. Can all this get any crazier?"

Erica giggled. "I used to say *beam me up, Scottie.*"

"Did Catrice respond, Brenn?" he asked.

"Yes. They are at the hospital, waiting for them. Mark, too."

Bernie nodded. "These poor people are going to be even more confused than we all were when we first arrived here. Now on to find the black gem. It's obviously not here. I guess we have to try the last tunnel."

CHAPTER EIGHT

Bernie wiped his sweaty face with his sleeve. The third tunnel was hot as hell. The farther they traveled, the warmer it got. It was as if someone had turned a heater to full blast, and what was that weird stuff all over the sides? It looked wet, almost as if the tunnel walls bled. He touched the stuff oozing from the rock. He grimaced and wiped his hand on the base of his shirt. The substance was thick and slimy, much like a garden slug's goo.

He studied the rock. It wasn't smooth, which it would be if it were carved out by any type of equipment or tools. When they accessed the tunnel, chunks of rock and debris littered the ground in front of it, like part of the cavern wall had collapsed. He sure as hell didn't think it was man-made like the other tunnels and caverns they had traversed.

"I don't think this is a mine shaft."

"It does not appear to be," Tanoth agreed.

They pushed onward, the tunnel taking a decline. They were moving deeper beneath the planet's surface.

"Stop!" Aldis yelled.

The group came to a sudden stop. Bernie could hear rocks shifting and sliding from the front, then silence. "What's going on?"

"The tunnel takes a severe decline. We will have to slide down the shaft one at a time," Brenn answered.

Bernie watched as one by one the team in front slipped into the opening, then disappeared.

When it was Julia's turn, she grabbed his hand and leaned forward to peek down the tunnel. "Are they fucking crazy? That is one hell of a slide! It's almost a direct drop! Are they trying to get us killed?"

He turned her to face him. It wrenched his heart to see the fear in her eyes. He caressed her cheek. "Everything will be fine, Julia. I'll be right behind you."

Jonathan stepped beside Julia. "He's right, Mom. I won't let anything happen to you. Neither will the others."

Julia looked at her son and nodded, then took a deep breath and entered the tunnel. Bernie waited for her to disappear. Her squeals echoed back up to him as she slid down. He braced himself for the downward spiral, following behind her.

Julia was right. It was one hell of a drop. The slimy floor of the tunnel made it easy for his body to slip downward at a high speed. It almost made him dizzy. When he flew through the opening at the end of the slide, he knew he was going to hit the ground hard. He closed his eyes and stiffened his body, but when he landed, he was cushioned from the rock. It was almost as if he were supported by a soft, billowy mattress. *Their magic! They must have used a spell to break our fall.* He stood, then quickly joined the others.

Julia moved to stand beside him and took his hand. "That scared the living hell out of me."

"I heard." Bernie chuckled and squeezed her fingers. It warmed his heart that Julia sought his comfort. "I wouldn't want a repeat anytime soon."

He studied the cavern they had fallen into. It was huge. Definitely not man-made. Long, spiking stalactites hung from the ceiling. Deposits of gleaming crystals threaded through the rock walls and formations of crystals jutted from the cavern floor. He couldn't see a way out except for the tunnel they had slipped through.

He stumbled as the rock floor suddenly shifted. The cavern walls shook. Several stalactites broke free from the ceiling and dropped to the ground.

"Find shelter! Now!" Aldis yelled.

Bernie scanned the cavern and spotted a small alcove. Gripping Julia's hand tighter, he yanked her to the opening. "Get inside!"

Luckily, she didn't argue. She nestled inside, then yanked his shoulders, pulling him into it with her. He wrapped his arms around her and held her protectively against him, feeling the slight trembling of her body.

A rumbling sound echoed in the cave. Pockets of rock, crystals, and debris flew from the ground. Four massive heads with long, tentacle-like feelers emerged from crevices in the rock floor. Bone-like mandibles jutted from maws as wide as the creatures' heads. Rows of pointed teeth lined their mouths. Two yellow eyes glowed on each side of their gaping jaws. Their bodies reminded Bernie of a snail, but the monsters had hundreds of legs running the length of their long bodies like a centipede. A greenish phosphorus glow surrounded their bodies, and they projected a horrific stench from two antenna-like antlers that came out of the knobs at the top in squirts of yellowish mist. It smelled almost like rotten eggs. Their tails ended in a four-pronged pincher made of bone. Their pointed ends looked as though they could cut through steel.

"What in the hell do you feed the bugs on this planet!"

Erica yelled.

The centipedes were fast. One rushed to the crevice where Bernie and Julia were sheltered, its huge feeler stretching toward them. He shot at it with his fleet weapon. The feeler pulled away, but its massive head shifted and blocked the opening. It peered at them with two of its glowing yellow eyes. Its mandibles snapped, digging into the rock and trying to make the hole bigger.

Julia screamed and fired her fleet weapon over his shoulder at the creature's eyes. Its head thrashed, but it dug deeper into the rock, yanking large chunks from the rock face. Bernie joined her efforts, shooting steadily at the creature. It wouldn't budge, and the rock kept crumbling away, making the opening wider and wider. It pushed at the crevice, trying to inch its head into the hole. He began to feel nauseous and lightheaded. What they squirted into the crevice appeared to have the same effect as a leaking gas pipe on Earth. That was how they could defeat other creatures or, in this case, the human invaders, he realized. He wondered how miners could have ever worked these tunnels in the company of such beasts. Or, maybe they had developed over the centuries that the mines and caves lay undisturbed by human invasion. Surely, no miners could have survived down here in the company of those monsters…

Suddenly he felt a wall of heat. The huge slug burst into flames, its writhing body burning quickly into a pile of ash and smoke. Bernie shook his head a moment. He'd thought for sure they were going to be goners, but somehow the dragons had shifted and saved the lot of them.

Hesitantly, he shuffled back into the cavern just in time to see the dragons shift back to their humans. Reaching for Julia's hand, he assisted her out of the alcove and pulled her against his side. She leaned into him, her arm around his waist.

"Holy fuck, that was something else."

"Oh, baby, you ain't seen nothing yet," Erica responded.

"I'll have nightmares for the rest of my life." Julia stepped away from Bernie.

He looked around the cavern. "There are no tunnels. I don't see any place where the gem could be hidden." He watched Tanoth examining the walls.

Tanoth turned to them. "There are a lot of gems embedded in these walls, but none are black. This cavern was mined, by my estimation, centuries ago."

Bernie turned around and looked at the wall. "These look like diamonds," he said as he brushed some dirt off protruding gems.

"What are diamonds?" Ciara asked.

"A very precious gem on Earth. These seem to be quite large. They would fetch a fortune back home. Like millions."

"The most precious gem on Ierilia is the purple zamphonia. It is only found in one realm, and the mine is heavily guarded by our warriors," Brenn informed Bernie.

"Enough talk of precious gems and their value. What do we do now?" Biryn barked.

Brenn patted him on the shoulder. "Calm down, Biryn. Ciara, can you talk to—"

He didn't get a chance to finish his sentence. Bernie had encountered a huge protruding diamond, and when he wiped the dust off it, the rock face rumbled, then opened to another cave. Startled, he jumped back.

Brenn and Aldis were the first to step into the cave. "It looks clear," Brenn called out.

Reaching for Julia's hand, he pulled her into the cave with him. "Oh my fucking God! Look at this! It's breathtaking!" Stalagmites and stalactites in a myriad of greens, blues, oranges, reds, and yellows hung from the ceiling and protruded from the walls and floor.

"It's awesome and reminds me of a picture I once saw in high school. They were called speleothems. They're formed by thousands of years of mineral deposits, then dissolved by water seeping through the cracks. The water evaporates, and the minerals accumulate over the centuries, which forms the speleothems," Julia said.

Bernie rubbed his chin. "Fancy remembering all that from your school days. You must have a photographic memory. How do we find the black gem among all these formations? There are so many colors."

"But there is one that stands out from all. Look closely." Ciara walked to the far wall.

Bernie suddenly saw it. A vivid glowing red, it jutted out from the wall. When Ciara grasped it, a partition opened above the stalactite. Inside it, resting on a golden glowing cushion, sat a small gold box, its filigree unbelievable. On top were two small statues of a tiny purple dragon and a golden lion. When she opened the lid, he saw the black gem. "Holy shit! That's got to be the largest black fucking diamond in the whole of creation!"

Erica, Laura, and Julia all uttered soft exclamations, echoing him. "Hell, take that back to Earth, and we could live in sheer luxury for the rest of our lives!" Erica whispered.

Removing it carefully from its hiding place, Ciara held it in her hands. The partition closed again, and the red stalactite disappeared.

"We have it!" Ciara stated proudly. "Biryn, we can go back to the palace now to wake the queen."

"How do you propose we climb up that steep, slimy tunnel?" Bernie questioned.

Astiana chuckled. "Now that our mission is successful and

completed, we will take us back, just like the eight people from Earth."

"Right. I forgot." He glanced at Erica and grinned. "Beam us up, Astiana."

CHAPTER NINE

Because of their involvement in the mission, Tanoth, Bernie, and Julia were allowed to be present when Cylena was woken from her forever-rest slumber.

Cylena looked as if she was just in a deep sleep. Hirsuta, Cewrick, and Icaras sat on each side of the bed. Biryn rushed to the queen's side, Icaras respectfully stepping aside but still hovering behind the king.

"Do you have it?" Icaras asked.

"Yes. We can wake her now."

The king bent and tenderly kissed his wife's forehead. Astiana stepped forward and placing the grimoire on the foot of the bed she opened it to the pages where she had found the spell. Then she handed the golden box to Biryn.

"Place the gem on her forehead, Biryn."

He took the box from Astiana, carefully removed the diamond, and placed it on Cylena's forehead.

"This spell is slightly different from the one we used for the Russian people. Now we must join hands and chant it. I will chant it once. After I am finished, it will remain in your memory, and we must all chant together. You, too, Cewrick and Icaras." Astiana closed her eyes and began to chant while the magick users clasped hands and stood around the bed.

Catrice had joined Bernie and Julia at the back of the room. "I hope this works," she whispered.

Bernie whispered back, "After what I've seen and experienced during our excursion, I'm sure it will."

After Astiana stopped chanting, she nodded to the circle surrounding the bed. "Now."

He watched and listened to their chant. The black diamond on the queen's forehead began to glow, its radiance increasing in intensity as the chant became louder and continued. His heart almost stopped as black vein-like spidery lines appeared on Cylena's face, chest, and arms. "Oh my God! What's happening to her?"

"Hush," Catrice hissed.

The black diamond appeared to sink into the queen's forehead, and the black lines increased in width and color until she resembled a zombie. At least, on Earth, sometimes zombies appeared that way in old movies. Her skin was now a chalky white, the black lines starkly standing out against it.

The chanting was almost deafening now. The diamond rose slowly, radiating a golden glow. The black lines turned into pure gold. They seemed to move beneath Cylena's skin. It was as if the gem was a living entity, rotating slowly, sending its tendrils beneath her skin.

The glow disappeared, the queen's coloring returning to normal, a healthy blush now on her cheeks. The magick users stopped chanting, and Biryn took the gem from Cylena's forehead and placed it back into its box. He handed it to Ciara. "Please have Dunmore bring this to my room? I will take it to the royal treasury later and lock it away safely."

Cylena opened her eyes to look at the crowded room. "What happened? Why are there so many people in the room? I began the birthing. That is the last I remember."

"That is the cue for us to leave," Bernie said, happy that the mission was now a complete success.

Only Biryn, Hirsuta, Cewrick, and Icaras stayed in the room. Biryn looked at his beautiful queen. "My love, I will tell you everything later. After you birth our little prince."

Cylena moaned and grasped her belly. Catrice hurried to her, holding her stethoscope. "I need to examine Cylena. Could you all, except Biryn, please step outside? Please ask Jason to join me?"

Catrice placed the stethoscope on Cylena's belly. "The infant's heart is strong and clear. Now to examine you to see how far you are. Please raise your legs?" She draped a sheet over Cylena's raised knees.

Biryn held Cylena's hand. "I am right beside you, my love."

Cylena groaned. "I would like my mother to witness the birthing."

"I will call her after Catrice has finished examining you." He stroked her forehead.

"Amazing. She's almost fully dilated. It won't be long. Her labor must have continued even though she was in some kind of stasis," Catrice said.

"Stasis?" Cylena managed to utter in between groans.

"Later, my love. Do not worry. Everything is fine." Biryn took a cloth that Catrice handed him and wiped the perspiration from his mate's forehead.

Catrice walked to the door and opened it a crack. "Hirsuta, the queen would like you with her for the birthing."

Hirsuta took the chair on Cylena's other side and grasped

her daughter's hand.

Catrice stood at the foot of the bed. Biryn heard her encourage the queen from afar. His mind was fully focused on his mate and the pain she was experiencing birthing their son.

The scream that came from between Cylena's lips terrified him. "Is she okay?" he shouted.

"Yes, she's fine. She's pushing. The baby's head is crowning," Catrice told him. "Try and hold for a few minutes, Cylena. Push when I tell you to."

"Crowning?" Biryn asked.

"It's an Earth medical term. Push again, Cylena."

Biryn's blood ran cold at Cylena's scream when she pushed. "Can you give her something for pain?" He looked at Catrice, whose head he could barely see as she concentrated on the birthing.

"Too late for that, Biryn. I can see his head. He has black hair. One more push, Cylena. Now!"

Biryn thought Cylena would tear his hand off as she pushed again. One loud scream, then the squalling of an infant.

Catrice held the baby up for Hirsuta and Biryn to see. "A beautiful, healthy boy. He's big. Must be more than eight pounds. Would you like to cut the cord, Biryn?"

"Eh...no. I will leave that in your hands." He turned to Cylena. "It's over, my love. We have a beautiful son. He has your black hair."

Cylena smiled wanly. "Can I see him?"

Catrice wrapped the infant in a waiting warm towel and handed him to Cylena. But as she was busy disposing of the afterbirth and cutting the cord to save for its stem cells, Cylena groaned.

"What's wrong, Cylena? It's all over. I just need to check if you need stitches, but it's behind you," Catrice told her.

"No…the pain…it has not gone. I still need to push."

"No more pushing. It's over. You have the baby in your arms," Catrice tried to reassure the queen.

"Take the infant, Mother. Something is not right."

Biryn looked at Catrice. "What is wrong?"

"I don't know, Biryn. Let me examine her." Catrice pulled the light closer to Cylena's legs. "Holy shit!"

"What is it? What is the matter with her?" Biryn asked in an agitated voice.

"Nothing. Oh my God! She is birthing another one."

Hirsuta smiled. "Twins?"

"Yes. The head has already descended, and she is ready to give birth. Push again, Cylena."

Cylena groaned, then pushed. A softer cry sounded in the room. "And we have a sister for the prince. She is much smaller, maybe about five and a half pounds." After Catrice cut the cord, she wrapped the infant in a towel and handed her to Biryn. "Your daughter, Your Majesty!"

Biryn gingerly held the small bundle and looked down at the now lustily crying infant. "She has blonde hair. How could we not know?" He looked questioningly at Catrice.

"I'll be damned if I know, Biryn. She never showed up on the ultrasound, and I never heard a second heartbeat."

Cylena held her arms out. "A little girl," she said weakly. "The gods and goddesses have blessed us. No wonder I was as big as the palace!"

"Do we have names?" Catrice asked.

"Yes, our son is Eliya, and Aylie for the princess," Biryn told her.

Jason had come in and busied himself washing the boy while Catrice finished examining Cylena. "Amazingly, she doesn't need stitches. But I'm sure she needs to rest now. It's a hard job bringing a baby into the world, let alone two."

"After I hold my son and daughter," Cylena said. "And then I would like to rest in my own bedroom. We have one cradle ready. We need another bed for our daughter, Biryn."

"Let me get you cleaned up while Jason washes the little ones," Catrice said.

Jason did not take long. When both babies were washed, diapered, and dressed, then each bundled in a blanket, Biryn held his arms out.

"Let me introduce the prince and princess to the team." He smiled broadly as Jason placed a baby in each arm. Then Biryn headed for the door. Jason opened it wide enough for the king to slip through.

"Meet Prince Eliya and Princess Aylie," he announced proudly. He looked at Cewrick. "You can go in to see Cylena now, Grandfather."

"Twins? Wow. Aw, they're beautiful. The princess is so tiny. Congratulations, Your Majesty," Julia said.

"The queen?" Brenn asked.

"She is fine. She will be returning to our quarters soon to rest. Why don't you all go to my dining room? It is close to midnight, and we've not eaten. Brenn, please tell Dunmore to order a meal for us?"

"Can I see my sister now?" Icaras asked after briefly looking at the babies.

"Yes, of course, Uncle Icaras," the king told him, grinning from ear to ear.

A light meal awaited them in Biryn's quarters. "I didn't realize it was so late," Julia said as they sat at the table.

"It's been quite a day. I don't know about you, but I'm exhausted. I can't wait to crawl into bed," Bernie told her.

"I feel much the same. I never ever want to go on another of these trips. It was interesting, enlightening, thanks, but no thanks. Some of Ierilia's dangerous underground creatures are going to give me nightmares as long as I live." Julia pulled a face.

"You persisted in wanting to go along," Erica reminded her.

"I suppose. I have no idea how you and my sister can enjoy these trips so much."

Bernie laughed. "Don't worry. We're not part of Biryn's team. This was our first and the last."

Brenn cleared his throat. "Eh...Bernie, Julia, Tanoth, what you've experienced today, and what happened to the queen, has to remain between us. We were merely on a geological expedition. Upon our return, the queen began the birthing."

After he stopped talking, the loud tolling of bells sounded. "Seems the news of the birth of the little royal ones has been announced. The city is rejoicing," Aldis commented and walked to the balcony doors. "There is already a huge crowd of people outside the palace walls, hoping for a glimpse of the prince and princess."

Just then, the doors opened, and Jason wheeled Cylena, a baby in each arm, into the room, accompanied by Catrice and Biryn and followed by Icaras, Cewrick, and Hirsuta. Bernie noted the queen looked bright and happy and seemed none the worse after her sleep ordeal and birthing two babies.

Taylith raised his glass of wine. "To the queen!"

All joined in. Then another toast. "To Prince Eliya and Princess Aylie. May the gods and goddesses bless them," Ciara said.

"Cylena, our people are outside rejoicing and waiting. Are you up to a moment on the balcony?" Biryn asked.

"Yes, of course, just for a minute. You hold them so the people can see the twins."

Biryn, an infant in each arm, stepped out onto the balcony,

81

followed by Jason pushing Cylena in the wheelchair. A loud roar came from the crowd. Flags waved back and forth, and the bells continued their tolling.

After they let the crowd gaze at their king holding the twins for a few minutes, Jason wheeled Cylena back inside, and Biryn followed them into their bedroom.

After a little while, Biryn joined the team. Bernie raised his glass to the king. "How does it feel to be a daddy?"

"Daddy?"

"Oops. That's what little ones call their father on Earth."

"I like the sound of that better than father. What do they call a mother?" Biryn asked.

"Mommy," Erica and Julia both replied.

"I think maybe we will adopt these words. I will discuss it with Cylena. I want to thank all of you for helping to find the grimoire and the gem. I do not know what I would do without you. Bernie, maybe you would consider joining the team? Julia?"

Bernie shook his head. "Thank you, Your Majesty. I hope you won't be offended if I decline. I'm glad I was able to help, but it is not for me."

"Or me," Julia agreed. "But if you truly need my help, Your Majesty, I will not say no."

"Good enough. Again, I am truly thankful for your assistance. You are both now members of my extended family."

The bells were overpowering loud, so Aldis closed the balcony doors again. "Zohmes and Odoxon must surely have run out of tricks by now."

"Lord, let's hope so," Erica said while helping herself to bread and cheese.

"Tanoth, what about you? Would you like to become a warrior in my army?" the king asked.

"Thank you, Sire. I, too, must politely decline. I am much needed in the mines, and now upon finding these new mines with the magickal ore and unknown gems, I am going to be very busy." Tanoth held his glass up.

"Can you update me on your findings? I am curious about the ore. As for the gems, I like the name diamonds. We will add that to the Ierilian language, too. We need to keep all of what we discovered just between us. Please remember that. Not a word to anyone, family, no one. Not until the mine entrances have been unearthed and we know more." The king poured himself another glass of wine. "After we eat, I will go and lock the grimoire and the black diamond in the royal treasury. I hope we never have to use them again."

CHAPTER TEN

With the king's assistance, Bernie had managed to bring in a lot more workers for the excavation of the temple. The beautiful building was rapidly coming to life. The excess soil was taken away to get dumped far from the new town. The workers toiled from sunup to sundown to get the work done in record time, but it would take several months yet before the excavation was completed and everything restored to its former beauty.

King Biryn had told him that the temple and its buildings would be part of Initiation Genesis, that they could use it for their community center and temple. Bernie had designated the new site he'd chosen for the community center to be a theater or perhaps a youth center, and he'd already stopped construction of the church. But that was looking too far into the future. After all, when they had children, it would be many years before they entered their teens. He'd have to make that decision later. The restoration of the temple was first on the list. James van der Veen, an accountant but also an ordained minister, was ecstatic when Bernie showed him the temple.

On the other side of the mountain, Tanoth was overseeing

the unearthing of the entrances to the mines. He was in constant touch with Bernie and reported the progress. As was suspected, the ore was the same from which the four swords had been fashioned. Bernie knew no other weapon could ever hold the magic of the four swords. They had been infused with their powers by the gods and goddesses, and maybe even by I Am. Tanoth had also visited Genesis and, with permission from the king, had brought him several of the diamonds. He'd had one cut and polished. It was beautiful. Bernie had a jeweler set it in a shiny gold band that he intended to give Julia.

It had been more than a month since he had gone with the team to look for the grimoire and gem. Since then, Julia visited him almost every day, and he was getting close to taking their relationship a step further. He strongly felt she was ready. Sometimes, Jonathan accompanied her. Bernie had taken quite a liking to the young man and enjoyed his company. He was everything a man could want in a son. He chuckled. A son? He doubted Jonathan could accept him as a father figure, but they had really formed a great friendship.

Tonight, he planned to take his relationship with Julia to a new level. He'd prepared a special dinner, had set the table with candles and flowers, then placed candles everywhere in the dining room. He glanced around. He was sure it was a romantic ambiance.

That week, they had opened their grocery store. Laura's vegetables and fruits she'd seeded and planted had thrived under the Ierilian suns and in its soil. She'd harvested quite a few for new seed but was able to stock the shelves in the general store with an abundance of vegetables, tomatoes, strawberries, watermelon, cantaloupe, and many herbs and spice plants, among them garlic. Many of the other fruit trees and shrubs would take longer to bear fruit, especially the trees. But everything grew so fast on Ierilia. He wouldn't be surprised if next summer, the trees were all fully grown.

Bernie had bought all the ingredients to make his own spaghetti sauce. He'd made the pasta the day before. It was tricky, making it all by hand, but he'd managed. The meat was also a challenge. Without a grinder, he'd cut very thin slices, then began chopping like crazy, until what he had looked close to ground beef.

"Holy fuck! If my nose is correct, I smell spaghetti! Real spaghetti!"

Bernie swiveled to face her. He'd not heard her come in. "Julia, you startled me. You're early. I wanted to surprise you."

"Well, surprise me you have. If what you're cooking is for real, man…I'm not leaving. I'll move in permanently!"

He smiled. "Our grocery store opened a few days ago. Your sister's hard work is paying off. With the help of all the seeds NASA sent along with us, we now have Earth vegetables and fruits. Among them were true potato seeds. I can't wait for Laura to harvest our first potatoes."

"I love Ierilian food, but I can't wait to taste real Earth food."

Bernie poured her a glass of red wine. "Come out to the balcony. It's a little early for dinner. The suns setting over the ocean is a sight to behold."

Julia took the offered glass and reached out to take his free hand. Together, they went to the living room and out onto the balcony. Bernie placed his free arm around Julia's shoulders and loved the way she leaned against him.

"You weren't kidding. Look at that colorful sky and the reflections on the water. It's breathtaking." She sighed.

"It is. And how romantic is this, watching this glorious

sunset and drinking a glass of wine." She didn't answer, but neither did she pull away. For a moment he could have bitten off his tongue. *Don't rush it, Bernie.*

"Oh, look! I see several boats."

"Maybe they're fishing boats? They have sails. Again, it's astonishing with all their modern technology how much of their methods are medieval."

"You know something? I hope they never change. I don't want any of Earth's bad influences to taint this gorgeous planet and its people. Many of their customs may be historical to us, but hell…whatever they're doing, it works."

Bernie pulled her a little closer. "Yes. Except for the fallen god and the evil sorcerer, Ierilia's gods weeded out the troublemakers centuries ago."

"Dealing with Zohmes and Doxie is bad enough. Hopefully, one day in the future, they can best those two. For now, they've been quiet for a while. Everything has been peaceful since Cylena woke and had the twins. Oh…they're so beautiful. They're starting to smile now. Eliya is still way bigger than his sister and resembles Biryn. And Aylie looks a lot like her grandmother, Hirsuta."

Bernie looked down at her and saw sadness cloud her face. "You're thinking about what you missed with Jonathan."

"Yes. The images I was given are in my mind, but it's not like experiencing it in real life."

"Honey, you're young. You can have more babies. But I need to finish cooking dinner."

Bernie began to make the spaghetti sauce while Julia sat on a stool at the center island chatting.

"Hey, something new I can tell you. Tanoth was sent on a geological mission to the area where the Initiation Two crashed, to test the soil. Guess what! He found another survivor. She'd been there for months."

He diverted his attention back to Julia for a moment. "I think I met her briefly yesterday morning with Tanoth. They visited the temple and market. Then they left to spend the day and night at the beach. I don't remember her being part of the relocation program though she looked vaguely familiar." He frowned. "She would have been rejected because of her age."

"She is Hannah's little sister, Isabella. She was too young to apply, barely fifteen when Hannah put in her application. And this is the shocker. She was a stowaway."

"Good God! How is that even possible?"

Julia told him the whole story. "Travis lives in Genesis now. You can get more details from him since he was part of plotting it all."

"Master thief, huh?" Bernie joked.

"Yes. That's how she survived. The king demanded to meet her. Izzy was terrified, of course, thinking she'd get sent to the gallows or something."

Bernie began to fry the meat and added his spaghetti to the pot of boiling water. "And?"

"The king meted out his punishment. When he heard that she'd taken a course in childcare, he hired her to assist Cylena with the twins. She's their nanny now."

Bernie chuckled. "Hardly a punishment. I recall meeting Isabella briefly once on Earth. That's probably why she struck a chord in my mind. At the time, she was just a kid, about sixteen or so. How old is she now?"

"She's eighteen, going on nineteen."

"Think what a great movie that would make on Earth." Bernie strained the spaghetti and brought the plates to the dining table. He returned to fetch the bowl with the sauce and a bowl of salad he'd made. "Come, milady. Allow me to escort you to dinner."

Julia giggled and took his arm. "Well, I'm hungry enough

to eat a horse, and then some. Wow, you even made garlic bread!"

She hadn't been kidding. When they finished eating, there was no spaghetti, sauce, or garlic bread left, and the salad was almost gone. Bernie picked up the dirty dishes. "I'll be back shortly with dessert."

"Oh, wow. Dessert, too? I'm stuffed."

"I think you'll want to eat *this* dessert."

Julia exclaimed when he set the bowl of lush red strawberries topped with whipping cream in front of her.

"Strawberries? For real?"

"Yes, honey. Like I told you, your sister has been busy in between her excursions and over the last weeks."

Julia picked up her bowl and peeked over the rim. "Is it rude to lick my bowl?"

Bernie burst out laughing. "Go right ahead. Don't forget, there is plenty more where this came from. Our people are having a ball buying at the grocery store." He filled her glass with wine. "Now to retire to the living room. The dishes can wait until tomorrow."

"I don't know how you did it all, but man alive, I'm stuffed." Julia rubbed her stomach.

"It took some imagination, seeing I don't have a pasta maker or a meat grinder. Those are something I need to look into getting designed and made."

They went to the living room and sat together on the couch, looking out of the open doors at the moons and the starry sky. "Isn't Polarium gorgeous?" Julia commented.

"Yes, and to know its rays are magical makes it really special."

"Apparently Isabella received much comfort from the star. I wonder if that's where all the gods and goddesses live."

"Maybe." He pulled her against him. "Julia?"

"Yes?"

"We've spent a lot of time together. Do you feel the chemistry between us?" Bernie asked softly.

"Yes," she whispered.

He set his glass on the coffee table, then took her glass from her fingers and set it beside it. He turned to her and took her into his arms. Tilting her head back, he looked into her eyes. "I've steadily been falling head over heels in love with you. I didn't want to rush you after John, and—"

"Just shut the fuck up, Bernie."

For a moment, her words took him aback, but when she placed her lips on his, he could hardly believe it. Was it the dinner? The wine? Pushing those thoughts to the back of his mind, he returned the kiss and tasted the sweet nectar of her mouth, her lips, her tongue as she explored the deepest recesses of his mouth. She suddenly drew away.

"Bernie, you've suffered your own losses. We both have," she whispered against his lips. "I've fallen in love with you, too."

"I didn't dare hope...I..."

"Hush. Just love me," she said in a husky tone.

He got up off the couch and, pulling her to her feet, scooped her into his arms. He carried her to his bedroom and deposited her on the bed, then quickly took off his shirt and pants. She had already taken her clothing off. He lay beside her and gazed down at her body. "You're so beautiful," he murmured.

She giggled, her eyes twinkling with mirth. "Even after bearing a child?"

"Stop it. Before we continue, I have a major question." He felt beside the bed for his pants and the pocket that held the little velvet bag. He pulled it out and brought it up to the bed. Pulling open the string, he took out the ring and held it in front of her face. "Will you marry me, Julia?"

Her hand flew to her mouth, and she gasped. "Is that…is that a real…"

"Diamond? Yes. From the mines we discovered. Tanoth had it specially cut and polished for me, and I had a jeweler in Cront set it in a gold band."

"Bernie…I…I…don't know what to…say…"

"*Yes* would be good enough."

"Yes, oh yes, I will, but I never expected a ring fit for a queen. Holy shit, it must be at least four carat." She quickly kissed him on the lips, then held her hand out to him. "Put it on."

He slipped the ring onto her finger and lifted her hand to his face. He kissed each of her fingers, her hand, up her arm, to her neck. Finally, he whispered against her lips, "You have made me —"

She kissed him. Hard. Her fingers tangled in his hair, pulling him closer. He broke their kiss and gazed down at her. She was exquisite. Her long, golden hair was splayed around her head like a halo, her creamy skin flushed with passion. He traced a finger from her luscious lips, down her neck and chest, and stopped to tease a hard nipple. A sharp pulse of need burned through his veins straight to his cock. He bent his head and sucked the tempting little morsel into his mouth, his other hand teasing the nipple of her neglected breast. She moaned and arched against him, her hips brushing against his aching erection.

He pushed up and heaved himself over her and off the bed. "I'll be back in a minute."

"Why? Where are you going?"

"Just wait." He sent her a grin and left the room. He wanted this night to be perfect, one she'd remember always. Once downstairs, he grabbed candles, put them in a bag. He ran to the kitchen and got the bowl of whipping cream and the strawberries. He also tucked a bottle of chairi wine under his arm. Last, he put two glasses in the bag.

He glanced at her when he got back to the bedroom. She lay curled up on her side. For a moment he was afraid she'd fallen asleep, but when she heard him, she rolled onto her back and gazed at him.

"What is all that stuff? I thought for a minute you'd gone to get some condoms, but that looks too bulky for those."

Bernie chuckled. "Condoms? Do we need those? Unless you're afraid you'll get pregnant right away. I do have some." He set the candles in various places in the bedroom and lit them. Then he took his other loot back to the bed and set the wine on the bedside table, along with the two bowls. He clapped his hands, and the lights turned off.

"Wow, you did think of all kind of modern conveniences," she murmured and accepted the glass of wine he'd poured.

"To us." He clinked his glass against hers and, linking his arm through hers, sipped.

"To us and our future together," she said softly before drinking from her glass.

The soft flickering of the candles' flames set the romantic atmosphere in the room, their scents permeating the air around them.

Bernie took the empty glass from her and set both glasses on the bedside table. He took a lush, big, ripe strawberry out of the bowl. He bit the top off, spit it out, then crushed the berry. He painted her nipples with its juices, spread it down her belly to her clit. When he'd coated her swollen netherlips with more strawberry, he reached and took the bowl of whipping cream in his hand. With his other, he slathered the sweet delicacy all over her breasts, her stomach, her belly, her clit, and between her folds.

She'd lain very still while he was busy, but he heard her draw in her breath several times, especially when he touched her between her legs. He set the empty bowl on the bedside table and leaned over her. "Ready, my love?"

"I was fucking ready half an hour ago." She moaned and squirmed. "I've read this stuff in old romance novels, but I never — "

He kissed her long and hard, his tongue dancing with hers, exploring every sweet crevice of her mouth. He kissed her chin, down her neck, and slowly to each breast, where he licked the cream and strawberry juices off, then sucked her nipples into hard pebbles.

He continued down her stomach, her navel, kissing her down to her clit. She moaned hard when he sucked the cream and strawberry off and ran his tongue around the throbbing little nub. Her legs parted further, her hips raising up, opening her folds to his gaze. He lifted his head for a moment, taking in the soft pink flesh, then crashed his lips down and licked her clean from top to bottom.

"My God, Bernie, you're killing me. Take me! I can't stand it anymore! Put that gorgeous cock of yours inside me!"

Teasing her until she lay writhing, he entered a finger, and another, his thumb on her throbbing clit, while he watched her face, her sparkling, hungry eyes.

He could hardly contain his own lust. It was time, or he'd explode all over her. Kneeling between her spread legs, he placed the tip of his cock at her entrance and pushed. Slowly at first... He continued to inch in until she raised her hips and he was buried within her completely. He felt her walls close around him, holding him tight. She wound her legs around his waist and pushed up.

Leaning on his hands, he gazed down at her and began to thrust.

"Fuck! Yes…oooooh, yes… I love you! Fuck me hard, lover. Harder…"

It had been too long for him. He was ready to burst. Tremors shook him as he felt imminent release building up. She moaned and writhed beneath him.

"I'm coming…I am…Bernie… Yes! Yes! Yes!" she shouted as they came at the same time.

A last few strokes and he collapsed on top of her. With his head beside hers, he lay quiet for a few minutes, catching his breath. After his heart had stopped pounding, he lifted his head and looked down into her eyes. "I love you, my darling. I never knew it could be this good…"

A fleeting moment of pain attacked his heart because it almost felt like a betrayal of his wife, whom he'd loved so much. But he had to be honest. Sex between them had never been like this.

"Neither did I," Julia whispered near his ear. "I bet the sheets are a mess."

They stayed up half the night, showered, and made love again—this time without fruit and whipping cream. They talked, planning their wedding, which Julia wanted to be held in the temple, until they drifted off.

CHAPTER ELEVEN

Bernie startled awake. He looked at the time. "Fuck! My crews will wonder where the hell I am. I'm never late," he muttered, waking Julia.

"And I'm supposed to be at work. Did I tell you that I am back to my job at the science center?"

Bernie looked around on his way to the shower. "No, you didn't. We'd both better get cracking."

"The dishes—"

"Can wait. I won't be long." Bernie entered the bathroom. Just as he placed his communicator on the vanity, it went off. He read the text message.

Grimoire and black diamond are in Zohmes and Odoxon's hands. Meeting at the palace at lunch.

"How the hell did that happen?" he muttered while showering. "The king said they'd be in a safe place where no one could get to them. Why do they need me?"

The message had clouded his happiness. Julia slipped into the shower as soon as he stepped out. He wanted nothing more than to get back under the steady stream of water with her and take her into his arms, but not now. They didn't have time. He noticed she looked disappointed when he continued to dry himself.

He dressed hurriedly. Julia joined him soon after. "What's wrong, honey? I know something is bothering you. I can see it on your face and in your eyes."

He combed his long hair, then turned to her. "Nothing for you to be concerned about, sweetheart. I'm just annoyed that I'm late for work."

"Oh, okay. Do you have time to take me to the science building? I'll probably get shit, too, for being late."

"Yes, but first I have to give my crews instructions. Just wait for me on the landing pad near my flyer. I won't be long." Bernie was glad the king had gifted him with a flyer. He'd drop Julia off, then hasten to the palace. He didn't want to trouble Julia with what he'd just learned.

"Hey, before you go, when I told you about Isabella, there was more to her story, but you didn't let me finish. The grimoire and black diamond were stolen by Zohmes and his accomplice. I bet the king and the team are off on another mission soon," Julia called out just as he was about to step out of the front doors.

They had sent her the message, too? He didn't answer her and hurried to meet with his foreman.

Jim met him at the temple's site. "I'm not used to you being late. Are you okay?"

"Yes, had a late night. Okay, most of the temple has been dug out now. I think we can get cleaning crews in there. Get the men to start excavating beyond the temple. I have a meeting with the king I need to attend. I'll be back this afternoon," he told Jim.

Bernie joined Julia at the landing pad and smiled. Even though Zohmes and Odoxon had stolen the grimoire and black diamond, he couldn't help the happiness that filled his heart. The woman he had at first thought he had no chance of a future with had agreed to marry him.

She gazed up at him with those sparkling blue eyes and returned his smile. Damn, she was beautiful—and she was his. He wanted to shout it from the rooftops. He tilted her chin and gave her a quick kiss. "Are you ready, sweetheart?"

She playfully nipped his bottom lip. "I'd much rather curl back up in bed with you, but I guess we'd better get moving. I'm late as it is."

He pulled her into his arms, kissed her soundly, then released her reluctantly. "So would I, but can't keep the king waiting." Strange. She knew about the theft of the grimoire and the black diamond, but she didn't mention anything about the meeting. Maybe she hadn't received the same message.

He opened the flyer door and boarded behind her, seating himself at the console and punching in the coordinates for the science building in Cront.

Once the flyer was in the air, he directed his attention to her. "How did you know that Zohmes and Odoxon stole the grimoire and black diamond?"

"Zohmes possessed Isabella and made her steal them," she said vehemently. "I was at the palace when they brought her and Tanoth back from their trial by fire for taking the grimoire and gem."

Bernie was shocked. All of them had been told by Erica exactly what a trial by fire entailed. "You didn't tell me that. Trial by fire? But they weren't hurt?"

She shook her head. "Thank God, they weren't. The trial by fire will only hurt the guilty. Isabella was shaken up, of course, but she went through it bravely. Damn, I would have been terrified beyond words. I imagine the king will fill you in when you get to the palace."

Too soon, Bernie caught sight of the science building. After adjusting the controls, he landed the flyer. "Can I pick you up tonight?"

She grinned. "I'd like that. I'll message you when I get done with my shift."

After Julia was safe on the grounds of the science building, Bernie made his way to the palace. It didn't take long. Transport here was so much easier than driving in the heavy traffic he was used to on Earth. He hadn't lived far from the training center, so most of the time he'd either walked or ridden his bike. He'd rarely used the old clunker inherited from his father, and gas was so expensive. When he reached the palace, he landed in the courtyard and exited the flyer.

The guards at the palace entrance waved him through, but to his surprise, the king's personal aide, Dunmore, waited for him in the grand foyer. It was a good thing, too. Bernie had no idea where this lunch meeting was taking place. He had visited the palace on several occasions, a couple of times for the wedding celebrations, but more so after he'd become ruler of Initiation Genesis. Those meetings were held in the king's private office in the throne room.

"Good afternoon, Lord Henderson. I will escort you to the king's quarters. He is expecting you."

"Thank you, Dunmore."

Dunmore led Bernie through a series of halls and up two flights of stairs. He stopped at a large ornately carved door, opened it, and motioned for him to enter.

"Please join the team in the sitting area. His Majesty will join you shortly."

Bernie entered the sitting area. The balcony doors were opened wide, letting the sweet-perfumed air in from the gardens below.

"Afternoon, everyone."

Erica was seated near the balcony doors beside her mate, Laro. "Hi, Bernie. How is the excavation going?"

"Things are progressing much faster than we anticipated. We are sending cleaning crews into the temple today, and the excavation teams have begun digging beyond the temple."

"We can hear about the excavation later. I want to know how your date went. Did Julia like the surprise dinner you cooked?" Laura sat forward in her chair, an eager expression on her face.

Julia and Laura looked a lot alike, though Julia's hair was more of a honey blonde and her eyes were a brilliant blue instead of green and Laura was slightly taller.

Bernie shook his head and grinned. "You will have to ask your sister when she gets off work." He was sure Julia would want to tell Laura herself about their engagement.

He turned when an interior door opened in the chambers. Biryn and Cylena, holding hands, entered.

Biryn looked very much the proud new father as he grinned broadly. "The twins are now sleeping soundly." He turned his attention to Dunmore. "I see everyone is here. Please call down and have lunch served."

They seated themselves at the king's dining table. Bernie felt kind of lost without Julia by his side, and for the life of him, he couldn't figure out why he should be present for such an important meeting.

While Brenn introduced the members of the team he hadn't yet met, Dunmore poured glasses of wine and served them to everyone, except for Cylena. He placed a glass of milk in front of her along with a cup of hot tea.

Biryn took a sip of his wine. "Bernie, as you now know, the grimoire and black diamond are in the hands of Zohmes and Odoxon. Because you assisted us in retrieving them, Initiation Genesis and your people may now become targets of Zohmes and Odoxon's wrath."

So that's why he'd been summoned. That was all his

people needed—a bullseye on their back because he had angered the crazies. "Julia mentioned that Isabella was involved, but she didn't give me any of the details. What happened?"

Bernie listened in shock when Biryn and the others explained what had happened to Isabella and how Zohmes got his hands on the book and gem. Neither the girl nor Tanoth had breathed a word of it when they had arrived at Initiation Genesis, and he had shown them around. All Tanoth had said was he was under royal command to show Isabella around Ierilia for the week.

"That poor kid." He caught Biryn's gaze. "But a trial by fire? Wasn't that a little extreme? Was there no other way?"

Biryn took a deep breath and set his wineglass on the table. "No, there wasn't. We had to know the absolute truth, and the evidence against her was more than incriminating."

"Isabella will be fine. She isn't a child. She proved that by surviving all those months on her own. What I am more worried about is what the hell are we going to do about the grimoire and the black diamond," Laura stated.

"Zohmes will not let the grimoire and gem out of his sight. We would do better preparing ourselves for the havoc he will wreak. The spells within the book will give him the ability to recreate his army tenfold, and with the black diamond? They could become invincible," Astiana warned.

Ciara set her glass on the table. "Rania has not spoken to me. I have asked her, but she said she could not help us at this point. The goddess did say we have to address another matter. We need to take Hirsuta to the Clyss so she will once again be the powerful sorceress she once was. This must be done before the team searches for the grimoire and black gem."

Bernie ran his fingers through his hair. "I still don't know why I'm here. I'm not part of the team and have no magical skills or anything. I would be of no use on such a mission. I'd be more of a hindrance."

Cewrick frowned. "You are the ruler of your people now, Bernie. You heard what the king said. Zohmes and Odoxon will have marked Initiation Genesis. You do not want to defend your new realm?"

"Of course. I was trained in all manners of warfare, but with so many on the team with magical abilities, I don't think I could contribute much." Bernie emptied his wineglass in one gulp.

Brenn's communicator buzzed. "A text message from the science center." He scanned the message, then furrowed his brow. "Several people watched as Julia disappeared in a vortex of smoke and flames."

Jonathan jumped off his chair, knocking it to the floor. "Again? What the fuck does the idiot want with my mother now?"

Bernie felt the blood drain from his face. He held the edge of the table to steady the dizzy spell that attacked him. *Julia? His Julia?*

Cewrick answered. "He wants you, Jonathan. He knows you are his son."

"So why didn't the fucktard take me?" Jonathan shouted.

Astiana stood and placed her hand on Jonathan's forehead. Her touch calmed him, and he picked up his chair and sat. "You are gifted. Your magick is as powerful as Zohmes' and even more so. He cannot possess you."

"So now we have a grimoire and black diamond to get back, but more important, my mother. Ciara, can you try to talk to Rania? Please?" Jonathan begged.

Bernie finally pulled himself together. He pushed his plate away. There was no way he could finish the food now. His

Julia, his bride-to-be, suddenly gone. They'd been so happy, only to have it come crashing down around their ears. "I will assist you in whatever way I can," he said loudly. "There is no way in fucking hell that asshole is going to take away my fiancée!"

Laura smiled grimly. "I knew it. I had a gut feeling. When did this happen?"

"Last night. She said yes and wears my ring. I left it for Julia to tell you," Bernie said softly.

"When is the wedding?"

"When the temple's restoration is finished. She wants to get married in our new church." Bernie gladly accepted the wine Dunmore poured for him.

"We need to wipe the spectators' memories," Astiana said.

"Yes. I will go to the science building with Ciara to question them. Ciara will attend to their memories," Brenn said.

Aldis set his fork on his plate. "We need to rescue Julia first and then worry about the grimoire and black gem."

"Where could he have taken her?" Jonathan wondered. "We know of many of his temples now."

Liana, who had not uttered a word and just quietly consumed her lunch, now spoke. "Ciara or I can talk to Rania. Rania communicates with me, too. The goddess can guide us. Maybe Taylith, Ciara, and I can scout the region where Zohmes has taken Julia."

Cylena sighed. "It is time to feed the twins. I wish I could help, but I guess I am not allowed on missions from now on."

Biryn grasped her hand. "No, my queen. You will stay by the side of the prince and princess."

"Taylith and I will call on our friends to guard the queen and the twins while we are away." Liana held her glass up for more wine.

No one had noticed Ciara slip away. She returned and sat. "Rania spoke to me. Zohmes and Odoxon have placed Julia into the forever slumber, knowing her son will not stop until he finds her. The grimoire and the black diamond will not be far from her, but they are not on Ierilia."

"What is that supposed to mean?" Biryn demanded to know.

"That is all the goddess told me, and all she is allowed to reveal." Ciara sipped from her glass. "First, we must take Hirsuta to the Clyss. The team must be present for this."

"So that goddamn devil has put the same spell on my mother as he placed on the queen? I'll kill the bastard. I swear on all I hold dear, he's history!" Jonathan shouted.

Ivran finally said something. "I do not think I am needed on this mission. I truly need to spend some time with my mate and my child."

"Rania told me the whole team needs to go. That means you, too, Ivran," Ciara told him.

Laro sighed. "I was just thinking the same, but I got my answer."

"The only person exempt is the queen. All must go. Rania said it was important. You each have your own magick and gifts." Ciara sank to her chair.

Aldis put his datapad on the table. "Did Rania give any other specifics?"

"No. Oh, yes, sorry. She mentioned Lord Cidus."

"Why would she mention Cidus?" Brenn queried.

"He is in league with Zohmes. Maybe he has information for us? Or his son? Perhaps we should pay a visit to Wildevein first and talk to Evior," Aldis suggested.

Biryn hit the table with his fist. "It is decided. We leave at sunup for the Clyss. Then from there, we go to Wildevein. We will meet here at the palace."

Bernie left the palace and flew home. His house suddenly felt very empty. Julia was supposed to come over again that evening, and he'd looked forward to cooking a special dinner for her using their new Earth vegetables. He sighed, his heart aching for what she was going through. What had already happened to her was bad enough, then to suddenly have a grown son, but now that evil bastard was trying to get the son by taking her? It made him ill to the stomach. Was the team ever going to be able to get rid of the bastard and the sorcerer?

CHAPTER TWELVE

He got up before sunup. Bernie had packed his backpack the night before but had no idea what to take and really didn't care. All he cared about was finding Julia safe and unharmed. He decided what he'd packed would have to do. The team would help him add whatever else he needed.

While he flew to the palace, he left a message for Jim that he was going to be away for a few days. A few days? Lord, how long were the rescue and the retrieval of the grimoire and black diamond going to take? He didn't give much of an explanation, except he'd come down with a bug. After he sent the message, he chuckled. *As if…* The flu was an unknown virus on Ierilia. He was surprised Jim didn't question it. Maybe he thought his boss was suffering from a major hangover.

They'd landed on paradise. There was no flu, no cancer, no multiple sclerosis, no diseases that were rampant on Earth. Since he'd been on the planet, he hadn't even seen anyone sniffle. Except for the plague virus that Zohmes and Odoxon had gotten their hands on from one of their ships. It still angered him that the Earth government would send germ warfare secretly on one of the ships meant to save their people. And for that asshole, Barry, to give it to Zohmes and Odoxon was inconceivable.

He would have to watch Barry. The man was disgruntled at having been usurped from a position of leadership. To him, their relocation mission continued as before, but things had changed dramatically when they crash-landed on Ierilia. The last thing they needed was for the man to stoke unrest and cause a rebellion.

Bernie landed his flyer in the courtyard of the palace. The dragons and Brenn had just arrived as well. After joining them in the courtyard, they made their way to the king's rooms.

The others were already with Biryn when they entered. They were seated around the table, their packs beside them, and everyone was dressed in battle gear. He felt ill equipped in his tunic and pants with just a few survival items in his backpack.

Aldis set his datapad on the table and glanced up at Bernie. "I have requested battle gear, supplies, and weapons for you. Dunmore will escort you to a room to change."

"Thank you."

Relieved to know that Aldis had anticipated his need for the gear, Bernie followed Dunmore to one of the suites down the hall from the king's quarters. He entered, changed, then hastily returned to Biryn's rooms. Bernie joined the others. "Has anyone received any other information? Any ideas where Zohmes and Odoxon could be holding Julia?"

Ciara shook her head. "Rania has already shared what she could."

Jonathan stepped up to him and clapped him on the shoulder. "We will find my mother. You can count on that."

"I contacted Evior last night. He agreed to gather any information he could from his father before we meet today.

Hopefully, he will have the information we need." Biryn stood and grabbed his backpack. "Now that we are all here and prepared, we can move out."

Bernie had been to the Clyss on a couple of occasions for weddings. He had studied the surroundings each time he had been there, but it always looked the same. The weather never changed, though the seasons did change around it on the other side of the surrounding mountains. The planet's magic was rampant in the Clyss. He possessed none, but even he could feel the air charged with magical qualities. The valley was gorgeous, full of lush foliage and colorful flowers. Birds and small animals played in the trees and near the sparkling water. The waterfall and basin, from what he had learned, were magical.

"So, what now?"

Erica leaned against the hovercraft. "We wait here, but be prepared to be flabbergasted at what you see."

Cewrick and the other magic users escorted Hirsuta to a clearing near the pool of water. They joined hands, and Bernie could hear their chanting echoing throughout the valley.

When their god, Izarus, appeared, he struck the poor woman with lightning. Hirsuta staggered from the force of it, almost falling to the ground.

Bernie looked at the spectacle in shock. "Holy hell! Is he trying to kill her?"

Brenn chuckled. "No, just watch. She will be fine."

Laura scrunched her nose. "Lucky for me I got a shower of magical sparkles instead of the electrical shock."

"Weirdly, it doesn't hurt. It's just a little jarring," Erica piped in.

After the god vanished, Hirsuta entered the water of the basin and disappeared beneath the surface. She seemed to be immersed for an eternity. Then suddenly she popped to the surface. An aura of power surrounded her, so strong, she seemed to be surrounded by an electrical current.

They returned to the hovercraft, Hirsuta none the worse for her experience. After they loaded up and strapped in, Aldis punched the coordinates of Wildevein into the console.

Bernie peered out of the window of the hovercraft as it took off. He found it truly amazing that the Ierilians had managed to design technology and transportation that didn't pollute the air. Earth had the capability, but by the time they had chosen to implement sustainable energy, it was too late. Earth was already polluted beyond their ability to reverse it, but energy wasn't the only problem.

His thoughts turned to Julia. God, he hoped she was okay. The pain of her loss speared him straight through the heart, and with it, a burning rage boiled deep within. Somehow, he would find her, and he would make the bastards pay for hurting her.

He clenched his hands into fists and took a deep breath. "Where are we meeting Evior?"

"At the base of the Dreaded Peaks where we camped before infiltrating Zohmes' temple. Evior spends a lot of time in the forest. It will not raise Cidus' suspicions if he meets us there," Biryn said.

"If you know that Lord Cidus is in league with Zohmes, why haven't you arrested him?"

Taylith cast Bernie a dark look, his eyes changing to those of his dragon. "I would rather burn the sick bastard to a crisp for what he has done to his people...and what he was going to allow Zohmes and Odoxon to do to Zandria."

"We do not have the proof we need yet, Taylith. Even Zandria cannot tell us who abducted her." Astiana's voice held a hint of sadness.

Bernie had met Zandria through Julia and Laura. She had been to Initiation Genesis a couple of times to purchase vegetables and fruits from the grocery store. The young woman had chosen not to return to her home and was now a member of Taylith and Laura's staff at their estate. His stomach dropped as the hovercraft started a swift descent, then landed.

He studied the mountains after they exited the craft. They were foreboding. The crests rose in sharp crags and peaks, their summits hidden in a vast blanket of fog. The team had rescued Julia and Niquine from one of Zohmes' temples hidden inside the topmost peak. That was where her son Jonathan had suddenly appeared from the future.

"We need to shield the area from Zohmes' spies." Cewrick began to chant, Hirsuta joining in.

Bernie couldn't see the shield that enveloped the area, but he could feel it. The air was charged with power. It felt almost like a living, breathing entity. Would it fry a creature that tried to breach it? Like an electric fence?

At the sound of rustling leaves and vegetation, his attention turned to the forest line. A young man stepped through the trees. He couldn't have been more than twenty, maybe early twenties. Age was hard to gauge on Ierilia. His blond, curly hair brushed his shoulders, and his eyes held a pain that went well beyond his age. He was accompanied by an older woman, with waist-long, curly, flaming-red hair. The only evidence that she was older were the silver strands in her hair and the wisdom in her eyes. When he thought about it, no one on Ierilia looked over forty. He'd seen none that were stooped and wrinkled. Did people not age on this planet? The two stepped through the shield unscathed.

"Evior," Biryn called out to the young man.

"Your Majesty." Evior glanced around, a fearful look on his

face. "I do not think it is safe to talk here. Father has grown suspicious of my questions. But I am not alone. The lady with me is Tabeka. She is a seer and a healer who lives near Wildevein. Her daughter Iridia and I have been close friends since we were children. Tabeka thinks she might be able to help."

Biryn gestured at the ground near the fire they had started. "Please, sit. Join us for some nourishment."

Brenn handed them both a stick with a piece of meat on it. They had caught a nemka. Bernie thought it looked similar to a rabbit, and it tasted something like chicken. He took a drink from his wine and listened to Biryn asking questions of the two.

"Tabeka, it is nice to meet you," Biryn said. He introduced each member of the team, adding a short explanation about the people from Earth.

"Your Majesty, it is an honor to meet you. To meet all of you," she responded.

"Do you work for Lord Milhella?"

"No. Twenty-five years ago, my family cast me out and abandoned me. Cidus allowed me to live on his property for a while until I moved to a cottage on the other side of Wildevein."

Bernie noticed her answers were not given too freely. She sounded stiff and seemed hesitant to answer questions.

Biryn took a bite of his meat. "Who was your family? Where were you from?"

"Our realm is Hakania. My father is its ruler. At the time, my family was trading in Wildevein and other villages in the Sirona Realm."

"I have met Lord Quasico of the Hakania Realm. I did not know he had a daughter."

"My father ordered my name never to be spoken again. But

110

please, it is a subject that pains my heart." Tabeka's voice became soft.

"How can you help us?"

"Evior asked if I knew of another of Zohmes' temples."

Biryn threw his stick on the fire. "Pray tell me, how can you know of Zohmes' affairs?"

Tabeka shivered as if she were cold. "All that live in the Sirona Realm know of Zohmes and his wicked ways. He is a god to be feared. So many of the young women have gone missing over the years. We all know what happened to them. Thank you for saving Zandria from an equal fate. As Evior told you, I am a seer. One of my visions showed me a dark planet, one that Zohmes has transported to just beyond our atmosphere. It orbits Ierilia, but Zohmes has a shield around it so it cannot be seen by your astronomers or any of your spaceships."

Bernie drank some more of his wine. "You've got to be kidding me. A planet?"

"Hush, Bernie. Let her talk," Erica warned.

"It is a dark, foreboding planet, surrounded by gaseous rings. On it, I saw a glimpse of Zohmes' army he has created. He has many soldiers, thousands upon thousands. He built a temple on the planet within its mountains. He called the planet Zonomia."

"Figures," Bernie muttered.

Jonathan grunted. "How powerful can he be to place a planet in orbit around Ierilia and hide it?"

"Very. But your powers are much greater, Jonathan, once you know how to use them all," Astiana told him.

"Why would mine be greater? My mother is from Earth."

Astiana took a drink from the wineskin. "He is your father, even if you do not like it. You have also inherited the magick from your forefathers. When your magick comes to its full potential, it will be much more powerful."

Tabeka nodded. "I have seen you in visions, a woman by your side. In the end, you two will be the ones to defeat Zohmes and send him back to Yanata, and you will send Odoxon back to Wuits Peak. But that will be many years from now. Zohmes and Odoxon will continue to reign terror for a long time. His obsession to once again rule Ierilia consumes his brain."

"I want to kill the bastards!" Jonathan exclaimed.

"They cannot be killed," Hirsuta told him. "Zohmes must return to Yanata and be bound there for eternity and Odoxon must be sent back to his cave."

"Zohmes escaped from Yanata before. Unless the gods and goddesses know a different way of binding him there." Jonathan took a bite of his meat.

Tabeka stood. "Thank you for the food and wine. That is all I can tell you. Unless King Biryn or anyone else has more questions, we should leave, Evior."

Biryn shook his head. "I have no more questions. You have helped us tremendously, Tabeka. Thank you, and if you ever wish to move to another realm, one that is safer for you and your daughter, you are welcome in Cront."

"Iridia does not want to leave here, especially since she is close friends with Evior. But thank you for the invitation. I will pray to the gods and goddesses that your mission is a success."

Astiana nodded her head in acknowledgment, then said, "Your departure from this realm may come sooner than you think, Tabeka. We will meet again soon."

Tabeka looked at Astiana. "My daughter—"

"Will be with you."

After they had left, Aldis stood. "Biryn, we are going to need our space fleet. I will contact Admiral Maroth. We must return to the palace to get ready."

"No fucking way in hell am I getting on a spaceship into outer space!" Erica shouted. "It was terrifying enough getting on one and going how many miles beneath the surface of the ocean..."

"Or me," Laura mumbled.

CHAPTER THIRTEEN

He felt the same as Erica and Laura and wasn't happy about getting on a spaceship either. Their ship crashing on Ierilia had happened not *that* long ago. Not that any of them had experienced the actual crashes since they had been in stasis, but just the thought of getting on a spaceship again sent shivers down his spine. Bernie put on the skinsuit, then the tight spacesuit. To save Julia, he would brave anything. Even going into outer space.

They had all slept at the palace, so they could get up before sunup and begin their journey to the mysterious planet. Aldis had made all the arrangements with the admiral. A fleet of ten stealth fighters would accompany them to Zonomia.

He headed to Biryn's quarters. His night had been rife with nightmares about Julia, and he hadn't slept much, but his adrenaline was high. He couldn't rest easy until he had her in his arms again. After he knocked, Dunmore opened the door.

"Good morning, Lord Henderson."

Lord. Could he ever get used to being called that? "Morning," he replied and headed for the dining table, which was already set with a hearty breakfast. "Morning, everyone."

Not everyone had arrived yet. But heck, it was still very

early. The suns had not yet peeked over the horizon. "Aldis, have you spoken with the admiral? What is the plan? Tabeka couldn't give us coordinates, so how in the hell do we find that planet?"

Astiana chuckled. "Bernie, you forget the company you are in. You heard me tell Jonathan that his powers are greater than his father's."

Jonathan had just come in. "Don't call him my father. Please! I've asked you all so many times. Just refer to him by his name."

Biryn and Cylena were last to sit at the table. "Good morning, team. We cannot tarry too long with breakfast." Biryn looked at Astiana. "Do we know if the gem and grimoire are in the same location?"

"Biryn, I am sure Zohmes has hidden them well. Perhaps not in that temple. As I have said before, Odoxon probably knows the incantations from centuries ago. That is how he was able to bespell Cylena. But together with the black diamond, the grimoire is more than dangerous now. It contains spells that are too abominable to imagine. The gem will make those spells stronger and is often needed to undo many of them."

Bernie managed to eat a little bit. His stomach was too tied up in knots. Erica and Laura were playing with their food, too. Jonathan suddenly grasped his head. Bernie saw his eyes roll back until only the whites showed. They began to glow.

Hirsuta stood and walked to Jonathan, then placed her hand on his forehead. "He is experiencing a vision."

Bernie sighed. Sometimes the hocus-pocus just creeped him out. Right now, Jonathan resembled some kind of alien. The light coming from the whites of his eyes had turned a greenish yellow and was flaring outward.

Jonathan snapped out of it, and Hirsuta returned to her

chair. He wiped his forehead, though there wasn't a drop of perspiration on it. "Damn, that was riveting."

"Riveting? As in how?" Erica asked.

Taylith handed Jonathan a glass of eldalas spirit. "I know it is very early, but you look like you need this. Erica, when I, or they, have a vision, you are not just shown the images by I Am. They are experienced as if you are a part of them."

"Thanks. After what I just saw, yes, I can use a shot. It is quite disorienting." Jonathan took a drink from the glass, then set it on the table. "First, I saw the coordinates based on Polarium. We need to fly west of the star to the Oxinia solar system and continue on that path to the star Triola. From Triola, we fly east. I Am told me I would be able to see the planet and its gaseous rings through the shield Zohmes and Odoxon have around it."

"I have made note of this for the fleet pilot. At least we will not be flying blind," Aldis interrupted.

Jonathan continued. "I saw the planet. I thought we'd seen everything, but this place is beyond horror. We will not be able to breathe the air. The army Zohmes has amassed are indescribable creatures. They stand twice as tall as us. I saw thousands upon thousands of them."

Astiana pushed her plate away. "He has used the black diamond and one of the spells. After the war and the loss of soldiers he incurred, he could not have amassed that many in such a short time."

Hirsuta laughed sarcastically. "Who knows how long this planet has been orbiting Ierilia? He could have placed it there before his banishment to Yanata and had an army in place already."

Bernie frowned. "Then why didn't he use that army on Ierilia as well to fight his war against us?"

"Maybe the creatures can't breathe the air on Ierilia?"

Laura suggested. "Can you describe them more?"

Jonathan thought for a moment. "They sort of resemble the snopia insect, except for their size, and they walk upright."

Bernie quickly searched his datapad and found a picture. "Ants."

"Ants? Oh, yummy," Laura said. "Chocolate covered?"

Bernie laughed. He was amazed he could under the circumstances, but he imagined twelve-feet-tall ants covered in chocolate. He saw the questioning faces around the table. "We have a similar insect on Earth. In some restaurants, they deep-fry them in hot oil and cover them in chocolate. It is considered a delicacy. I've never eaten any. And they're only for the rich that can afford to go to fancy restaurants that are still open. And I wouldn't want to eat any, even if I was given the opportunity. I laughed because if these are twice the size of a man, I was imagining them deep-fried and covered in chocolate."

This caused a few giggles.

Jonathan continued. "These things have four legs and four arms, antennas on their bulbous black heads, and huge, glowing, yellow eyes. They make loud clicking noises when communicating with each other. A long stinger comes out of their egg-shaped black chest, which almost looks like it is made of leather. The stinger excretes a yellow poison. That's how they kill. They're very fast."

"So that is what we are up against." Laro pulled a face and shivered. "Sounds appetizing."

"If the air is unbreathable, we will not be able to call on our dragons," Liana said.

"Or our lions," Ivran added.

"No. You have to remain in human form, wear spacesuits, oxygen tanks, and helmets. I do not know what the atmosphere will be like in the temple. I presume it is breathable because Zohmes and Odoxon are there. We will find out when we get there." Aldis stood up, indicating it was time to head to the hovercraft and go to the ISEC, which Bernie had learned stood for Ierilian Space Exploration Center.

Bernie took a food package off the tray and quickly put it inside his pack. He wondered how long this mission would take while he slung the pack over his shoulder, his mind once again on Julia, his heart one big ache.

Bernie followed the team to the waiting spaceship. Nearby were ten stealth ships waiting to take off after them. He stood still for a moment, looking at the ship. It was quite large. It kind of resembled the SR-71 Blackbird—the most advanced plane ever built on Earth, except this ship was much bigger. Aldis had told him how it took off, and he'd watched holographs. It would feel almost like flying in a plane, except at incredible speed.

His heart thumped hard, and his stomach roiled. Visions of the ship plummeting through space and crashing on some planet filled his mind. Or worse, getting torn apart by an asteroid. Glancing at Erica and Laura, he noticed the grim expressions on their faces and knew they were feeling the same.

His feet were lead as he climbed the steps and boarded. Aldis led them to the passenger lounge. Bernie was surprised at the ultra-modern futuristic design of its interior. Large viewports were on both walls. The seats looked comfortable. Everything was sleek and streamlined. He was surprised to see a team of engineered soldiers already seated.

"Please take a seat and strap in," Aldis told them. "After we have ascended you can all unstrap and walk around. Those of you that are interested, I can take you to the bridge and introduce you to some of the crew and the captain. Below is engineering. Disaldo Que is our chief engineer. Also, there are plenty of cabins if any of you wish to rest a while. Just let me know, and I'll take you to one."

The door closed, and the ship's engines fired. Bernie closed his eyes. He hated flying in airplanes, let alone on this thing. At least on the Initiation Six, he'd been in stasis upon take-off and during the crash.

It wasn't as bad as he'd thought it would be. He felt a bit of a rush, a slight pressure to his chest, but once the ship settled, he could have just been on a cruise ship or in a hotel. The only evidence that they were in space was the black void dotted with stars he saw through the viewports.

"That didn't take long at all," Erica remarked. "I was terrified. Still am a bit."

Aldis smiled. "None of our ships have ever crashed. Our pilot is the best in the fleet. He will get us to our destination safely. You can take your safety belts off now and walk around. There are refreshments for you at the bar in the corner over there." He pointed to the far corner where a young man was busy setting snacks on the countertop.

Bernie undid his straps and stood. His legs felt wobbly, but he knew that was the fear sinking down to his feet. "How fast will we get there?" he asked, looking at Aldis.

"Hard to say. The coordinates Jonathan received from I Am were not the usual and quite vague. A day, a few days. I really cannot tell you. Jonathan will join the captain on the bridge as he will be the only one who can see through the shield hiding the planet from our view."

Cewrick and Hirsuta joined them. "I hope everyone realizes we cannot use our magick on that planet. We draw our magick from Ierilia and Polarium. The gaseous rings Jonathan described, and having to wear the monstrous suits I saw hanging on the wall upon entering, prohibit our use of magick. We will have to rely on our own resources and skills in fighting." Cewrick placed his arm around Hirsuta and pulled her against him.

"Then why did all of us have to come along?" Hirsuta asked. "I am not a skilled warrior."

"I do not know. Maybe we are able to use our magick inside Zohmes' temple," Cewrick suggested. "He must have made it livable. Also, he would not be able to use his own powers. It is unlikely he and Odoxon would reside somewhere where their magick is of no use."

"You are probably right," Icaras said.

After two days in space, Bernie was actually beginning to enjoy the trip, in as far as he could, because his worry about Julia was foremost on his mind. But he'd seen so many wondrous sights through the viewports—nebulas, star clusters, even a black hole and a comet. Objects one only saw in science fiction movies and fantasy shows on Earth, or on pictures taken by NASA robots and the Hubble. Seeing these things so close up was breathtaking.

This was their third day. The rays from Polarium were getting brighter by the minute. He knew they would change course soon and head in the direction of Zohmes' planet.

He decided to finally go to the bridge. "I'm going to the bridge. Want to come along, Erica? Laura?"

They glanced at each other, then walked toward him hesitantly. "Okay, I guess. If anything, it'll be interesting to see their technology," Erica said and looked at Laro, who joined them.

So far, they'd not been anywhere but the passenger lounge and their cabins. Bernie led the way. "How are you two feeling?" he asked.

"I'm okay now," Laura said.

"Yes. Me, too. It's not as bad as I thought it would be," Erica added.

They stepped onto the bridge. Technical equipment and electronic boards lined the walls, technicians and navigators controlling it all. The captain and his number one were seated in the center. He stood to greet them.

Like everything else on the ship, the bridge was ultra-futuristic and streamlined. Huge viewport windows from floor to ceiling took up the whole front of the bridge. Bernie walked to stand close to them but quickly stepped back. Vertigo attacked him, a feeling he'd plummet down into that black void. He quickly moved away from the viewports.

"I've seen enough," he told the others and left the bridge. He just hoped they would soon change course and arrive at their destination that day.

CHAPTER FOURTEEN

I t took almost another night and part of the next day before Jonathan came into the passenger lounge to announce that he'd seen the planet. "The captain said we should be landing in about two hours, so better sit and strap in."

As he'd predicted, the ship landed almost two hours later, on a remote spot on Zonomia in a valley surrounded by dark, craggy mountains. The sky was almost a blood-red, with purple streaks here and there, the atmosphere polluted by gases. Plumes of it shot up about forty feet high from small red and green bubbling craters on the surface.

The engineered soldiers were fast getting into their suits, but most of the team members needed help getting into their spacesuits. On Earth, they were always shown as white, but on Ierilia the material was a silver color. The boots were heavy and would keep them grounded. The helmet was last, then the tanks. The crew helped with those.

"Aldis, do we know where we're going?" Bernie asked before they placed the helmet on his head.

"Jonathan said I Am will guide him. Your fleet weapons are strapped to your wrists. Do not hesitate to shoot anything that crosses our paths. The fleet is on standby up above. At my command, they will annihilate whatever army Zohmes has here. Be sure to turn on your communicator system so we can hear and talk to each other," Aldis responded.

Bernie felt claustrophobic after the helmet snapped to the suit. The oxygen tank was rather heavy. He wondered how the women would manage. It was hard going down the stairs to the surface. He turned to assist Laura, who was behind him and struggling to move her feet.

"Damn, these things are weighed with lead," she muttered.

"To keep us grounded. Imagine floating away in this muck." Bernie chuckled when Taylith lifted her off her feet and deposited her on the ground.

Jonathan took the lead, followed by several soldiers, the other soldiers bringing up the rear. He skirted the base of a mountain and led them to a pass to the other side. Walking on the surface was tricky. Bubbling pits appeared constantly, where before there had been none. It was as if the planet sensed their presence. Or maybe Zohmes knew of their arrival and was busy producing the bubbling goo.

On the other side of the mountains was an expanse of reddish dirt and more bubbling pits. "Where is this temple?" Bernie asked. He wondered if the bubbling goo could be lava.

Jonathan pointed to a ridge of jagged mountains. "It's located within the next mountain range. We have to cross this valley first."

Aldis warned, "Be careful. Whatever it is, it appears to be boiling. We do not know what it can do to us."

They need not wonder for long. One of the soldiers stepped into a suddenly appearing pit of red liquid. He sank waist deep into it. Two of the other soldiers immediately went to his assistance and dragged him out. The bottom half of his body was gone, some of his entrails dangling from the gaping part of his upper torso.

Bernie felt sick at the sight of the soldier's mangled body. The man had not uttered a sound, but he'd learned they felt no pain. He watched as Aldis strode toward them and shot the soldier through the forehead. He turned to the team. "They feel no pain, and he would be unable to regenerate his body after this much damage," he told them.

Bernie could not quell the nausea. They were engineered, sure, they felt no pain...nevertheless, it all seemed so cruel and heartless. He didn't know much about the soldiers, only what he had seen of Dunmore, but they looked human, acted and talked like a human. What he had seen of the mangled body, even the entrails looked like human innards.

The team managed to get through the maze of bubbling pits without further incident, the men helping the women. Walking wasn't too bad now that they were on the ground, though lifting one's feet and taking one step in front of the other was still a chore.

When they finally got to the mountain ridge, Bernie looked up at the craggy, sharp peaks. Could there really be a temple located here?

Jonathan led them through the first layer of peaks to the other side. There was a narrow path winding around one of the peaks, barely wide enough for one person. He began up it, the soldiers following and the team behind them. They had to walk sideways. Bernie dared not glance down once they got up higher, until they'd shuffled along the narrow ledge for quite a while. He looked down, and vertigo attacked him again. They were up so high the ground and its pits were miniature. He stumbled. A strong arm steadied him.

"Easy there, soldier," Ivran told him.

Bernie leaned his helmet against the wall of the cliff. "Thanks."

The narrow ledge led them to a plateau. Bernie heaved a

sigh of relief when they stood on it. The cliff wall facing them was very smooth. Almost like it had been sanded. Engravings were etched into the surface, but there was no evidence of an entrance.

"This is the temple," Jonathan announced. "We need the four swords."

Erica, Biryn, Taylith, and Brenn drew their swords they'd had strapped to their spacesuits. "What do we do?" Biryn asked.

"I Am said to look for a large eye. It is the key to opening the entrance."

The four approached the wall and, after searching all the engravings, spotted the eye. The points of the swords touched, and they aimed them at the center of it. It began to glow as the swords came close. Then, suddenly, a hidden panel slid open to display a chamber.

All hurried inside. The panel closed. Lit torches in sconces illuminated the inside of the chamber. They faced another wall with similar engravings. Without waiting to be told, the four holding the swords pointed them at the wall. An eye, like the previous one, began to glow. The points of the swords touched it, and another panel opened.

After they rushed through it, the panel closed behind them. They stood in a dimly lit corridor. Aldis held his tester up. "We can breathe here. You can take off your helmets."

Bernie tried to lift his foot but couldn't. "How about our boots? I can't move. And how do we take Julia back with us? She'll need a suit."

Aldis chuckled. "We have extra suits with us, Bernie. You worry too much."

And he did. He had noticed some of the soldiers pulling a cart with them that had barely fit on the narrow ledge they'd just traversed. Aldis would know to come prepared for anything and everything.

They stripped off their interfering gear and left it near the wall in the corridor from which they'd just come.

"Do you think Zohmes knows we're here?" he asked.

Astiana answered. "Nothing seems to escape him. I am sure he knows. Be prepared."

"To save Julia, we need the grimoire and the black diamond first," he said.

"Bernie, the spell to take her out of the forever slumber we already know. We do not need the grimoire for it," Cewrick said.

"But the diamond?"

"That was mainly needed for my daughter. But we do need to retrieve it because Zohmes and Odoxon can use it to cast many evil spells when using it in combination with the grimoire's content."

They followed the corridor. It was dark, gloomy, and long. They finally came to a door. It was a dark metal, again with etchings, but it had a handle. Jonathan turned it slowly, then edged the door open.

"It looks as if this is the main part of the temple where he holds rituals and such. There is an altar. It's empty. I don't see anyone," he said.

"Almost too easy," Bernie murmured. "If he knows we're here, wouldn't he have done something by now?"

"At least we know the magic is working, Bernie. Our swords' magic worked just fine," Erica said.

"If we can lure Zohmes and Odoxon out onto the planet's surface, maybe we can get rid of them forever," Laura suggested.

"That would be just too uncomplicated, wouldn't it? So where do we find Julia?" Bernie demanded to know.

"We need to go through the temple. Behind the altar is an

entrance to his castle. My mother is inside it," Jonathan said.

"Jonathan, I will take the lead now," Brenn told him. "Do not forget, he is merely using Julia. This is a lure for Zohmes to get a hold of you. He wants his son."

Brenn took point and led them into the ritual room. An ornately carved altar built of what looked like black marble flanked the wall across from them. Blood-red candles set in carved skulls were on each side of the long altar top. A large chalice stood in the center, a dagger beside it. The dagger was silver, its hilt topped by a small skull with red glowing eyes.

On the wall behind the altar, a large red glowing oval appeared. It reminded Bernie of a portal. It was ringed with odd symbols, and the center was as red as blood. It pulsed with life, the red liquid flowing through it in swirls, like a whirlpool. Now and then it looked as if the liquid or plasma formed a face, then dispersed in an explosion and switched direction.

Bernie thought his eyes were playing tricks on him, but the shadowed image of a face appeared again. "That is ghoulish as hell."

Erica patted him on the shoulder. "You haven't seen macabre yet." Bernie cast her a sidelong glance and pointed to the weird portal. "How in the hell are we supposed to get through that?"

"It is a doorway, like the temple at Dreaded Peaks. We will have to walk through." Taylith stepped toward the swirling red mass and drew his sword. "I will take the lead."

Bernie couldn't believe when Taylith just stepped through the glowing substance and disappeared. Brenn hastily followed, then Cewrick. One by one the team vanished through it. When it was Bernie's turn, he hesitantly took one step, then two... He pushed through the portal, expecting to be covered in the bloody red gunk. All he met was a slight resistance before he joined the team in a large cavern-like room.

He glanced around looking for an exit but couldn't find one. It looked as though they were stuck unless they left the way they had entered. He turned his attention back to the entrance.

The last person to emerge from the doorway was the soldier helping with the cart of supplies. As soon as he stepped free, the red glow dissipated, and the portal disappeared.

"That's just fucking great. The bastard's trapped us here," Erica complained.

"There has to be a secret door. Maybe another portal like the one we came through?" Bernie felt along one of the walls close to him, hoping for a fissure or crack in the wall that would signify a secret door. All he felt was the smooth surface of the marble wall.

He scanned the room again. The others had joined him in his quest to find a doorway. "There is nothing here."

Astiana touched the area that had housed the portal and chanted softly. The space her hands touched began to glow softly. Symbols appeared beneath her fingertips. She ran her hand along the wall. Everywhere she touched, strange hieroglyphics became visible.

Astiana turned to the group. "It seems we are in a room with no feasible way of escape. Zohmes has bespelled it the same as he did the doors of the temple in Dreaded Peaks. No key will release us from this trap."

Jonathan leaned against the wall beside Liana. "There has to be a way out. If he placed a spell on the room, then we should be able to break the damn curse."

Bernie started forward as smoky black hands pushed through the wall on each side of Jonathan. A flame-laced fog enveloped his body, the misty hands and arms clamped tightly around him.

"Oh, fucking hell...no!" Jonathan yelled. He struggled against the apparition that held him, his body starting to sink into the wall.

"Jonathan!" Liana shoved her hands into the smoke, grabbing Jonathan by the shoulders, trying desperately to hold him in place.

Laura grabbed one of Jonathan's arms. "Let him go, you fucking bastard!"

Bernie grabbed Jonathan's other arm to help Laura, but even using all their strength, it was hopeless. The power pulling him into the wall was too great.

Cewrick pointed his staff at Jonathan and began to chant. The crystal at the top flared to life, glowing brightly in the dimly lit room. Ciara, Taylith, Hirsuta, Biryn, Icaras, and Astiana joined in the chant while Laura and Bernie helped Liana fight to keep Jonathan in place. It was no use. The smoky substance thickened, flames shooting from it, so hot, Bernie was sure his face was blistered and every hair on his head gone. Sinister laughter echoed around them as the specter yanked Jonathan completely through the wall.

Bernie was in shock at what he had just experienced. How in the hell could he, a man from Earth, without any type of magical power, hope to fight and win against a sorcerer and a god? If Zohmes and Odoxon retaliated against Initiation Genesis and his people, he had no hope of protecting them on his own...or Julia. And now the Ierilian Satan had her son. He glanced around the room. The whole team looked shaken by what had just transpired.

Laura's face was pale, and she leaned against Taylith. "Where the hell did he take my nephew?"

Liana stood beside them, a thunderous expression on her

face. She held Laura's hand for a moment. "Do not worry, little sister, we will find Jonathan and Julia."

"Come, we must try to break the containment spell." Hirsuta took Cewrick's hand.

Bernie watched as the other magic users joined them and clasped hands. The murmur of a spell in multiple voices filled the room, growing faster in cadence and louder in volume. The hidden symbols etched on the walls and the ceiling above began to glow, the room illuminating in an eerie greenish light. A breeze began to whip around them, growing stronger as the chanting voices grew louder.

Suddenly, the floor began to rumble and shake, causing Bernie to lose his footing. His knees hit the ground hard. Sharp steel rods thrust through the floor, surrounding him completely. The bars curved and bent, closing at the top. A chain clanked loudly, and the ground rolled and shuddered, then the cage lifted.

Erica helped him to his feet. "I really hate those gut sucking intestinal parasites! Is there a better word for hate? I detest the bastards! Loathe them."

Bernie noticed Ivran and Laro were trapped along with them. The lions tried to squeeze their big bodies between the bars. But they were too close together. Even Erica, as small as she was, couldn't fit through. The sound of chains rattling, the echoing of metal clanking against metal throughout the cavernous room was deafening. The cage rose higher and higher. When the clinking of the chains ceased, all Bernie could hear was the psychotic laughter of their jailer.

Bernie peered through the bars. The cage they were trapped in hung high from the vaulted ceiling, the floor at least forty feet below. Other cages hung in varying degrees around them. The whole team was effectively contained like a bunch of parakeets. "Now I know what a bird feels like.

Anyone want to begin chirping?"

"Is everyone okay?" Aldis called out.

Bernie was relieved when he heard everyone acknowledge Aldis' question. So much had happened in a very short time. First Jonathan disappearing, then the interruption of the spell with the entrapment of them in the cages.

The cage began to pitch side to side, swinging hard. The rumble of rock scraping together resounded from below. Bernie grabbed hold of the bars and looked down. The floor opened to reveal a bubbling pit of what looked like red lava, the same substance that had eaten away the bottom half of one of their soldiers. Once the slabs of rock stopped moving, the medieval birdcages slowed their momentum, coming to a standstill.

Erica peered through the bars. "We really pissed off the crazies."

CHAPTER FIFTEEN

Bernie sat on the metal floor of the cage. They had been
stuck for what seemed like hours. No matter what spell
the magic users had tried, nothing worked. He wiped
his brow with his sleeve. Though the room was huge, it had
turned extremely hot. Even the skinsuit didn't help. The
boiling pit below them acted like the hot coals in a sauna.
Bernie took a deep drink from his waterskin. "We can't just
sit here. We need to figure a way to get out of these damn
cages."

"What the hell else can we do? Bend the bars? They won't
budge." Erica flopped down beside Laro.

Ivran ran his hand along one of the metals bars. "Wait...
Bending the bars might work."

"And just how in the hell are we going to do that?" Erica
gave Ivran a sidelong glance. "Besides, have you seen what is
bubbling below us, waiting to eat the flesh off our bones?"

"We have magick users. Maybe they can shield us from the
pit below." Laro peered through the bars.

Bernie shook his head. "You do realize that is one hell of a
drop, even if we could escape this cage. And Erica is right.
We'd fall right into that stuff and get eaten alive."

Erica snapped her fingers. "Oh! Remember Dreaded Peaks! The magic users kept Ciara and Taylith in the air while they shifted so they wouldn't hit those damn spikes."

Erica screamed when the cage abruptly dropped several feet and swung back and forth sharply. Then the momentum slowed. The loud clank of large chain links scraping against metal gears resounded in the cavernous room. Bernie jumped to his feet, his heart pounding in his chest. The bastard was going to lower them into the acid lava in the pit.

"Okay...this shit is about to piss me the hell off!" Erica gripped the bars of the cage.

Bernie managed a sarcastic chuckle. "As if you weren't pissed off already?" He heard the others talking in their cages, but they hung too far apart to understand what they were saying. He hoped someone would come up with a solution. Fast! He heard Astiana now chanting loudly.

Their descent stopped abruptly, and a blinding light so intense it rivaled the suns filled the room. Bernie shielded his eyes to try to see what was happening. The glowing symbols etched into the ceiling and walls seemed to burn away to ash, and a great flaming thin rod carved new ones. He recognized the symbols. They were the same that he had seen carved into the doorframes at the underground temple.

Wind whipped around the room, turning into a whirlwind, the breeze twisting and turning, gaining speed and velocity. Suddenly, Bernie felt as if he were sucked into a vacuum. His vision blurred, and dizziness overtook him. He thought he would pass out.

Maybe he did. The next thing he knew, he was sitting on a solid rock floor.

"Sound off! Is everyone fine?" Brenn called out. "Biryn?"

Murmurs of assent filled the room as each team member replied.

"Well, that was fucking awesome," Erica said in a sarcastic tone while rubbing her behind. "Maybe next time have some pillows catch us?"

Bernie rubbed his eyes to clear his vision and studied his surroundings. They were no longer caged. They were still in that cavernous room, but everyone was free. The pit beneath them was hidden again by the floor, and the walls and ceiling were covered in glowing blue glyphs. "What the bloody hell just happened?" Laura inquired.

"I Am has chosen to aide us," Astiana stated. "He has shown me the way out."

Bernie's gaze trained on Astiana. The goddess stood in the center of the room, her arms straight down by her side, and she was looking up at the ceiling. A whisper of a chant spilled from her lips. Her long, blonde hair whipped around her face, and sparks of light rained down upon her. She looked forward, her eyes illuminated by an unearthly light. She raised her arms in front of her and clasped her hands together briefly, then pointed to a section of the wall. Lightning flew from her fingers, striking the wall before her, and a doorway appeared.

Relief filled Bernie when the door slid open. "About damn time. We need to get the hell out of here and find Julia and Jonathan."

He grabbed his pack, slung it over his shoulder, and headed for the door. A hand grasped his shoulder.

"I will take the lead with Astiana and Hirsuta. We do not know what kind of traps Zohmes and Odoxon may have planned for us." Cewrick held his staff in his hand. The crystal emitted a shimmering light even though it didn't seem as if the sorcerer was casting a spell. "Biryn, stay close to Hirsuta and me. It appears Zohmes right now is only interested in his son, but I would not find it strange if he attempts to attack you, too. I think in the future it would be best if you let us handle these missions. We must protect the crown at all cost."

"My challenges are far from over, Cewrick. Each mission is yet another test of my endurance and ability to rule Ierilia. I would like nothing more than to live a peaceful existence with my beloved and raising the twins."

"I hope to God it's the last expedition I'll ever be on," Bernie muttered. "Now where do we go from here?"

Astiana turned to face them. "Beyond this doorway lies the castle Zohmes has created on this planet. Our magick is alive and well within this mountain range. Bernie, I Am has granted you limited power. You are able to shield your body if you concentrate, just like the other people from Earth. I Am showed me the castle. This mountain range is hollow. There was some kind of structure here previously. I Am did not dwell much on that, but if there was, it means the planet was once habitable. Zohmes created the mountain range around the structure, then changed it and the atmosphere to suit his foul taste and needs. We must tread carefully. Zohmes will have guards stationed throughout. He must know by now that his plan to bury us in the pit of flesh-eating liquid failed. He will be furious."

"What other joyous treats does he have in store for us?" Bernie uttered.

After they had stepped through the door, Bernie was sure he had walked into a different dimension. The interior was state-of-the-art design, futuristic, gorgeous in a macabre way. The walls and decorations were all in black, red, and gold. The furniture was black. He could hardly imagine Satan living in such a place. Then again, what normal person would want to live in a black-and-red environment? Or was it all an illusion to fool them?

They followed a corridor. Most of the doors were open,

showing them comfortable rooms. They appeared empty. Why would Zohmes create such a castle and have no one in it?

None of it made sense. To escape the horrors he'd just experienced, to this? "Is this real, Astiana?" he called out.

"Do not believe anything you see. Like you, I believe this could all be an illusion," she called back.

Bernie could hardly believe he'd been so happy just days before. He could still feel Julia in his arms, smell her sweet scent, hear her voice. *Hang in there, honey. We are coming.*

The corridor seemed endless. Finally, Cewrick called to them to stop. "We have come to a door. Let me open it first to see what lies waiting for us beyond."

It was nothing detrimental. Once they all stepped through the door, they stood in a huge greenhouse. Vegetables, plants, and fruit trees were scattered throughout. They noticed young women kneeling to weed the vegetable beds. "Damn, do a god and a sorcerer even need food?" Bernie questioned. "Or is this just another illusion? And the people I see working here look normal. Kidnapped from Ierilia? They don't look unhappy."

Astiana answered. "They are probably under a spell. We do not know who all Zohmes has imprisoned on this planet. He may not need sustenance, but his prisoners do. It could be real."

Bernie plucked off a fruit that he recognized and bit into it. "Tastes real." He wiped the juices off his chin.

Hirsuta admonished him. "Bernie, you just played with your life. Things may look real but could be an illusion to fool us. Do not touch, eat, or drink anything. Much of this food could be authentic, but do not forget, Odoxon or Zohmes can make anything appear in less than a second and it could be poisoned."

"Sorry. It looked like a fruit from Ierilia I've eaten before. Didn't hurt me. So far, I'm fine." The greenhouse was very large. It amazed Bernie that the god would have created this, but who knew how many unfortunate souls Zohmes had kidnapped to work for him.

At the end of the greenhouse was a double glass door. Cewrick opened it to show them another shorter corridor. "How long do you think Zohmes has had this temple? When did he transport the planet?"

"All we know is what Tabeka told us of her vision. Looking at the vegetation in the greenhouse, it must have been here a while," Biryn answered.

"Where would he have found time, though? He occupied Cewrick's body for centuries."

Hirsuta turned to answer him. "At night, while Cewrick slept, Zohmes was able to leave the host. He had plenty of time to create all his temples. I believe he thought we would never find this one."

"I bet he built this to escape to if things on Ierilia get too hot for him," Bernie muttered.

At the end of the corridor were two stairwells. Cewrick pointed his staff at them both. The one on the right lit up in a bright white light. "This one."

They climbed the winding stairs. The walls again had many hieroglyphics carved into the marble. Sconces hung on the sides of the stairwell, lighting their way. When they came to the top and Cewrick opened the door, they stepped into a large room. Laboratory equipment stood scattered throughout it. Two men in white suits worked at a long bench, one bent over a book, the other gazing through a microscope.

"Okay. We've found two mad scientists. That one reminds me of the crazy scientist in the movie *Back to the Future*," Bernie said, pointing at the one leaning over the book. He had a mop of white hair that looked like it hadn't been brushed in years. "Now what?"

The men ignored the group and continued their work. Laura walked along the walls, looking at large jars. "This is sick," she called out. "Look at what's in these containers."

Bernie was sure his stomach was producing boiling acid. Looking at the content in the vessels made him feel nauseated. Bile crept up to his throat. The jars contained fetuses — a mix of human and insect or animal. *How did they get their hands on human fetuses? Maybe from the women in the greenhouse?*

Further down there were glass cubicles the size of a phone booth. Inside them were grotesque figures floating in a clear liquid, half human, half insectoid. Bernie felt his blood run cold as he gazed at a man whose upper body looked human, but his bottom half was a scorpion. When he looked closer, the man's hands were more like a scorpion's claws. He appeared to be alive, his eyes gazing back at Bernie. A tube protruded from his mouth and two tubes from his nostrils. They were attached to some machinery at the back of the cubicle. "I think we've found where Zohmes creates his soldiers. I feel sick to the stomach."

They saw a lot of empty cubicles. *Probably waiting for the next experiment*, Bernie thought. "Let's get out of here. I can't hack looking at this stuff."

He had no sooner spoken when a black cloud descended, enveloping each of them. His stomach somersaulted. His head spun. Then everything went dark.

When he opened his eyes, he was inside one of the cubicles. A tube in his mouth and tubes inside his nose almost choked him as he tried to breathe. He thrashed wildly. His efforts didn't help. He stopped wasting his energy and looked through the water. It was blurry, but he saw each of the team inside a cubicle. They were pickles in a jar. Now what?

After his eyes became accustomed to the liquid, he could see clearer. The two men in white outfits walked toward the booths. They stood before each one, a datapad in their hands, and made notes. After they gazed at Bernie for a while and made their notations, he noticed one holding a large hypo. He injected something into the cubicle through a small round gelatinous circle. Drowsiness attacked him. He tried to fight it but found himself drifting off to sleep.

Bernie had no idea how long he had been out. He'd forgotten where he was and fought the tubing and the liquid, then remembered. He was a pickle in a jar. When his vision cleared, he looked at the other cubicles and saw everyone awake. What about their magic? Surely one of them could get them out of the stalls?

The two scientists, at least that's what he assumed they were, approached, accompanied by a man dressed completely in black, a black cape lined in red draping from his shoulders. There was no mistaking who this was. Zohmes in person. His fiery hair was in disarray, as always. Bernie could hear nothing, but he saw the bastard laughing evilly, his eyes a glowing amber.

Zohmes stopped to stand in front of Biryn, a sneer on his face. "You are worthless. There is too much of your great-grandmother in you. Such a waste of potential, just as Rithar was. But Jonathan..." A maniacal grin split his face. He resumed walking, pausing to stare at each cubicle, his satanical laughter filling the room. It was strange. Now, Bernie could hear everything. His stomach clenched, and he balled his fists. Murder wasn't in his makeup, but oh man, he felt like choking the life out of the maniac.

"You are now mine. Soon you will all serve me. And you," he stopped to gaze at Cewrick, "have thwarted me once too

139

often. You will remain here forever."

The voice resounded through his brain, followed by that horrible laughter. Bernie tried to lift his hands to his head, wanted to cover his ears, but his arms felt like lead.

Zohmes had not counted on Cewrick's strength. The sorcerer's staff that lay on a counter suddenly lifted and glowed. It sent a shaft of green lightning directly at Zohmes and the two scientists, then again at the cubicle that held Cewrick. The glass broke into a million small shards, and the fluid spilled out in a rush. Cewrick pulled the tubing from his mouth and nose and grabbed his staff. Before Zohmes had a chance to react, Cewrick, with one wave of his staff, had released Hirsuta, Biryn, Astiana, Liana, Icaras, Taylith, and Ciara. Linking hands, they chanted while Cewrick continued to attack Zohmes.

Zohmes disappeared in a cloud of reddish smoke, his laughter echoing throughout the laboratory. The two scientists lay unconscious on the floor.

Damn, did you forget about us?

But no, after Zohmes disappeared, Cewrick released the rest of the team.

"I hope that killed him." Bernie searched for his clothes. He had not realized that they were all naked. The scientists must have stripped them while they were unconscious, or maybe Satan had whisked their clothing off when he had the scientists place them in the cubicles. Though it was embarrassing, at least their clothing was dry.

Icaras shook his head vehemently while getting dressed. "Unfortunately not. Nothing can kill him. Not even that pit of bubbling red acid. He will be waiting for us as we continue to look for Julia and Jonathan."

"He must have hidden them well," Liana said while tying her wet hair back into a ponytail.

"At least we didn't find them in the lab. Heaven forbid those scientists would have experimented on them," Bernie grumbled.

"He will not harm Jonathan, Bernie, and he will keep Julia alive as a pawn to intimidate her son."

CHAPTER SIXTEEN

Bernie wasn't so sure that Zohmes wouldn't hurt Jonathan. Maybe he would try to possess his son to double his powers.

They left the laboratory, leaving the two scientists lying inert on the floor. "Are they going to be okay?" Bernie glanced back at them. "The poor guys are under Satan's spell. They probably don't even know what they're doing."

"They will be fine," Ciara assured him.

"We will have our work cut out for us to save all the people he has here," Biryn commented.

"How long do you think we were pickled?" Bernie asked.

"Pickled?" Laro asked while Laura and Erica giggled.

"Sorry," Bernie mumbled. "On Earth we have a long, green vegetable that can be pickled, meaning in vinegar and spices, in jars. That's what I felt like in that cubicle. A pickle."

"Quite a long while. We are lucky they had not begun experimenting on us while we were unconscious." Astiana grimaced.

"I don't know why you couldn't have worked your magic right away," Bernie told Cewrick.

"My magick did not work. The thick glass walls interfered,

and there was something in that fluid. It was I Am that helped me, or we would still be a pickle, as you call it."

At the end of the corridor, there were four entrances to stairs. All had a field of greenish and purple plasma shielding entry. The substance could not withstand the energy emanating from Cewrick's staff and was gone in a second.

"Now, which entrance to take," Erica said.

Cewrick's staff did not light up any of the four. "I suggest we begin with one. Heaven only knows what we'll find at the top," Laura suggested.

At the top of the first stairs, there was a corridor with several doors. They opened one after another only to see some bedrooms, then a living room, and even a kitchen. "I believe we have found Odoxon or Zohmes' living quarters. We need to go back and try another," Biryn said and turned to go back.

A strong wind sent them tumbling back into the room. Bernie scrambled up. Before them stood Odoxon. Old, stooped, his beard almost reaching the floor, and a very wrinkled face, he looked like something out of a horror movie. Bernie had never seen him but had heard about the sorcerer, and he knew immediately who it was.

Cewrick jumped up and pointed his staff at him. "Your powers have weakened, old man. You are no match against all of us."

Odoxon's body flew across the room and landed with a thud on the stone floor. Red glowing circles encased him from head to toe.

"He will not bother us for a long while," Cewrick said with grim satisfaction.

Double doors faced them at the top of the second stairwell, also protected by a field of plasma. Cewrick made short work of disintegrating it. He and Aldis pushed the doors open and stopped dead in their tracks.

A naked Jonathan hung upside down from the ceiling, intravenous tubing attached to the carotid artery in his neck. The end of the tube led to a large glass container. It was almost filled with blood.

"My God! He is draining the lifeblood from him," Laura yelled and began to run toward Jonathan, but it looked like an invisible shield stopped her. "Something is blocking me. I can't get through it to him. Do something!"

"So this is what he is attempting. Zohmes thinks by taking Jonathan's blood and infusing it into his own body, he will have all his son's powers, too." Astiana looked grave.

Jonathan was unconscious. Bernie looked at his chalk-white face. He hoped they weren't too late.

"We need to get him the hell out of there." Laura tried punching the force field. "Jonathan!"

Taylith pulled Laura away. "We do not want to alert Zohmes and Odoxon that we have found Jonathan." She leaned against him, tears streaming down her cheeks. "We will free him, sweetness."

Cewrick touched the shield with his palm. A glowing dome formed. When he removed his hand, the light faded. He turned to the team.

"Join hands. Quickly! There is not much time before all his blood is drained. He cannot kill Jonathan, but he can cause enough pain and damage that will send his spirit out of his body."

Bernie stepped back as Biryn, Taylith, Ciara, Astiana, Liana, Icaras, Cewrick, and Hirsuta linked hands and began their spell. The shield illuminated brighter than it had when Cewrick had touched it, but their spell did not seem to be working. The light dimmed and faded away, and the shield was still effectively in place.

Liana kicked the invisible wall. "Those bloody bastards are

going to pay for this."

Bernie would find the dragon's use of Earth terms funny if the situation weren't so dire.

Jonathan jerked, and the chains holding him began to rattle. A black smoky mist encircled his body, hiding him from view. Flames undulated through the mist, growing in intensity, and that psychotic laughter filled the air.

"Let him go!" Liana slammed her fist into the shield. Fire streamed from her hand, fizzling and popping as it surrounded the force field.

The curling black fog separated from Jonathan. His skin was an ashy blue color, and he appeared to be dead. Bernie's heart clenched at the thought of having to tell Julia what had happened to her son. But he'd been told quite a few times that Jonathan couldn't be killed.

The smoke solidified into the form of a man. A black hand laced with fire reached down and grasped the jar of blood beneath Jonathan, then lifted it to the contorted face of Zohmes. The god smiled and brought the container to his lips, drinking deeply of Jonathan's blood.

Utter chaos ensued. The magic users focused on the shield, and Bernie joined the others in their attempt to breach the shield and free Jonathan.

A radiant flash of light filled the inside of the dome. It emanated from Jonathan. His eyes were open, glowing brightly. He reached his hand out and clasped his fingers around the smoky figure's leg, his lips moving as if he were chanting a spell. Zohmes dropped the jar of blood and tried to turn, but it looked to Bernie as if he were frozen in place. Tendrils of ice spread from Jonathan's hand, winding up the black leg he held.

"You dare to try to bespell me, boy?" Anger distorted Zohmes' face. "You are no match for me." His body changed shape, again becoming a haze of smoke and mist.

"You shall not harm him!" Bernie heard Cewrick yell.

"Do not test my patience, Cewrick," Zohmes sneered.

A sickly green vapor surrounded Jonathan, and he began to cough and gasp as if he was choking. His body writhed, struggling for air, then hung limply again.

From the corner of his eye, Bernie saw Cewrick point his staff at the black fog. The room suddenly shook. All the dark energy felt like it was sucked from the room as if they were in a vacuum. Cewrick focused his staff at the forcefield. Waves of sheer power shot from the crystal at the field, slamming it with all its might. Pure, clean energy blasted throughout the room. Bernie stumbled, the shock of it smashing into him. The shield surrounding Jonathan burst into millions of particles showering down to the floor. When the room finally cleared, Zohmes was gone.

Laura ran forward, grabbed the intravenous tubing, and withdrew it from Jonathan's vein. Pressing hard on the small hole it left, she yelled, "Get him the fuck down!"

Taylith, Biryn, Icaras, and Laro rushed toward them, removed the chain, then lowered Jonathan to the ground. "Guard the door," Brenn commanded the warriors that had accompanied them.

"Shield the room. Laura is going to need time to heal him." Taylith stood behind Laura, his hand resting on her shoulder. Liana sat on the floor beside Laura and cradled Jonathan's head in her lap.

Bernie studied Jonathan. He was too still. All life had drained from his body into that flask. "I don't think Laura is going to be able to help him."

Erica patted him on the shoulder. "Don't be so negative. You'll be fucking amazed at what our Laura can do. Just watch."

Bernie was mesmerized when Laura placed her hands flat on Jonathan's chest. A brilliant rainbow of glittering colors showered down, encasing them in a luminous glow. Jonathan's pallid skin began to change as his lifeblood slowly replenished. The mask of death had left his face. He was no longer pale, and soon, his skin had a healthy flush. He suddenly sat up and took a deep, whistling breath, sucking much-needed air into his oxygen-starved lungs.

Liana leaned down and placed a kiss on Jonathan's parted lips. Was it a kiss? Had she blown her own lifeforce into his mouth? Bernie drew in a breath at the tears that soaked her cheeks and the expression on her face. Could it be? Jonathan and Liana? A dragoness and a demigod? The Ierilian gods and goddesses were having fun throwing together these odd couples.

"The book of knowledge knows all, Bernie," Astiana said softly behind him. "It was written that the people from Earth would crash here and that our people would find lifemates among them."

Bernie couldn't help feeling more than awed by what he had seen Laura do. Had she really brought Jonathan back from the dead? "I'm astounded by Laura's capabilities. How is it that she has such powerful magic now?"

Astiana squeezed his arm. "I Am favored her and gifted her with special abilities, and she is also mated to a dragon now and has his soul shard."

He shook his head. "I'm feeling somewhat bewildered. By all accounts, Jonathan should be dead after Zohmes drained him of all his blood."

"I understand. In time, you will learn much about Ierilia's magick and Polarium that powers it." She raised her voice a little. "Jonathan is healed. We need to continue on to find Julia."

"He needs to rest, Astiana," Liana protested, her arm linked through Jonathan's.

"I'm fine now. Thank you, Aunt Laura, for bringing me back from the dead. Where the fuck are my clothes?"

Liana let go of his arm and hurried to the side of the room. Jonathan's clothes lay in a pile on the floor. Running back, she handed them to him. He turned his back to them while he quickly dressed.

Bernie scratched his head. "I thought you were a goner."

Jonathan turned around and grinned at him. "I was. But the bastard can't kill me. I Am spoke to me while I was out of my body. The god said there is more deity in me than Earth DNA, and Zohmes cannot kill me or possess me, but if you guys hadn't come, my spirit would have dwelled outside my body in the realm of dreams for who knows how long."

"Enough talk. Before Zohmes and Odoxon recover from this failed plan of theirs, we need to find Julia." Biryn headed to the doors.

At the top of the third stairs, they found another hallway and more doors. The rooms were empty except for the last one. The door was locked, but Cewrick made short work of that. When they entered, the smell of sewage greeted them, and a figure stood up from a cot. The room was all black — the walls, the ceiling, the floor — and the black, sparse furnishings were falling apart and old. A bucket stood in the corner that he presumed was for the man's excretions. Bernie was beginning to think this planet had to be the hell he'd learned about on Earth.

"Cidus? What in the gods' names are you doing here? How did you get here? Zohmes?" Biryn shouted.

"I thought you were in league with that bastard. Why did he lock you up?" Erica questioned. "Wait. You couldn't have grown your hair and a long beard in such a short time. Biryn, this can't be Cidus."

Bernie gazed at the man. Hair that looked like it had once been blond hung to below his waist, tangling with a long, filthy beard. Tattered clothing clung to parts of his body, and the stench that came from him told Bernie the man hadn't seen water in years.

Bernie suddenly felt itchy all over and wondered if lice were a universal problem. He shuddered inwardly.

"I am Lord Cidus Milhella of Wildevein Manor." The man calling himself Cidus spoke slow, soft, as if not used to conversation.

"Impossible. Cidus is alive and well on Ierilia," Cewrick said. "This must be another illusion." He turned to leave the room.

The man held his hands out beseechingly. "Please, do not leave. I am real. The man calling himself by my name is my twin brother, Jatron. Many years ago, Zohmes captured me and put my brother in my place. I am the real Cidus."

Taylith stepped toward the man and looked back at the team. "The twins I saw in my vision. Remember? I am sure this man is furious at his brother."

Cidus' blue eyes that had seemed dull and lifeless suddenly flared with hatred. "What Zohmes and my brother have done to me is unthinkable. And for what reason? I did not even know I had a brother until Zohmes appeared in my room at Wildevein Manor, accompanied by Jatron."

"Yet Zohmes kept you alive all this time. I wonder if he had yet another of his thwarted plans in mind by doing so. Are you well? Can you walk?" Ciara asked.

"He fed me well, and I walked this room a hundred times a day to keep up my strength, and I exercised. My thirst for vengeance fueled my determination to stay alive."

"We will take all Zohmes' prisoners back with us. How, we

do not know yet." Brenn rubbed his chin. "We came here to rescue one woman and find some missing artifacts. We did not bring enough space gear for so many."

Bernie grunted. "We've found a lot more people than we bargained for. Now...where is Julia?"

They left the room, Cidus accompanying them. Bernie tried not to walk too close to the man. He smelled like decaying corpses. His stomach lurched at the thought of Julia held in a room like the one they'd just seen.

Beside him, Astiana began to chant, and Cidus' body was enveloped by a soft glow. The dirt and grime that caked the man's clothing and body disappeared. When Astiana quieted and the light dissipated, Cidus had been cleansed as if he had showered and his ragged clothing laundered. Bernie sighed in relief. The stench permeating the air was gone.

"Thank you, my lady," Cidus told the goddess.

At the top of the fourth set of stairs was a single door. It wasn't locked. Bernie entered right behind Cewrick, his heart beating a mile a minute in fear that Julia wouldn't be there. But she was. The large room was black from ceiling to floor. Julia lay upon a red altar in the center, her hands folded on her chest. His heart skipped one beat...then two. If not for the pink flush to her skin, she appeared to be dead.

Bernie rushed to her side, grasped her hands, and kissed her lips. A wave of relief coursed through him. She was warm, her lips soft to the touch. A corpse would be pale, cold. The body stiff and unpliable. They were stuck in a twisted version of *Sleeping Beauty*, except he was no prince and it would take a hell of a lot more than a kiss to wake his princess.

Jonathan stood on the other side of the altar, his face twisted in pain. His eyes had an eerie glow. He reached down and caressed Julia's cheek. "That bastard is going to pay for this."

Bernie turned his gaze to the team, the burn of tears in his eyes. "Do something…please."

"The spell." Ciara stood at the foot of the altar. Linking hands, the team of magick users began to chant the spell they had learned from the grimoire.

When the echo of the chant faded, Julia opened her eyes and sat, then threw her legs over the side of the altar. "Bernie? Jonathan?" A look of confusion crossed her features when she glanced around the room.

Bernie helped her to stand. When she was steady on her feet, she hugged Jonathan, then turned to Bernie. "Where the hell are we? The last thing I remember, I was at the science building, ready to resume work."

"Long story, honey. We need to get the hell out of here now." He held her tightly against his chest for a moment.

Ciara looked at them all, a gloomy expression on her face. "Rania just informed me that the grimoire and black diamond are no longer on this planet."

"Great, then we can go home," Laura muttered, hurrying to hug her sister.

CHAPTER SEVENTEEN

Bernie had no idea how they were going to take Cidus along or any of the other people they'd encountered. They only had enough spacesuits for the team, the soldiers, and Julia. They didn't find that many other prisoners—just the two scientists and the few people they'd seen in the greenhouse. But still too many to get to their spaceship without the atmosphere of the planet killing them.

He sighed, leaving the worry on how to save the others to the magic users. They headed back the way they had come as fast as they could. Just before they got to the greenhouse, Bernie heard a sound from behind one of the doors in the hallway. "We checked all these rooms, didn't we?" he called out.

"I thought we did," Erica said.

"I just heard something behind this door." Bernie let go of Julia's hand and turned the knob. There was no light in the room. It was hard to see two feet in front of him. When his eyes adjusted to the darkness, he gasped.

"Fuck, how could we have missed seeing these people?"

A young man and woman in black spacesuits crouched in a corner of the room. Several of the team had come in behind him. Erica lit her glimmer stick and held it up, causing the two to shield their eyes.

They looked to be either in their late teens or early twenties—it was hard to tell. They were dirty, their hair hanging in oily strings. Their bodies were emaciated, and their eyes were filled with terror. When Erica stepped toward them, they grasped each other, the woman burying her head against the man's shoulder.

"Who are you?" the male asked.

"Bloody hell, he speaks English," Erica murmured.

"My name is Erica. How is it you speak English? How did you get here?"

Bernie stepped toward them and gently disengaged the woman from the man. "Don't be afraid. We are friends."

The man stood. "My name is Liam Alexander, and this is my sister Emma. We were in stasis on our ship. When we woke up, we were here. Some horrible alien has kept us prisoner."

Bernie shook his head in disbelief. "That's impossible. All the ships and members from the relocation program are accounted for."

Liam gave them a defiant glance. "We were not an official part of your relocation mission." He grasped his sister's hand and pulled her up to stand beside him. Erica brushed her hand through her curls and shook her head. "We can talk about this later. Zohmes and Odoxon are probably hot on our tails."

Bernie agreed. They had to get the hell out of dodge before the crazies caught up with them. He motioned to Liam and Emma. "Come with us. We will get you to safety."

Liam stood stiffly for a moment, almost as if he would argue. Emma nudged him. He turned his gaze to her, then relaxed and nodded. "We will go with you."

Bernie couldn't believe the young man would hesitate to escape from his dire circumstances. They left the room and joined the rest of the team. Erica ushered Liam and Emma to join the rest of people they had found in the castle.

Cewrick and Hirsuta led the group, with the rest of the magic users placed strategically throughout their entourage. Bernie couldn't believe their luck when they had finally exited the castle door and entered the hollow mountain. Why hadn't Zohmes and Odoxon tried to stop them? Their escape almost seemed too smooth. They hurriedly made their way through the tunnels toward the temple entrance. Bernie held his breath as he stepped into the cavernous room. He had no wish to become caged again. Twice trapped on this mission was enough.

Cewrick stopped and turned to the group. "We are safe here. I Am placed a shield around this room."

Bernie gazed at the extra people they were now tasked with getting off the godforsaken planet. "How do you propose we transport these people to the ship? You can't use your magic outside that door. The air isn't breathable, and we don't have enough spacesuits."

Aldis clapped him on the shoulder. "There are extra suits on the spaceship. When we know it is safe, I will have one of the warriors bring them to us."

As if that would fix things. They still had to get everyone out of the temple and off the planet unscathed. The team may not have found the grimoire or the black diamond, but Bernie knew Zohmes had to be furious that they had thwarted his plans.

"We must be prepared for a trap. Zohmes and Odoxon will not allow us to go free without a fight." Taylith gestured to the people they had found in the castle. "This room is protected by I Am. They should remain here until we secure safe passage and obtain spacesuits for them."

"Hirsuta and I will stay with them to protect them until you return." Astiana placed her hand on the wall. Instantly the hieroglyphics I Am had etched into it blazed to life, and a doorway opened. "Be careful. Zohmes will be incensed at losing Jonathan, and the pawn to get him here, his mother."

A fist squeezed Bernie's heart at those words. The devil could still try to get to her. He clasped Julia's hand. "Julia, I want you to stay here with Astiana and Hirsuta."

She tilted her chin and gazed up at him, a determined look on her face. "Not on your life, Bernie. I am *not* leaving your side."

"Wait a minute," Liam called out and took a step toward Bernie. "I don't want to stay with these people. They scare the shit out of us with their magic tricks. And we don't understand their language. Take us with you."

Erica approached the young man. "Liam, we can't. We haven't enough spacesuits for you all right now, but not to worry. There are more suits on the ship. And first, we have to see what waits for us beyond that entrance. We don't trust the bastards that captured you. They could be up to something else."

Emma took her brother's hand and pulled him back. "They know what's best, Liam. Better listen."

The lad still seemed reluctant, Bernie noticed. What the hell? He should be glad they had rescued him and his sister. How they managed to be on a spaceship and crashed here was still a puzzle, but they'd probably get the full story once they were safely home.

Brenn led the team through the portal Astiana had opened. They waited until it closed again. Once they cleared the altar and entered the passageway, they followed it to the room to the main entrance. Bernie's senses were on hyperaware. He could hear every creak in the floor, see every shadow. Something wasn't right, but he couldn't put his finger on it. Where in the hell was Zohmes? It was strange that they could just leave the place without the asshole trying anything else.

"Everyone, get into your spacesuits. Stay on high alert," Aldis called out.

Bernie pulled Julia to the cart and retrieved a suit for her, then grabbed his and quickly got into it. "Do you need help, Julia?"

She scrunched her face at him. "This is the easy part. What I really need is a weapon. I have a sick feeling that Zohmes isn't going to just let us walk out of here."

Jonathan handed Julia a fleet weapon. "He's not, Mother. But he is about to find out just how pissed off I can get."

Bernie could feel the rage emanating from Jonathan. Energy crackled around him like a lightning storm. His hair whipped around his face, and his eyes were eerily lit from within, flames dancing in the blue of his irises. Julia's son was kind of scary. At that moment he seemed more Zohmes' offspring than Julia's.

"Whatever they have planned, they won't get the best of us." Liana put her hand on Jonathan's shoulder. He seemed to relax and the fire in his eyes faded.

They finished climbing into their spacesuits and securing their headgear and oxygen tanks.

"Let's get a move-on." Brenn grabbed his pack and hoisted it to his shoulder. "Remember, magick will be useless beyond that door, so have your weapons ready."

The four swords touched and pointed at the door, the tips barely grazing it. It opened to a blazing red sky. A wind as fierce as a hurricane almost swept them off their feet.

Bernie took a deep breath. When his visor cleared, he saw an army of thousands advancing toward the entrance. They were not any of the warriors Zohmes had previously used to attack them. These were crazy ant-resembling soldiers like Jonathan had seen in his vision and tried to describe to them. Standing at least twelve-feet-tall, they had ant-like heads. Antennas protruded from their skulls. Glowing yellow eyes bulged from their heads. Stingers protruded from their chests. Bernie thought they looked like giant ants walking upright. They carried spears and made loud clicking noises, so loud, it penetrated their communication system.

"I need to get back inside to contact the fleet," Aldis shouted.

Just as the swords opened the entrance and they were all ready to run back in, a huge face appeared above the ant army. It was Zohmes, surrounded by a ring of fire, his eyes blazing and sending bolts of red lightning at the team.

Bernie was about to scoot back inside, Jonathan beside him, when from the corner of his eyes he saw Jonathan turn around to face the army. "Jonathan, what the hell are you—"

"Oh my God! He's taking his helmet and gloves off!" Bernie shouted back at the team. He tried to stop Jonathan, but no use. Breathing that toxic air would kill him instantly. He tried grabbing Jonathan again, but the young demigod was unmovable.

To his astonishment, Bernie didn't see Jonathan collapse. He stood facing the fearsome face and raised both hands toward it.

"You fucking bastard, motherfucking cocksucking asshole god! Take this!" Jonathan shouted.

Flames erupted from his hands. Streams of fire that blazed beyond comprehension were aimed directly at the leering face. Zohmes' satanic laughter echoed around them again, deafening them all.

"Whelp! You dare to defy your father!" Bolts of lightning

struck back at Jonathan, but he masterfully diverted them to hit the advancing ant soldiers instead.

Bernie stood rooted to the ground. The god and the demigod fought. Jonathan suddenly chanted, his voice booming, sounding too much like Zohmes. It was unnerving. The face exploded into a million particles.

Just at that moment, the fleet appeared above them and attacked the horde of ant warriors. The giant ants were no match against the fleet weapons. Within minutes, the laser fire raining down on them had turned them into ashes.

"Is he dead?" Julia asked behind Bernie, her hand on his shoulder.

"We can't kill him, Mother, but I sure as hell bested him and gave him something to think about. The fucking bastard. Oh, how I wish I could annihilate him forever," Jonathan said, turning to her.

Julia stood before her son and touched his face. "You can breathe this air. It's unbelievable."

A loud rumbling sounded as if an earthquake was threatening. "Now what?" Bernie mumbled.

He need not have feared. The sky cleared. The craggy peaks that surrounded the temple crumbled into dust at the base. Instead of the dark temple, they stood at the entrance of a beautiful castle, its golden peaks shining in the rays of the three suns that appeared in the now-mauve sky.

The scenery around them changed from craggy mountains and peaks and red desert with bubbling red lava pits to verdant green, lush with beautiful floral trees and flowery shrubs.

Bernie sucked in his breath. "Unbelievable. It's gorgeous. So it was all an illusion?"

Cewrick joined them. He gestured at the beauty that now surrounded them. "Zohmes bespelled this planet. Jonathan, through his magick and spell, broke the curse. The boy is so much stronger than his father or any of us. Just wait until his full powers come into force."

"But from where did the bastard get the planet, and who lived here? And there is this castle. Surely there must have been inhabitants?" Bernie wondered.

"Maybe Zohmes and Doxie baby killed them all," Erica suggested.

"Rania has enlightened me. Zohmes moved the planet from another universe to this one. He more than probably captured the people that lived here but might be keeping them prisoner elsewhere."

Bernie sighed. "Great. Another mystery to solve. We still have to find the grimoire and the black diamond, and now a whole world's population as well?"

Jonathan suddenly grinned. "You can take your helmets off. You can all breathe now."

CHAPTER EIGHTEEN

They walked back into the castle. Instead of the horrible room where they'd been caged, they saw a beautiful entrance hall.

Liam rushed toward them. "What the hell happened here? First, we're in hell, and now we're in paradise? What the fuck is going on?"

"Calm down, young man." Bernie patted Liam on the shoulder.

Liam shrugged his hand away and gave Bernie a look of disdain. Bernie shook his head. The young man reminded him of Barry. He had no doubt Liam would prove to be a handful when they returned home.

"We defeated the demon that kept you prisoner, and some of us removed the evil spell from this planet. Be glad. We can now leave and go home." Erica tried to stay patient.

"To Earth, I hope. I should never have agreed to this crazy plan to start with!" Liam shouted.

"To Ierilia. To the people that saved us all. You can come with us now. Spacesuits are no longer needed," Laura assured him.

"I want to go home to Earth!" Liam persisted.

"Impossible," Julia told him.

They all took off their spacesuits and gear and placed them in the cart. Then, leading the group of freed prisoners, they walked back out onto the steps of the castle.

"What is that sprouting up from the ground?" Astiana pointed to a spot in the center of the valley.

The trunk of a tree slowly became visible. It was no ordinary tree. The trunk was the color of pale flesh and almost transparent. Bernie watched in awe as it reached a tremendous height and began sprouting branches and silvery leaves.

He looked up. The fleet was hovering high above. But it seemed they had no further need of their assistance. What was that tree?

"We need to go to it," Hirsuta suddenly said.

"Why?"

"Rania told me it houses the inhabitants of the planet. It was their method of escape from Zohmes and Odoxon's attack."

Bernie focused on the tree, then on the valley. He hadn't noticed before, but now he saw villages dotted here and there. "Who needs to go?"

"Those with magick. Let us do this so we can return home," Hirsuta said and began to walk down the white marble steps.

It didn't take them long to get to the tree. Though Hirsuta had instructed those with magic to go with her, Bernie had gone along, Julia firmly by his side. He stood before the massive trunk large enough to fit a house inside, maybe two. It was a pale pink color, transparent. Veins that looked like they were filled with blood threaded throughout the trunk and branches, making it appear to be a living entity. When he looked closer, he was sure he saw faces, hundreds of them.

Jonathan stepped forward. He spread his arms wide and

leaned against the trunk, his face resting against the pulsing membrane. A soft chant issued from his lips. His body glowed, a soft white light engulfing him.

Astiana and the other magick users linked their hands and stood close to him, chanting along.

Within minutes, people began to appear, coming out of the tree, one after the other. Bernie backed into a throng of jubilant men and women, all shouting and praising the team for releasing them.

They appeared human in body structure and build, but that was where the likeness ended. Their skin reminded Bernie of fire opals. It was incandescent, glowing with a myriad of swirling colors. Their hair was a shimmering silver, the men's clipped short, while the women wore long, tiny braids decorated with colorful beads. They had pointed ears and large almond-shaped eyes, the palest of blues. Once the people had quieted down, a man and woman came forward, both dressed in blue silken robes trimmed with silver-embroidered foliage along the edges of the collar, hem, and sleeves. Silver crowns in a leaf design graced their heads. The design was delicate, the leaves looking paper thin and much like the leaves from the tree. When they spoke, their language was lyrical, like a song, and Bernie couldn't understand a word of it.

"Get a couple of translators," Biryn ordered.

Brenn retrieved one from his backpack, then grabbed one from Aldis, and turned them on.

He offered them to the man and woman. "Pin them to your robes. The translators will calibrate to your language and allow us to understand you."

The man pinned the device to his robe and spoke first. "I am Rathal, and this is my consort, Esyae. We are the rulers of Atromia. On behalf of my people, I thank you for releasing us and returning our planet to its true state."

"I am King Biryn of Ierilia, the planet yours now orbits." Biryn introduced the rest of the team. "Can you tell us what happened?"

Rathal's jaw clenched, his eyes filled with anger. "Our planet was under threat of attack by offworlders. Their technology was far more advanced than ours, and we had no way to defend ourselves from their weapons. Zohmes and his assistant, Odoxon, aided us to defeat the offworlders. We did not know that they had ulterior motives. They cursed Atromia, bringing death and destruction to our world. Many of our people were lost before we escaped to the Iyathi Tree, the tree of life."

Pain clouded Esyae's face, her eyes glistening with unshed tears. Her body trembled. "Those creatures Zohmes brought with him killed our son."

Bernie couldn't believe the Atromians had trusted the bastards. The aura of pure evil surrounding Zohmes pulsed around him like a living entity. But he knew Zohmes could change his countenance. He'd done that more than once and fooled Julia into thinking he was John. He had probably done the same when he'd approached these people and offered his help. If they had seen him in his true form, they never would have trusted him. He squeezed Julia's hand, silently thanking God and the Ierilian gods and goddesses that they had found her and that she was now safe. And for all they knew, the God they had grown up believing in could be I Am.

Astiana grasped Esyae's hand. The woman visibly calmed. "Your people are safe now. Zohmes and Odoxon no longer have a stronghold on your planet."

"Your people have great power. You defeated Zohmes and the old sorcerer. You changed our planet to its natural state. Can you return us to our rightful universe?"

Astiana shook her head. "Zohmes is not defeated. We only thwarted his plans by driving him from this planet and freeing your people from his spell. We do not have the ability to return your planet from whence it came."

Brenn studied Rathal. "If you will allow it, and with the king's permission, I would like to leave a unit of our fleet warriors here. They will be able to notify me if your people need assistance."

Biryn nodded his agreement. "Of course. We will do whatever we can to help. And in the future, I would like to invite you both to visit Ierilia. We are close neighbors now."

Rathal gave Brenn a guarded look. "I am not so trusting as I was before Zohmes tricked us. He had hidden his evil so well, even the Iyathi Tree did not recognize him for what he was."

Esyae grabbed Rathal's arm and gazed up at him. "Rathal, these people freed us. If not for them, the Iyathi Tree would have eventually perished, along with our people. And Zohmes would have continued to destroy our planet."

Rathal sighed. "Of course. You are right." He turned his attention back to the team. "I will allow it. Due to the circumstances of our capture, there are several empty cottages available your men can use." Rathal gestured to one of the Atromian men. "Elas will assist your men in getting settled."

Brenn inclined his head. "Thank you." He returned to the group of warriors, Elas following.

They didn't have to walk far. The rest of the team, the warriors, and the people they had saved from Zohmes and Odoxon had joined them near the tree. Understandable. The light show was quite a spectacle when the magic users had released the Atromians from the tree.

Bernie couldn't help but notice Elas was as large as Brenn with much the same bearing. He had to be a warrior of some kind. His clothing was a strange mix of modern and medieval. His pants were the same dark blue color as Rathal and Esyae's robes. Tall black boots covered his feet and legs all the way to his knees. The silver shirt was form-fitted and sleeveless. A wide leather belt encircled his waist, and a knife with a large curving blade filled a sheath at his side. They were truly a unique people. With their pointed ears, on Earth, they would be regarded as elves. He wondered if they had powers. After all, that living tree was something else.

Brenn retrieved a translator from one of his warriors and activated it for Elas. Once Elas attached it to his shirt, Brenn assigned several of the engineered warriors to Elas for security detail on Atromia.

After Brenn returned to the group, Biryn turned to him. "We must return home to Ierilia. Zohmes will be furious that we have undermined his plans, and I will not leave my people without our protection."

Bernie had the same concerns. He had no doubt Zohmes would try to wreak havoc on Initiation Genesis for his part in rescuing Julia. As for Jonathan... The man might have Zohmes' DNA, but he was also Julia's son, and by all counts, that made Jonathan his future son as well. As powerful a magic user Jonathan had shown himself to be, Bernie still felt protective of the young man. He would do everything within his power to keep both Julia and her son safe.

Aldis placed his communicator back in his pocket. "The spaceship has already landed in the clearing near the castle."

They said goodbye to Rathal and Esyae, then escorted the survivors to the ship.

"I'm not getting on another fucking spaceship!" Liam shouted.

Bernie grunted. "And you keep yelling you want to return to Earth? Impossible. This is another universe. How do you think you'd get there? Catch a bus? Get on a train? Grow up, young man. You're going to Ierilia with us, and that's where you will make your future, along with the rest of the people from Earth."

The sister pulled at Liam's arm. "Stop it. We should be grateful these people saved us from that satanic maniac who was starving us to death."

"Emma, they're taking us to yet another planet. God knows what kind of aliens wait for us there. I mean, look at the people on this planet. They're elves, for God's sake!"

Bernie grimaced. "Most of the people you see with me are Ierilians. A few of us are from Earth. All of the people from the relocation program are living on Ierilia. You'll be among friends."

"I just want to go home," Liam mumbled, pushed his sister's hand away, and began to walk toward the waiting ship.

Bernie sighed. It would seem they had a rebel on their hands. That was all they needed.

Julia linked her arm through his. "He'll come around. He's young."

"Honey, with Barry constantly stirring up trouble, the last thing we need is a young upstart."

CHAPTER NINETEEN

And he'd been right. After they arrived at the space center, the lad kicked up a fuss about going to the hospital. Erica and Laura tried to calm him, but nothing helped. He refused to listen to reason and continued to yell obscenities and kept cussing at everyone.

Ciara finally stepped in and placed a spell on him. "I will remove the spell after the doctors have examined him and he is settled in at the compound."

"Settled? I don't have a good feeling about that young man." Bernie ran a hand through his hair. They still had to find out the story behind Liam and Emma, how they were in a spaceship and in stasis. Then there was the Russian crew to deal with. He sighed. Right now, all he wanted was a hot shower, a good meal, and to sleep for a week. He didn't envy the task Biryn had ahead of him dealing with the Lord Cidus switch. It shocked the hell out of Bernie when Cidus appeared on the bridge of the ship, clean-shaven, and his hair trimmed. From the holographic image Brenn had shown him, Cidus and the imposter brother were identical.

After the ship's medic declared Cidus surprisingly healthy despite the circumstances of his captivity, Brenn invited him to stay at his estate until they could deal with Jatron.

Their first stop was the palace. Biryn insisted they have a meal before returning to their homes. "I have ordered the kitchens to prepare enough food for all of us, and we need to discuss a lot of matters."

Bernie sighed. He ached to be with Julia. Admittedly, they were both very tired, and he would probably fall asleep as soon as his head hit the pillow. He just wanted to be alone with her and hold her in his arms.

They all went to their respective rooms to bathe and change. He followed Julia to her room.

The soothing, perfumed water acted as a balm on his aching muscles. What was even better medicine was when Julia stepped into the tub with him and told him to sit forward.

"I think you're in need of a good neck massage." She wiggled in behind him and began to massage his neck and shoulders.

"Sweetheart, you can do this all evening," he murmured.

"I think the king might get a little upset. We can't be too long. They'll be waiting for us to have dinner. Don't worry. I'm coming to your place with you tonight." Her soft lips caressed his shoulder.

"I won't be much use to you. I'm so tired, I can't describe it. They can keep these missions. Of course, I had to be in on this one seeing the bastard took you. I can't believe you're so calm and upbeat after what you went through." Bernie reached behind and stroked her face.

"Thing is, I didn't suffer. One second I was at the science center, and next, I woke up on that slab with you all standing around me. If anything, I've had a long rest. Yes, the horde of giant ants was scary, but I'm fine. Really." She shampooed his hair and soaped him from head to toe, then washed herself while he rinsed off. As tired as he felt, her soft hands washing him, touching his cock, caused a half-erection. If she would have continued, he was sure he would have been hard as a rock. *No time for that, Bernie. You have a meeting to go to!*

They quickly dressed and hurried to the royal quarters, where they found everyone taking turns holding and cuddling the twins.

"Time for them to go to bed. Isabella, will you take them? After they are asleep, you are free for the evening," Cylena turned to tell her.

Isabella rescued the twins from a doting grandmother and grandfather and, carrying a bundle in each arm, left for the nursery. Bernie smiled. The girl seemed to have recuperated nicely after her ordeal.

"Food is waiting. Sit, everyone." Biryn tapped his fork on his plate to draw their attention.

In a way, Bernie was glad they were eating at the palace. He doubted he'd have had the energy to cook once he got home. Even though it had taken a couple of days to get back to Ierilia, he hadn't slept well on the ship. Worry for Julia and Jonathan plagued his mind. What Zohmes had done to Jonathan was nightmarish, and he was glad that Julia didn't know the details. He wasn't about to tell her either, not for a very long time, and he sure as hell hoped that no one else would.

Everyone was quiet while they ate, until Biryn pushed his plate away. "You all know what is next. We must find the grimoire and the black diamond. They cannot stay in Zohmes and Odoxon's hands."

"Until Rania gives us a clue where they are, it's like looking for a needle in a haystack," Laura said.

Brenn cleared his throat. "I think we also need to rest for a day or two. Bernie, Mark, and Erica need to deal with the Russians and the two young people from Earth we found on Atromia. Especially that angry young man."

"Yes, and I need to see what is happening at Initiation Genesis. By the way, is there any word on a name choice for our city?" Bernie looked at Erica.

Erica grinned. "Yes. The votes are all in. There were sure some weird suggestions, but the most votes were for Henderson, named after you."

"My God! Honestly? Bad enough that I'm now Lord Henderson, never mind having a town named after me," he exclaimed.

Biryn slammed his hand on the table and laughed. "I approve. Henderson it is. It shall be recorded as such."

"Damn, don't I get a say in this?" Bernie muttered.

"What did you vote for, Bernie?" Liana asked.

"Newtown. Sounded good enough to me. I saw Henderson on the list but didn't think anyone would go for it."

They talked a little about the mission while they had dessert. When they were finished, Brenn stood. "I think we should all head for our homes now. We are all tired. Tomorrow is another day."

Bernie took Julia's hand, and after saying goodbye, they headed outside and to his flyer.

He woke up to the aroma of bacon and eggs. Sitting up with a start, he noticed Julia was already up. It had to be her in the kitchen. He was not at a stage where he could afford to hire a cook and other staff.

After quickly showering, he hurried to the kitchen and found her busy making breakfast.

She turned to look at him and grinned. "Sleepyhead. Jim's already been here looking for you."

"Why didn't you wake me up?"

"You were exhausted. You know, this bacon isn't half bad. I wonder if the meat is from some kind of pig." Julia bit a piece off a strip.

"Who knows. You didn't have to do this, Julia."

"Hey, we're going to get married. Of course I'll cook for you. I can make breakfast, but there are some things you'll need to teach me. With the scarce rations we were allotted on Earth, it didn't make for cooking ambitions." She sidled up to him and shoved a piece of bacon into his mouth.

"I'll eat quickly and then go and deal with Jim. I also have to go to the compound to speak to the Russians and the two youngsters. That's if they've been released from the hospital." He tackled the eggs and bread.

"Would you like me to go with you? I don't start work again until tomorrow. Laura was smart enough to call me in sick."

Bernie frowned. "And they would believe that? People on Ierilia don't get sick. Sure, they have a hospital, doctors, and nurses, but I think mainly for injuries. Then again, I used that excuse for Jim, too."

Bernie finished his breakfast, kissed Julia, and hastened outside to find Jim. He hoped Jim hadn't run into problems while he was gone.

"Hey, Bernie. Good to see you're over your bug. Maybe too much of the Eldalas stuff? Though you'd have been over that in twenty-four hours. Having fun with the lady friend maybe? I ain't stupid. People here don't get the flu, or coughs and colds." Jim took off his helmet and wiped his brow.

"Good to be back to work. And my friend…Julia is now my fiancée. So what's up? Is the excavation going well?"

"Wow, congratulations! Nothing to do with work. I thought you should know that Barry has been stirring trouble.

The man is insanely jealous of you. He's been telling our people that he'll make a much better leader. Besides all that, he tells them that the king is lying, that there is a way for us to leave here and go back to Earth." Jim planted his shovel firmly on the ground.

"That's insanity. The election can't be undone. And you and I both know that returning to Earth is an impossibility. And who would want to anyway? Compared to home, this is the Garden of Eden." Bernie was angry. He'd known from the start that Barry was a troublemaker. But worse, now there was Liam. Heaven forbid those two got together. But it was inevitable.

"I have to go to the compound this afternoon to meet with the Russians. We also have two new arrivals from Earth." He watched Jim's brow furrow and his eyebrows raise in surprise.

"Yeah. Don't ask me. I don't know their story yet. I'll find out this afternoon. That's if they were released from the hospital."

"Two more stowaways? There was Isabella, and —"

"No. Not stowaways. I'll find out how exactly they got here and I'll tell you tomorrow. Meanwhile, is there anything to report?"

Jim shook his head. "Nothing. Everything is on schedule. We've finished digging out the temple, and the cleaning of it is almost done."

"Safe for me to take off for the afternoon?"

Jim grinned. "Go ahead. I've got everything in hand here."

Bernie hurried back to his house to find Julia ready to go with him. "You sure you want to do this, honey?"

"Yes. Did you contact Erica?"

"Yes, she and Mark will meet us at the compound."

"Good. I don't fancy dealing with Liam."

"That's if the hospital has released them. They could still be there."

"They were malnourished but seemed okay. Nothing that food can't cure." Julia entered the flyer with him.

They arrived at the common room in the compound almost the same time as Erica, Laura, and Mark, who had been brought up to speed on the new arrivals. To their surprise, the newcomers were already waiting for them, sitting at one of the long tables.

"Good afternoon, everyone," Bernie greeted. "We all speak English, so we don't need our translators."

They took a seat at the table. Bernie noticed Liam and Emma had been released from the hospital. Liam seemed rather subdued. Ciara's spell kept him docile. They looked clean now. The lad's hair was still in disarray. He was tall, gangly, and had an angry expression in his green eyes and a dissatisfied scowl on his face. The girl was petite and quite pretty. Her long, strawberry-blonde hair was clean and brushed. She had lovely cerulean-blue eyes and shapely lips.

Bernie cleared his throat. "First, you are all on a very friendly planet. The people here will do anything to help us. But you're far away from Earth. You're in a different universe."

"Names?" one of the Russian people shouted.

"Sorry. We will introduce ourselves, and after that, you can all tell us your names. I am Bernie Henderson, elected leader of the people from Earth."

They each introduced themselves. The Russians and Liam and Emma did the same.

"Now that we know each other's names, please tell me, Andrei, when did your ship leave Earth and where were you headed?" Erica asked.

173

"We on large ship. Russia want us begin colony on Mars."

"Mars? Wow. You can't breathe there," Laura commented.

"Our ship have supplies. We want build special containment shelters."

"How long ago did you leave Earth?" Mark questioned.

"It was two thousand forty-five."

"Wow, that was more than a hundred years before us. Strange that Russia kept it so quiet," Bernie said.

"We wish go home!" a young man named Vladimir shouted.

"I'm sorry. And what I'm going to say is for all of you. You are in a different universe, and there is no way to go back to Earth." Erica planted her bottle of water on the table.

Bernie heaved a big sigh. "Would you even want to? We all know the state Earth was in. Look at this planet. It's hospitable, clean, the people are great, and we can live a healthy, normal life here."

"My family! They on next ship!" Vladimir yelled.

"I'm sorry, Vladimir. We, or you, don't know if they ever launched another ship, and if they did, your family is long gone. Since you left Earth more than a hundred years before us, you have no idea the condition our planet was in when we left it."

"I want to go home," Liam suddenly announced, raising his voice a little.

"Emma, or Liam, how is it that you two were in stasis on a ship? You were not members of the relocation program, so what is your story?" Mark asked.

"Our father is a billionaire. He helped to fund the relocation program on the condition that they build a ship for Liam and me. It was launched from Vandenberg Air Force Base at the same time your ships were launched," Emma told them.

"But why wouldn't the powers that be just allow you into the program? Why the secrecy?"

"The program was already filled. Thirty-two people per ship. And it was kept secret because other rich people would be clamoring to go and demand ships built for them. They said, even with millions of dollars funding, they wouldn't be able to get all the supplies needed to build more ships. I never wanted to go in the first place. My father had them sedate me, and then I woke up with those crazy idiots. I just want to go home. I have a girlfriend there." Liam had an obstinate expression on his face.

Emma elbowed her brother. "I don't want to. I know what conditions were like on Earth, and I think we've landed in a paradise environment. We should be grateful. And Suzy is the biggest flirt. She had a dozen boyfriends before you, and she probably found someone else right after we left to go on a supposed vacation."

Erica stood. "There is no way anyone can go back to Earth. Ierilia's technology is much advanced, but they cannot travel to another universe. Matter of fact, even if it were possible since all the equipment on our ships was either destroyed or malfunctioned, we have no idea how long we were in stasis before crashing. For all we know, it could be the year four-thousand now. There may be no life left at all on Earth, and if there is, no one we knew will be alive. We have to deal with what is.

"We have been granted a realm on Ierilia, or in Earth terms, a state or province. Its name is Initiation Genesis, and its first city is called Henderson. Bernie was elected as the ruler of our realm. We all fall under the king's law, Ierilian law, just like the rulers of each of the realms. You are all welcome to come and live in Henderson. We have homes ready, but you will have to share for the time being. Mark is your liaison. You all need to learn the language and study Ierilian history. We will provide you with tablets. Are there any questions?"

Vladimir put up his hand. "If I may ask, is this town Henderson same to towns on Earth?"

"Not entirely. We have incorporated Ierilian architecture with our own. But I'm sure you'll all be happy and comfortable."

Bernie had a sick feeling in the pit of his stomach as he watched some of their faces and especially Liam's. This was not going to be easy.

Andrei, the Russian captain, pushed his chair back and stood. "For my team, we agree. We live in Henderson." He appeared to ignore some of the murmurs in Russian from his crew, shaking his head. Speaking Russian, he said something in a stern tone. He turned back to Bernie. "We do you want."

Bernie smiled. "Thank you. We must leave now. Mark will assist you with everything."

"We can talk you?" Andrei asked, looking at Mark.

"Yes. Any time. I live in Henderson, and you can call on me whenever you wish. You will all be given communicators that you can use to call or message me."

After they left the compound, Bernie had a heavy feeling. Even if Liam was under a spell, he still displayed rebellion, and some of the Russians were not happy. How was all this going to play out? There was the mission up ahead, finding the grimoire and black diamond, although he didn't think they needed him for that. The last thing he wanted was to go on another quest. He'd only go if it meant saving the love of his life, Julia, or her son. He grasped for her hand and squeezed it as they headed toward his flyer. "Are you staying the night with me again?"

"I love you! I love you! I love you!" Julia murmured the

words against his neck.

Bernie could hardly believe he had found love again and on another planet. Yes, he'd loved his wife, but the love he felt for Julia was so much more. It was like nothing he'd ever experienced. Was it the magic on this planet? He didn't know and didn't care. All he knew was that she was his heart and soul and he could hardly wait to make her his wife.

She stood on her tiptoes and quickly kissed him, then turned her head to look at the sprawling beach. "It is so enchanting here. I can't believe that this realm is really our new home. It is absolutely stunning."

She was right. The beach was incredible, and the view from his balcony was spectacular. The four moons hung heavy in the sky, casting their glow on the surface of the water. Trees, much like palms, painted their shadows on the silvery sand. Many of their people took to walking along the water's edge during the warm evenings. Polarium's brilliance made the beach appear magical, almost as if the scene had been plucked from a fantasy or dream. Julia had squealed with delight when he surprised her that evening with a romantic dinner on the balcony overlooking the ocean.

"Not half as beautiful as you are." He leaned down to claim her luscious lips. God, she felt so good in his arms.

She pressed her body closer to his and wound her arms around his neck, moaning when he deepened the kiss. She nipped, then sucked on his bottom lip, causing a blaze of need straight to his cock.

Pulling back, she gazed up at him, her blue eyes sparkling with passion. "I need you, Bernie. Make love to me under the stars?"

She grasped his hand and pulled him toward a chaise nestled in a darkened corner of the balcony, then nudged him to sit. His breath caught in his throat when she unlaced the top of her dress and allowed it to slip from her shoulders and drop to the floor. His heart pounded, his blood a raging fire coursing through his veins. She looked like a goddess. The light of the moons and the radiance of the magical star illuminated her form. Her silken hair was like a golden halo. It spilled in luxurious waves around her shoulders and down her chest, her erect nipples peeking through the strands, making him ache to taste them.

He pulled his shirt over his head and dropped it, then made short work of his pants. Her eyes trained on him, devouring every inch of his skin, down to his pulsing erection. When her ravenous gaze traveled back up, a wicked little grin played across her lips. She pushed him to lay back against the chaise, straddled his hips, and with one thrust impaled herself on his aching cock.

"Holy hell, woman." Bernie groaned and tamped down the urge to come. He had never seen this bold side of Julia, and fuck if it didn't drive his hunger to a boiling point. He laced his fingers through her hair, pulled her down, and kissed her hungrily. She rode him hard, meeting every thrust of his hips. A moan escaped her when his fingers skated down her back, to her ass, then grasped her shapely buttocks.

She pulled away from his lips and leaned back. "God, yes, Bernie… Yes, yes…"

She was breathtaking. Leaning back in wild abandon, she arched those beautiful breasts in front of his face. He couldn't resist. Releasing her ass, he grasped both of those enticing morsels and took first one nipple, then the other in his mouth. Her cries of pleasure filled his ears, her muscles clamping down hard around his cock. Her name escaped his lips as she took them over the chasm into absolute bliss.

Julia collapsed against his chest and murmured, "I love you, hot stuff."

He chuckled and brushed his fingers through her hair. "Hot stuff?"

She caressed the muscles of his chest, down to his abdomen. "Mmmm… You're sexy as hell. Don't even tell me you don't know it either. All the girls noticed these abs when we were in training." She patted his stomach. "And don't get me started on that well-formed ass of yours."

He grinned and chuckled. He couldn't help it. When they were in training, he had seen this playful side of Julia before. That was one of the things that had drawn him to her. Since John, she had kept the playful part of herself hidden away, and he hadn't realized how much he had missed it.

"You are pretty damn hot yourself." He tilted her chin and placed a tender kiss on her lips. "And I am a lucky man to have won you."

He shifted and planted his feet on the floor, then stood with Julia still nestled in his arms. She wound her arms around his neck and teased his bottom lip with her teeth, then gazed up at him, passion still burning in her eyes.

He winked at her while carrying her into the bedroom. "You keep that up, honey, and I'll be ready for round two."

"That is exactly what I have in mind."

Damn, the woman stirred his blood. He dropped her on the downy comforter and caged her beneath him. *Insatiable.* And he was a starved man. He leaned down and kissed her soundly.

CHAPTER TWENTY

Summer had arrived in all its glory. Cront and all Ierilia were preparing for the biggest festival of the year, the Celebration of Armistice, held in memory of when the fierce wars were eradicated. It was celebrated every year in Cront, in the arena, although from what he had researched, it was also celebrated in the villages, marketplaces, and in every major city of each realm.

With all the upheavals caused by Zohmes and Odoxon, this festival was something to look forward to, a happy, joyful occasion for a change. The god and his sidekick had been silent. The king and his team didn't trust it, and deep down neither did he. His gut told him the two were up to something.

Tomorrow, they were going to have their first annual general meeting in the temple. It was not something Bernie looked forward to. Unlike all the rulers of the realms on Ierilia, who had no advisors, he was going to elect some people to assist him. If they were agreeable, of course. Erica was one of them, for sure, and Mark. He needed two more people but hadn't made up his mind yet as to which two to choose. He would also ask Brenn if he would assist. Even though they had learned much about the Ierilian culture and laws, Bernie still had many questions. It would make sense to include an Ierilian on his advisory team.

Julia had returned to her duties at the science center. They spent their evenings planning their upcoming wedding, which would be held in the temple a week after the festival.

Now that it was fully restored, the building was quite something to behold. Built from white marble, white pillars at the top of the steps leading to the main entrance, the peaked roofs shiny gold, it was the first building one saw when entering Henderson. It would retain its name — Temple of Fertility. Part of it they were going to utilize for a community center. The worship hall was to be the church for those that believed, but it was going to be a place of worship, no separate doctrines like on Earth. He'd already had several discussions with James van der Veen. They had decided the temple would be a sacred house for Earth people and Ierilians to worship whichever god or goddess they chose. The altar would remain the same. James had also mentioned that he would adapt to Ierilian culture and worship.

Bernie chuckled. On Earth, after he became an adult, he was never a regular churchgoer, but now he just might attend… James' sermons could become very interesting since the minister was quite impressed with the various gods and goddesses of Ierilia, the healing, the magic, and that quite a few people could communicate with the deities.

"Penny for your thoughts." Julia startled him out of his musings.

"Just thinking about our wedding. All done with the dress fittings now?" he asked.

"Pretty much. Just seven days to go…"

"It's going to be a busy time. First the meeting tomorrow, then the festival, and a few days later our wedding. It was so generous of Brenn and Ciara, offering to have the reception at their estate. They've got that huge ballroom."

Julia sat on his lap. "Yes, and they're insisting on providing the dinner. I protested, but they wouldn't listen to me."

"It means everyone from Earth can attend, and then some. We owe the Ierilians so much. Just imagine if we'd crashed on an uninhabitable planet. Well, we wouldn't have survived that. But what about a hostile alien species? Instead, we now live in a wonderland."

"I still think that's what it is sometimes. We did all die, and many of us ended up here and are working our way to the realm of dreams. Those that we lost must have ended up in Yanata…"

"Really? It all feels very real. When do you get those thoughts?"

"Sometimes. And other times I think we're still in stasis and it's all one big dream."

"Crazy woman. Come here. I want to kiss you." He turned her toward him and claimed her lips. "No more of those wacky thoughts. Hear me? It's all real."

The community hall in the temple was jampacked. Many had to stand.

When Bernie scanned the crowd from the podium, he saw that everyone was present, the king and most of the team taking up much of the front row. He'd not written a speech. Hell, what did he know about such things? He was just going to play it by ear.

For just a split second the sea of faces all gazing at him swam before his eyes, and his stomach somersaulted. It reminded him strongly of when he'd had to deliver the valedictory when he'd graduated. Pulling himself together, he took the gold bell from the table and rang it several times.

The whispers stopped, and everyone waited.

Bernie stood up. He didn't feel comfortable sitting on a chair behind a table.

"First of all, a warm welcome to King Biryn and his team of brave warriors. Welcome to all my fellow travelers from Earth, some of whom have found love on this planet, so welcome to their partners as well."

Almost all stood and clapped. Bernie raised his hand to get them to sit down and quieten.

"On behalf of all the relocation travelers, I would like to thank King Biryn, the queen, and all Ierilians for their help, assistance, and kindness. You have made us feel at home."

"Speak for your fucking self!" someone shouted. The others began clapping again.

Bernie rang his bell several times.

"Please! Contain yourself, whoever just yelled. If you don't, we'll have no choice but to remove you from this meeting." He glanced at the sea of faces. The voice had sounded like Barry's, but he wasn't sure.

"I will begin with asking five of you to be my assistants. What the hell do I know about running a realm, right?"

This caused a few chuckles.

"As you all know by now, once a ruler, always a ruler, and the title is passed on to the firstborn son of the elected lord. There are no reelections like on Earth. But the five I have chosen can choose to leave at any time. I do, however, need some help and guidance. I have studied all your files carefully and have picked Captain Erica Martinez, First Officer Mark Harris, Captain Gordon Callahoun, and Captain Ethan Delaney for my council. I would also like to add an Ierilian member, General Brenn Mildash. If you all agree and accept, could you please join me up here on the podium?"

Bernie waited until they joined him. He shook their hands,

and they sat at the table. He was happy they'd all accepted. He was just about to speak again when Barry Sullivan jumped up.

"You fucking bastard! The president chose *me* to lead our people. I should be the ruler! What in hell do you know about running a town and state? I am the chief of staff and—"

Bernie raised his voice. "Barry, sit down!"

"I don't have to fucking answer to you! You're a nothing, an asshole, you are—"

"Barry, please take your seat!"

"Fuck you, Bernie." Barry grabbed his chair and flung it across the room. It hit the wall with a loud crash.

"Guards!" Bernie shouted.

Several guards rushed into the hall and quickly took Barry outside, but seconds later, Liam jumped up.

"I don't know what the fuck is going on, but I want none of this. I just want to go home, back to Earth!"

"Liam, we explained to you just recently that it's impossible. Be quiet and sit or we'll have you removed, too."

Liam muttered something, then left the hall on his own. To Bernie's dismay, he saw about five others follow him, and two of those were from the Russian crew. But at least it wasn't a major exodus. Overall, nearly all the relocation members were happy and satisfied where they were. What they were going to do with the usurpers, he had no idea yet. He'd have to discuss that with his new council.

He rang his bell and waited for the murmurs to stop. "Now that trouble has left the building, I shall continue. Henderson is growing fast. We still have quite a few empty stores, so if any of you are interested in starting your own little business, let us know. The excavation of what lies behind the temple is continuing. Once the mines are unearthed and opened, there will be work available for those who would like a job working in a mine. And I'm sure we all would like to work because we need money. As it stands, we've been given so much for free, it makes me feel guilty."

"Nonsense!" Biryn shouted.

Bernie smiled down at the young king. Young? It was easy to forget that Biryn was much older than him.

"Thank you, Your Majesty. We do, however, need to earn money, or as on Ierilia, gold and silver coins. There will be ample opportunity for all of you. We will also begin choosing more farmland soon and build a house, barn, and whatever else is needed, on those farms. Are there any questions?" Bernie looked over the crowd of familiar faces. After spending two years on Earth, training closely with them, he knew everyone by name. Many of them looked eager to work toward their future on Ierilia.

"What about a police station?" Lucas yelled from the back.

"We don't need police on Ierilia. If an infraction is committed, the military investigates. Anyone who commits a crime is judged by the king and the gods and goddesses. Punishment can be quite harsh, so that's why there is little or no corruption here."

"But they have military outpost," Andrei said in a booming voice. "Much like motherland."

Mumbling rose up from the group of Russians.

Andrei calmed them down. "No. Is good they have army. Maybe I join."

"What about a fire station? Surely fires occur here," Aiden questioned. From what Bernie knew of him, he had been in fire rescue on Earth.

"True. The council and I will discuss that option. Anyone else?"

"Yeah, what about cars? Motorbikes? Are we going to be able to manufacture those?" David said loudly.

"No. There will be no factories and pollution-causing vehicles manufactured on Ierilia. This planet has the cleanest air any of us have ever inhaled. The king does not want Ierilia to suffer the same fate as Earth. Do you remember the plastics and fossil fuels, excessive amounts of psychotropic drugs in our water and soil? Lead, in the same, that was being increasingly discovered, chemicals in the soil that leached into any of the fresh food that was still being produced? Any of that fresh food sprayed with pesticides?"

"You mean we are going to be stuck riding horses and using wagons?" Eva grumbled.

"Or stuck walking," Chloe commented.

Erica rapped her fingers on the table. "Like that has changed much from Earth. How many of you actually owned a fucking car?"

"There were trains and busses, and at least I had a bike! They don't even have those here!" a man in the back yelled.

"You can get a damn horse. They're faster anyway," Laura said. "And you'd have a pet."

"Who in the hell wants to shovel all that manure." Samuel Thorn pulled a face.

"Hey! That makes for great fertilizer for the gardens," Travis MacPherson called out.

Samuel shook his head. "Fuck you, Travis."

Aria's voice rose above the others. "Why would we want to ruin our second chance at a future by polluting this utopia? Besides, they do have flyers. They run everything on crystals and don't pollute the air. Nothing says we can't get a couple of flyers and use those as our public transportation, like trains, busses, and trams on Earth, except here, we'll fly."

Biryn stood and turned to face the crowd, holding his arms up to silence them. "Everyone be quiet, there is too much fucking going on in here."

186

For just a second there was complete silence, then an eruption of laughter. Biryn sank down in his chair, the expression on his face priceless. He must have realized his faux pas.

Olivia, who was seated in the back, stood. "I don't know why any of you are complaining anyway. You have seen the beach here, right? Seriously! We had nothing like this back home! Can any of you remember ever swimming in the ocean?"

An outburst of excited feminine voices sounded in a rush.

"She's right!"

"We couldn't even swim in the lakes and rivers on Earth," came from someone.

Erica motioned for the women to be quiet. "All right, let Bernie finish."

"More questions?" Bernie waited, but no one else spoke. "Before we end this first meeting, I want to tell you that now that you live here, your physiology will adapt. You will live much longer and healthier lives. Those of you that have any concerns or suggestions, please contact Mark, Erica, Gordon, Ethan, Brenn, or myself. I will see you all at the festival in a few days, and then at Julia's and my wedding. All of you are invited. This meeting is now concluded. Our next meeting will be in one month. Lunch and drinks are waiting for you in the dining room. Thank you all for coming."

He sank down on his chair and heaved a sigh of relief. Erica approached him and patted his back.

"You did well, Bernie. You were born for leadership."

Mark, Gordon, and Ethan came toward him. "Way to spring that on us." Gordon grinned and clapped Bernie on the shoulder.

"We'll turn Henderson into a dream town," Ethan said.

Mark rubbed his chin. "You said no cars or pollution-causing vehicles. I presume that includes planes, too? How are we going to stop evolution?"

Bernie stood and looked at them. "You heard what Aria suggested. We can purchase a couple of flyers for public transport. People can buy tickets, just like they did on Earth to travel by bus or train. Ierilia has managed to stop Earth's kind of evolution for thousands of years. The king is glad he knows what happened on Earth. We will not do to this gorgeous place what humanity did to our home planet. Enough said. Let's go and have some lunch."

Julia sidled up to him in the dining room. "I feel neglected." She heaved an exaggerated sigh.

"Aw, poor baby."

"That was awesome. I am so proud of you." She kissed him on the cheek, then concentrated on her strawberry pastry.

CHAPTER TWENTY-ONE

"**D**o you think there'll be some sort of carnival, Bernie?" Julia asked while she dressed for the festival.

Bernie smiled at her reflection in the mirror. The deep blue of her dress enhanced the pansy color of her eyes. Her gaze met his, and a wicked little smile played across her lips, making his heart skip a beat. Damn, he was a lucky, lucky man. She looked like a pirate's wench in her medieval style walking gown. She wore a flowing white blouse beneath a corseted overdress with long, black overskirts and a hint of her blue underskirts peeking from beneath. The corset top came to just below her breasts and laced up on each side in a crisscrossing pattern, accentuating her figure.

He slipped his arms around her waist from behind. "You mean as in a theme park, a Ferris wheel, bumper cars, and other fun rides, like on Earth in Disney World, Disneyland, amusement parks, and at fairs? Honey, I've got no idea, but probably not. We'll find out when we go to the marketplace, to Cront, and to the arena. Maybe we can introduce some of that for future festivals. If we use the Koriam crystals to power motors needed to run the attractions, it wouldn't cause any pollution."

She faced him and wrapped her arms around his neck. "We should look it up on our datapads. There must be information about these festivals. There are more than one in a year, but because of all the shit that's gone down, none ever happened since our arrival, until now."

"The games in the arena are going to be interesting."

"Yeah, right. And you put your name down for the horse race. That's a bit freaky. How well do you know how to ride?"

He smiled and kissed the tip of her nose. "I grew up riding, sweetheart. My grandfather taught me how and I am pretty damn good at it, too."

Bernie had purchased several horses from Laro's family in Xynnar to use as breeding stock on his estate. The Xynnarian's were lucky when they had returned to rebuild their homes that their livestock had been spared. They were able to round up most of the horses and jagos that had escaped their fences.

Julia patted his chest and gave him a coquettish grin. "I will be rooting for you on the sidelines." She pulled a blue ribbon from her hair and tied it around his wrist. "Now you have a token of my favor, my handsome lord."

He brushed his fingers across her cheek, then lightly kissed her lips. "We better get moving. Jonathan, Liana, Taylith, and Laura will be here soon."

Cront was a flurry of activity. Colorful banners, urns, and tall vases of foliage and flowers decorated the city. Floral garlands were strung from building to building. People flowed through the streets, dressed in their finery. Bernie couldn't help thinking that this is what a medieval festival would have looked like on Earth. The market overflowed with traders and their wares. Jugglers and performers roamed the city, entertaining young and old alike. Teenagers danced in a courtyard to a lively tune, while a puppeteer mesmerized a group of young children with dolls dressed as lords and ladies. Julia bubbled with excitement. "This is incredible!"

"So are you." He squeezed her fingers.

They strolled on until they came to the market. Traders gave away free samples, and they had all priced their wares down.

"Oh, look! Jasmine has set up shop to trade goods!" Laura pointed out a table laden with Earth's fruits and vegetables.

Large buckets filled with strawberries, tomatoes, cucumbers, and lettuce stood on the table. There were even raspberries, blueberries, and blackberries, and she'd cut up a cantaloupe and a watermelon and handed out wedges. So much of the produce that was in scarce supply on Earth grew abundantly in Ierilia's soil. Bernie chuckled when two youngsters turned, grinning from ear to ear, their hands dripping with the juice of the plump red fruit she had given them to sample.

Julia held his hand as they walked through the marketplace, drinking in the beauty of the scene. Taylith, Laura, Jonathan, and Liana had joined them for the day. What an unlikely group they were, two dragons, a demigod, he couldn't even guess at what Laura had become, and two mere humans. And now they were his family... Or soon to be officially.

They were to meet up with the others at the arena before the games were to start. Erica was already at the arena, warming up for the obstacle course. The horse race was scheduled before the obstacle course but wouldn't be held in the arena. It would begin just outside the arena and end there, but the route would take the riders to the open fields and roads. "Hey, there's Ciara and Brenn." Laura gestured to the couple.

191

Bernie knew that Cidus was staying with them while he healed, but he was surprised when he caught sight of Cidus and Tabeka holding hands. *That was fast work…* And Evior, as well as a lovely young woman, were standing close to him. Even with a smile on Tabeka's face, Bernie could see the troubled shadow that crossed her features when her gaze traveled to the young couple. He wondered about Cidus and Tabeka. They were from the same realm. Had they known each other in the past? The way Tabeka gazed up at the man beside her, it was easy to see the adoration for him on her face and love shining from her eyes. He bent down to Julia and whispered near her ear, "Cidus and Tabeka? See them?"

"Hush. I haven't had a chance to tell you. They knew each other before Zohmes swapped Cidus and Jatron. They were betrothed, and now they're reunited and betrothed again."

Ciara suddenly turned, looking straight at them. Her eyes lit up, and she rushed over, first hugging Liana, then Laura, and finally Taylith.

The young woman stepped up behind Ciara, her eyes filled with fascination. "You could be twins! Ciara, they are jewel dragons, too?"

Tabeka gave the young woman a frown. "Iridia, I taught you better manners." She looked up at Taylith and Liana. "Please forgive my daughter. She grew up listening to fairytales of the jewel dragons. None of us could have guessed those tales had been based on truth."

Iridia gazed down at her feet, looking chastised.

"It is all right, Tabeka." Ciara smiled patiently at Iridia. "Yes, Liana and Taylith are my cousins. Our fathers are twins."

Laura patted her on the shoulder. "I was just as excited as you when I found out dragons were real."

Bernie was a little shocked the first time he had seen a

dragon. Ciara was with Erica when he and his crewmembers had been rescued from the Yeavoth. He'd known she was different because of the scales on her face, but when he had first seen the dragons land in the Clyss at Erica's joining ceremony, it had freaked him out.

Brenn interrupted them. "We were just about to return home for the flyer. The horse race will start soon. It is the first event on the program. I will be racing Atom."

Ciara hooked her arms through Liana's and Taylith's. "Why don't you join us? There is no need to take another flyer."

Laura chuckled. "The three musketeers." She motioned for them to move forward. "Lead on, then."

It didn't take long to reach Brenn's estate. It was right on the outskirts of the city near the market and shops, making it easy for Brenn's staff to transport the fruits and vegetables produced on his estate.

Brenn fetched Atom from the stables and led him to the group waiting near the flyer. "I'll ride him to the arena to get him warmed up. Bernie, where is your horse?"

"Already there. I took him to the arena stables early this morning."

"Good. Taylith, you can have the honor of flying our family and friends to the arena. I will see you all there."

Bernie watched Brenn ride away. Atom was quite the horse and, from what he had heard, unbeatable. His own horse, York, was fast, but he doubted his stallion could beat the magnificent black.

They ascended the steps and strapped themselves in, while Taylith took the controls. It didn't take long to get to the arena. Bernie gazed out of the window. "Look, Julia, it's quite something." The arena, like everywhere else, was heavily decorated. Hundreds of colorful flags waved gently in the slight breeze. Banners in a myriad of colors hung from the arena walls. What they would have called balloons on Earth floated above the arena, or at least, something similar to balloons. They didn't seem to be attached to any strings. When they began to descend, he thought they sort of resembled giant soap bubbles, the sun reflecting on them causing them to shine with rainbow colors. Some kind of magic held them in place, he supposed.

After they left the flyer and neared the arena entrance, there was a huge banner displayed above it with the words *Festival of Armistice*. Two tents stood on each side of the entrance, the tables within set with glasses of juice, small dishes of fruit, and platters filled with cookies.

A lot of spectators waited on either side of the route. It had been marked with yellow ribbon, and guards made sure that no one stepped over those. When Bernie looked up, he saw a platform. The king and queen, each holding an infant, sat on two thrones overseeing the course. Guards stood behind and beside them.

"It's a pity we can't see the whole race. Just the start and the finish." Julia pouted.

"I have to go, darling. Root for me, okay?" He kissed her before hurrying to his waiting horse held by a stable boy. Most of the competitors were already mounted and waiting, the horses snorting impatiently. He mounted York and took his place. New competitors would ride first. The winners of previous competitions were in the last line.

His heart sped up, the excitement of competing taking hold of him. He had ridden his horse every day in Henderson to practice. He was so ready.

A horse suddenly reared, causing the other horses to become restless and dig their hooves into the ground. He steadied York. All horses settled again.

The king's voice boomed over their heads. "Let the race begin!" The horn sounded and off they were.

There were at least forty or more competitors from what Bernie had seen. At first, the horses bunched together, but then slowly separated, and he had space. He took it easy for a while. It was a long course and pushing one's horse too soon would tire the animal out fast. It seemed Brenn had the same idea. He was just in front of Bernie. Quite a few hopefuls had pushed their horses and rode far ahead.

They followed the yellow ribbons that marked the course. Bernie reveled in how York ran, the air whipping against his face, the fragrance of flowers and fresh air hitting his nostrils.

The ribbons changed color. They were now green, marking the second stretch of the course. He urged York on a little. Brenn still rode close to him. Red ribbon marked the last leg of the race. Bernie urged his horse on and so did Brenn, because Atom shot ahead in front of him. They had already overtaken almost all the eager wannabe winners. There were only three riders left just ahead of them.

"Go, Atom!" he heard Brenn shout.

Atom passed the horses in the lead easily. Bernie clapped York on the neck. "Come on, York. You're as good as Atom. Go, boy!"

He, too, overtook the other riders and was about two lengths behind Brenn. They were approaching the finish line. People lined up behind the ribbons shouted. Bernie thought he heard Julia's voice. Wow, if he won this race, that would be something else! Before he'd entered, he'd heard that Atom was virtually unbeatable. Brenn and Atom had won this race many times, Brenn not even entering it some years to give others a chance.

Suddenly, he slipped sideways. His saddle shifted and fell beside the horse, taking him with it. He vaguely heard screams, people yelling. York reared. Bernie's foot was caught in the stirrups, and York turned and raced back from where they'd come, dragging Bernie along on the ground. Several horses trampled over him. He tried desperately to pull himself upright, but of no use. A hard knock on the side of his head, then everything went black.

CHAPTER TWENTY-TWO

"**O**h my God! Oh my God!" Julia rushed onto the course, ignoring the horses that came thundering toward her.

"Julia, watch out!" Taylith yelled.

She jumped aside just in time, or she would have been mown down by a horse. "Bernie!" She ran after York. The horse still dragged Bernie through the dirt. He looked lifeless, limp.

Brenn had turned his horse and raced after York. He caught up to him and managed to grab the reins and stopped him. "Whoa...easy now."

Julia fell to the ground beside Bernie. He lay unmoving. Blood pooled from his head. His face was a mass of gravel burn, his tunic and pants shredded, the skin flayed from his chest, arms, and legs. "Bernie, honey, can you hear me? My God, he's not breathing!" She began applying CPR, pumped his chest, then held his nostrils and breathed into his mouth. Then she looked up at Brenn. "Do something!"

"Please, give us room," Brenn told the spectators all pushing to see what had happened. "Guards! Remove all these people. This race is over. There is no winner!"

The curious began to disperse, especially when their king approached and made his way to the scene of the accident.

Julia sat on the ground, Bernie's head on her lap, her hands covered with his blood. Tears soaked her cheeks. Visions of John's death flitted through her mind. Bernie's head wound looked similar. A good portion of his scalp had been ripped off, the skull exposed, and she saw a large crack in the bone. *A major skull fracture.* She had lost him, she knew it, and it felt as if her soul had been ripped apart. God, there was so much blood. The king approached, followed by Ciara and the other members of the team.

Laura sank down beside her. "Julia, honey, lay him down. Let me help."

"No. I don't want to let go of him. He's dead, Laura. That bastard Zohmes took my Bernie, too, just like he did John!"

"Calm down, Julia. Move away so I can heal him," Laura said patiently.

Julia felt the warmth of Jonathan's hand on her shoulder. "Everything will be fine, Mom. Let Aunt Laura help him."

Hesitantly, Julia gently took Bernie's head between her hands and lowered him to the ground. Jonathan took her into his arms when she moved aside. The team had formed a ring around them to shield them from prying eyes. Laura placed her hands on Bernie's head. Taylith, Ciara, and Liana had stepped behind Laura and placed their hands on her shoulders. Her hands lit up and glowed, and a soft chanting surrounded them. Slowly, Laura's hands moved down across Bernie's chest, his arms, his legs. The light emanating from her was so bright, it hurt Julia's eyes, but there was no way she would close them.

A gasp, a raspy inhaling of air, spluttering, bloody mucus dripping from Bernie's mouth. He opened his eyes, blinking a few times. "Wh...wh...what...h...happened?"

Julia pulled away from Jonathan, her tears like a waterfall as she bent to rain kisses on Bernie's bloodied forehead. "Baby, you're alive. You're okay. Laura healed you!"

He sat up and took her hand. "I don't remember exactly what happened. One minute, Brenn and I were racing to the finish line, I felt the saddle shift a little, and the next…well, that's kind of hazy."

Brenn approached them, accompanied by Biryn. "Glad to see you are fine again, Bernie. Thank the gods for the healing powers they gifted Laura. But we need to investigate because I discovered that Bernie's saddle was sabotaged. The straps were cut. This was no accident."

"Zohmes," Biryn said softly.

Brenn brushed his hand through his hair. "We do not know that yet. Trevain and his unit are on the way to inspect the stables to see if we can find any clues as to who did this."

"Cylena is returning to the palace with the twins to be safe. I have to remain for the duration of the games, but I will not chance something happening to the queen and the twins. Hirsuta and Cewrick have gone back with them and will remain at the palace with the queen." Biryn took a deep breath. "I will make an announcement that Bernie is fine, but there is no winner. The race is disqualified. We will hold it again at the next festival."

With Julia and Laura's help, Bernie stood. A bit wobbly at first, but then he was fine. "I think this is the last horse race I'll ever participate in," he muttered.

Brenn's words penetrated Julia's fogged mind. "Why would Zohmes do this to Bernie? For what reason?"

"I think I'd like to go have a bath and get into clean clothes," Bernie said.

"Maybe you should rest a while, Bernie," Laura advised.

"I feel fine, and I thank you for saving me. I'm forever in

199

your debt."

Julia looked at him. "Are you sure you're okay?"

"Yes, we don't want to miss the rest of the activities, do we? Let me hurry home to change. We haven't had this much fun since we got here."

Julia poked him. "You're fucking kidding me! You call this fun? If you insist on coming back to watch the games, I'm going with you to get some clean clothes as well. My dress is just a tad stained."

Bernie and Julia sat with the rest of the team to watch the games. He was determined that his accident would not spoil the rest of the festivities.

"Julia, stop fussing over me."

"Geez, Bernie, I thought I had lost you. You weren't breathing, and there was so much blood."

"I have a distinct memory of your lips on mine, breathing air into my lungs. You pulled me back, honey."

"No, Laura did. You don't have a mark on your head or body. The skin was practically flayed from your head, legs, arms, and most of you."

"Sweetie, let's try and put it out of our minds for now and just enjoy the rest of this day and evening. Brenn will investigate the incident."

Julia leaned her head against his shoulder. "The obstacle course is about to start. I am so glad you decided not to enter!"

Bernie chuckled. "And compete against Erica? Not a chance."

The participants were lined up at the starting point of the course. There were at least ten people on each team. Bernie was surprised that Isabella had decided to give it a shot.

Though he shouldn't have been. The girl was tough and had survived for months alone in a forest before Tanoth had found her.

Erica made quick work of the course. She tackled each obstacle with the same gusto she had for life and battle. The woman was small, petite, but incredibly strong, fast, and agile. The teams had lost quite a few contestants by the time they reached the last obstacle — a huge tower constructed of rapidly turning wheels and rope ladders. Erica grabbed hold of one of the ropes and slung herself up high enough that she bypassed two of the wheels. Even though Tanoth and Ivran were hot on her heels, she managed to best them and reached the top first. Happily, she waved the gold flag while waiting for the second and third place winners, a big grin on her face. Tanoth came in second, and Ivran made third. They, in turn, held up their flag, silver for second and blue for third.

Cheers rose up from the crowd. The games had ended, but the evening celebrations would go on long into the night.

They had managed to enjoy the games, though Bernie could not get the accident out of his mind. He had been so close to death. It scared the living hell out of him. When they left the arena and headed for the flyer, a young woman approached them and pulled Taylith aside. Brenn lifted his eyebrows and looked at Bernie. "Mm, that is Zandria, the young woman we rescued from Zohmes' temple at Dreaded Peaks. She works for Taylith and Laura."

Bernie glanced at Zandria and Taylith. The girl looked quite disturbed.

When he saw that Zandria had finished speaking, Taylith guided her to Brenn. Bernie noticed that whatever Zandria had told Taylith had riled him. His eyes flashed to those of his dragon.

"Zandria has information that will be useful in the

201

investigation of the accident. Zandria, everything will be fine. Once you speak with the general, go with Laura and Liana. I do not want you returning to the estate on your own."

Zandria nodded, then looked at Brenn. She wrung her hands together in an agitated way when she began to speak louder so they could all hear. "General, I was close to the stables at the arena before the races. I saw two men entering Lord Henderson's horse's stall. They behaved very strangely, so I followed them and peeked around the corner. They appeared to be inspecting the saddle."

"Did you hear them talking? Did they speak any names, Zandria?"

Zandria took a deep breath and continued. "They were talking, but it was too low for me to understand what they were saying. I am sorry... I do know. They did not speak Ierilian from the few words I did catch. I did hear their names because one of the men seemed to get angry at the other one. I heard the names Liam and Barry. I think they are from Earth, like Laura."

"Did they or anyone else see you?"

"No, I do not think so. The stables were empty except for me and the two men."

"Thank you, Zandria. Do as Taylith said and join Laura and Liana by the flyer."

Bernie waited until Zandria had joined the others before he spoke up. "It has been hours. There is no telling where those two assholes could be now."

Brenn pulled his communicator from his pocket and put it on speaker. "Trevain, send your men to locate Liam Alexander and Barry Sullivan. I want them detained."

"As you wish, General. Would you like them escorted to the palace dungeons?"

"Contact me first. I will be joining in the search."

"Yes, General."

Brenn stuck his communicator back in his pocket. "Bernie, contact Mark and have him meet us at my estate. And before you even ask, Taylith, I need you and the rest of the team to stay put on the estate grounds. I do not want to rouse suspicions. There will be too many innocents attending the celebration. I will not leave them unprotected."

Taylith gave Brenn a hard stare. "Agreed. But if you do not find them in a reasonable amount of time, Jonathan, Liana, and I will track them down."

Bernie shuddered. Damn, the dragon could be scary. Pair him up with his sister and Jonathan, and they formed a formidable trio. If he wasn't so angry with Barry and Liam, he might have felt sorry for them.

Brenn shook his head. "That is what I am afraid of. The three of you on the loose without Ciara's guidance."

Taylith chuckled. "You have much to learn about your lifemate." He clapped Brenn on the shoulder. "We need to get to the others."

When they returned to the flyer, Julia rushed to Bernie's side. He could still feel the unease emanating from her. He knew she was freaked the hell out. He would have been, too, if the tables were turned, and she was the one that had been injured.

Julia gazed up at him, an anxious look on her face. "How are you feeling? Is everything okay?"

"Baby, I'm fine. Let's get on this tin can and go party like there's no tomorrow."

The grounds at Brenn's estate were lit up like a Christmas tree. Lights blinked everywhere. Garlands of flowers were strung from tree to tree, sending their fragrance on the whispering breeze.

"I think I'll go with Brenn and Mark," Bernie told Julia as

they walked toward the house.

"No. You stay right here with me."

"Honey, Brenn, Mark, Trevain, and Brenn's other warriors will be with us. What can Barry and that kid do to me?"

"Stay here, Lord Henderson," Tabeka said behind them.

Bernie raised his eyebrows. "Why, Tabeka?"

"Tabeka, did you like the games?" Julia asked, trying to change the subject.

She shook her head. "I do not like anything to do with danger. I had a feeling of doom, but the goddess did not grant me a vision, so I could not warn you. I am so glad you are healed, Lord Henderson, but I still feel that something else will happen. The premonition has not left me."

Bernie groaned. "Please, Tabeka, stop it with the lord stuff? Just call me Bernie?"

"When I was a young girl, my parents taught me to address people by their titles. After they abandoned me, I lived a secluded life for many years. The old teachings are still present."

"Bernie from now on, please."

They ate, danced, ate some more, and had some eldalas spirit. Before they realized, a few hours had passed.

Brenn and Mark returned. Brenn pulled Bernie aside. "Bernie, we found Barry and Liam in one of the taverns, quite drunk. They are secured in the dungeons. The king will have a trial tomorrow morning."

"Did they admit to sabotaging my saddle?"

Brenn grunted. "They were too drunk to make any sense. It is a good thing we have a witness. Zandria will identify them tomorrow."

"So it wasn't a Zohmes trick after all. Barry thought with me out of the way, he'd be elected ruler. It's unfortunate he involved the young lad in his scheme. As for Zohmes and his sidekick, I still think the two bastards have been quiet too long. I wonder what they're cooking up."

"Let us put this aside for now and enjoy the celebration," Brenn said and walked away to join Ciara.

"I'm getting close to wanting to go to bed," Bernie murmured against Julia's cheek.

"Yes, I'm getting there, too. Are we going back to your place?"

"Brenn already invited us to stay the night because I want to be present at the trial tomorrow."

Julia scrunched up her nose. "Damn. I didn't bring any other clothing or nightwear."

He grinned. "You don't need nightwear, and I'm sure Ciara has a dress you can borrow."

"It's only a few days until our wedding. I have so much to do, and —"

"You are betrothed." Tabeka had obviously overheard their conversation.

"Yes. We will be joining in a few days," Julia told her. "Would Cidus, you, and your family like to attend the wedding? The joining ceremony will be held in Henderson, at the temple, and the celebration is here. Brenn and Ciara are hosting it."

Bernie noticed Tabeka studying them both, a serious expression on her face. Suddenly, her eyes rolled back in the sockets until only the whites showed. "Oh my God. She's having a seizure!"

Her daughter came running to them. "She will be fine. This happens when she has a vision or sometimes when the goddess speaks to her." Iridia supported Tabeka until her eyes turned back to normal.

"Your mother has the gift of foresight?" Julia asked.

"Yes, and of healing. Not like Laura. Mother works with

herbs and makes potions. Mother, what did you see?"

Bernie took in Tabeka's pale face. "Maybe you should take her inside?"

Cidus rushed to them, carrying a cup of wine and a small plate of fruit and cheese. "Tabeka, what is wrong?"

"Nothing, nothing. I am fine," Tabeka murmured.

"Bullcrap. I mentioned our wedding, and you go into some kind of trance?" Julia said in a raised voice. "If that bastard asshole Zohmes intends to do something at our wedding—"

"Do not trouble yourself. You will both be fine," Tabeka mumbled just before Cidus led her away.

"Oh, that's just great. Makes me feel really good! Maybe we should postpone it?" Julia looked up at him.

Bernie shook his head. "She said we'd be fine. I don't know what she saw. Maybe she'll tell Ciara. Otherwise, if she doesn't, tomorrow we'll tell Ciara what happened. Let's go to bed, hon. I'm absolutely bushed."

"If you say so." Julia peered up at him, a serious expression on her face. "After today's events, I would love nothing better than to get you alone. I have had quite enough of magic and visions for one day."

CHAPTER TWENTY-THREE

Biryn decided to hold the trial in the throne room. The whole team was present, including some of Biryn's advisors. Cylena had begged absence. She preferred to be with the twins.

There were no spectators allowed. Biryn was a king who preferred to hold private trials without the shouting and demands of an audience.

Several guards led in the two perpetrators. Barry and Liam looked bedraggled and dirty, but their faces were grim, their eyes spitting venom at Bernie.

The king's scribe read from the scroll he held. "Barry Sullivan, Liam Alexander, you are charged with attempted murder and causing extreme bodily harm. How do you plead?"

"Not guilty," both replied.

Aldis stood in the center of the room in front of a podium. "Zandria Zonogan, please step forward."

Zandria's face was as pale as a ghost, and she was obviously scared to death. She gazed at Taylith, who nodded encouragingly, then squared her shoulders and stepped toward the two men.

"Are these the men you saw tampering with Lord Henderson's saddle?"

She studied the two men, then looked at Aldis. "Yes, Captain. They are the men I followed into the stable."

Aldis pinned the two conspirators with a hard stare. "Barry Sullivan and Liam Alexander, how do you plead now?"

Liam burst out laughing, though it sounded forced. "I had sex with the wench and dumped her like the gypsy whore she is. She's nothing but a lying bitch."

Bernie couldn't believe the audacity of the young man. He obviously did not fear for his safety. If they were not in the midst of a trial, he had a feeling Taylith would put the fear of the gods or I Am into the lad.

Zandria raised her chin and gave Liam a disgusted look, then turned to face the king. "Your Majesty, I have never been with a man, and I would never let that serpent touch me. You can have your physician examine me to prove it."

"Ha ha, you can have sex without penetration. Tell them you sucked me off, woman," Liam sneered.

"Silence!" Biryn thundered. "I will not have you sully this young woman's name!" He waved his hand at Aldis. "Continue."

Aldis swiped his fingers across the screen of his datapad. "Were you or were you not in the stables with Lord Henderson's horse?"

"No!" both men yelled.

He peered at the perpetrators, a bored expression on his face. "Both of your DNA was found on the straps of the saddle. Do you still deny your guilt?"

Bernie shook his head at the incredulous expressions the men had on their faces. Obviously, they had not counted on the fact that Ierilian technology was quite up to date with DNA. Their testing was even much more advanced than

Earth's standards.

"We were just making sure it was secure," Barry said, an inscrutable expression clouding his features. "After all, how many of us could ride in a race? Most of us have never been on the back of a horse. And I don't know what the fuck all the fuss is about. Bodily harm? The man looks just fine to me!"

Bernie had trouble keeping his mouth shut. Julia's hand on his arm kept him steady.

Aldis returned his datapad to his pocket. "Your Majesty, I have no further questions for these men."

The king pondered for a little while. "I have listened to enough." He turned his attention to Barry and Liam. "I do not find it necessary to hold a trial by fire. The DNA results and eyewitness testimony are damning and conclusive. You are both sentenced to the mines. Barry for twenty years, Liam for ten years, to be taken there forthwith."

"For fuck's sake, do something, Erica," Barry yelled.

Erica stepped forward. "Sorry, Barry. You brought this on yourself. You were all apprised of Ierilian law and punishment. Be grateful you were spared the trial by fire. You went too far, all because of your jealousy and obsession to rule Initiation Genesis."

"Fucking bitch! I'll get you for this. If not now, if we are to live longer lives here, I'll get you in twenty years!" the man yelled.

Liam remained quiet. In a way, Bernie felt sorry for the young man. He had been raised a spoiled rich boy, and it had tainted his character. The parents were at fault. But that didn't matter. Ierilian law was harsh. If the king had sentenced them to the trial by fire, Bernie had a feeling neither Barry nor Liam would have survived it. The Ierilians had kept this planet peaceful for so many centuries, and he would never stand in the way of that. He supported the king's decision completely.

Attempted murder was no mean crime and only through Laura's magical healing intervention had he lived. He was glad Liam had received a lesser sentence. It showed Biryn's wisdom. He realized the lad had been influenced by the older man and Liam had to do a lot of maturing.

"Take them away and to the mines," Biryn ordered. "Be sure to inform the guards that Barry Sullivan is considered high risk."

After the prisoners were led out of the throne room, Biryn stood. "And now I have a meeting with Cidus, Tabeka, Evior, and Iridia. My team, my family, please join me in my quarters?"

Ciara placed her hand on Biryn's shoulder. "One moment, Biryn."

The king gave her a quizzical look, then nodded. "Yes, you are right, Ciara."

Telepathy. On Earth, some people had claimed to have that kind of ability, but Bernie had never seen or heard proof of the ability to communicate in one's mind until now. Although he had suspected that the members of Biryn's team had silent conversations quite often. The ability came as no surprise. These people had some pretty freaky powers.

Biryn took a deep breath, then glanced at Jonathan, Julia, and Bernie. "What I am about to tell you has been a closely guarded secret for centuries. The past was rewritten to hide the truth. I was not even privy to the information until recently." He gave Jonathan a lopsided grin. "I am sure you have pieced together the information for yourself, Jonathan."

"What... That I am your uncle?" Jonathan screwed up his face. "Yeah. I thought it was bloody weird, too."

Julia's eyes widened in shock. "You can't be serious! I was on the research team when Zohmes made his presence known. I found nothing in the data records indicating he was related to you, Biryn."

Bernie was just as shocked as Julia. Who would ever have guessed that Zohmes was related to the king? It should not have surprised him so much the way that evil god was so bent on ruling Ierilia. "Is that why Zohmes is after the throne?"

Biryn gave them a patient look. "Yes... He and Astiana were once the rulers of Ierilia. As I stated previously, the truth was hidden. Zohmes, to my ultimate distaste, is my great-grandfather."

Julia chuckled. "Wow! To think I gave birth to a son who's not just a demigod, but he also has royal blood flowing through his veins!"

Julia couldn't believe how fast the past couple of days had flown by. Tomorrow was her wedding day, and it filled her heart with joy. Julia fingered the satiny material of her wedding gown before closing the closet door. Tonight, she would stay the night at Laura and Taylith's, and he would fly them to the temple tomorrow for the ceremony.

Erica and Laura had planned a bachelorette party for her that evening to bring some of the Earth traditions to Ierilia. On Earth, the girls would have dressed to kill and painted the town red—a last hurrah with the bride's best friends. Right now, a quiet night with the women who had become her family, and some of their closer friends from Earth, sounded pretty damn good to Julia.

"Hurry up! Slowpoke!" Laura poked her head around the bedroom door. "Erica is waiting."

"I'm coming, I'm coming." Julia couldn't remember ever being so happy.

"Seriously, Julia. I have no idea what a bachelorette party is. I am dying to find out." Liana stood behind Laura.

Julia grinned at Liana. She really liked the dragon. The past couple of months they had become close, almost like sisters. Quite often Liana would accompany Jonathan to visit at Initiation Genesis, and she had a gut feeling that those two would end up together. "I imagine we'll just sit around, eat, drink, talk, and get silly. Nothing like the parties on Earth."

"That doesn't matter." She pulled a face. "I spent centuries alone in that forest. A little celebrating, no matter how small it is, will do all of us some good."

Laura grabbed her hand and pulled her from the room. "We have to go."

Julia linked her arms with Liana and Laura's and headed downstairs to the courtyard to meet Taylith by the flyer. He would transport the women to Erica's. Then he, Jonathan, and Laro would fly to Initiation Genesis for Bernie's bachelor party.

Mark had joined forces with Gordon and Jim and had planned some fun on the beach. After the rough few months they had, between her kidnapping and the murder attempt on Bernie, the lot of them were ready just to cut loose.

Taylith and Jonathan were leaning against the flyer when they approached.

"Are you ready?" Taylith gave Laura a quick kiss, then opened the flyer door.

"Absolutely."

They quickly boarded, and before Julia knew it, the flyer was landing in Erica's courtyard.

Jonathan unstrapped from his seat and opened the door. "We'll see you in a couple of hours."

Julia followed Laura and Liana out of the flyer just as Laro and Erica joined them on the landing pad.

"Why did you not just arrange a celebration together?" Laro gave Erica a confused look. "And with the Earth clothing you are all wearing, you truly look alien."

"Because, babe, it is partially an Earth-style wedding, and this is how we do things." Erica stood on her tiptoes and kissed Laro's cheek. "Go have fun with the boys." She had insisted they all wear casual Earth clothing for a change. Strangely enough, Julia found her jeans now uncomfortable after getting used to Ierilian clothing.

Erica led them inside the house. "I was beginning to wonder if you had chickened out. Everyone else is already here."

"Where is Tomas? He's a little young for a bachelor party," Julia asked Erica.

"He's at his grandparents until tomorrow morning. All the grandparents have their grandkids to themselves tonight."

"All?"

"Cewrick and Hirsuta have the twins while Biryn and Cylena have some fun."

"Oh my God! Cylena is here? I didn't think she'd be able to make it."

"Of course she is here. And Biryn is at Bernie's party."

Julia heard the women chattering even before Erica opened the door. What she had thought to be a small gathering wasn't that small at all. When she stepped through the doors out on the back porch, a loud cheer went up. All the women from the team were there, and also a bunch of their fellow travelers.

Someone shoved a glass into her hand, someone else a plate with fruit and pastries. To her delight, there was quite a bit of Earth fruit. She glanced over the large tables set with all kind of food—a mixture of Ierilian goodies and Earth delicacies. Preston Burnett from the Initiation Six was a baker before he joined the relocation program. He'd put his name down for one of the stores and had recently opened a bakery. There were big round platters with many of his pastries, both sweet and savory, small pies, sausage rolls, and a large cake.

Julia moaned in delight when she bit into one of the sweet treats. "Wow. Preston has outdone himself. I'll gain ten pounds tonight." She walked around to greet everyone and thank them for coming, starting with the queen. "Cylena, I'm so glad you could come. It's time you had some fun."

"I could not miss this, Julia. Especially learning some of your planet's customs. I find your clothing quite interesting, but it looks uncomfortable. Is this what everyone on Earth wears?"

Julia nodded. "Pretty much. Yes, the jeans are tight. I was used to them on Earth, but now I think I prefer Ierilian clothes."

Erica shouted to make herself heard. "Everyone, some quiet, please? I'm going to ask questions about our bride-to-be. Whoever has the correct answer wins a prize."

Julia wondered what kind of questions she'd throw out there.

"Question one—what is Julia's middle name?"

"Theresa!" Talia yelled. Several others had answered, too, but Talia was first.

"Winner. A bag of Preston's cookies. Question two..." She paused. "You know, this is not a fair game because many of these questions are Earth related, and our Ierilian family and friends wouldn't know the answers. We'll play a different game. Ready? Okay, there are one hundred charms in different colors and shapes, like this one," she held up a small silver dragon, "hidden in the kitchen and living room. The one who finds the most will win a prize, and you all get to keep the charms."

In no time flat, everyone except Julia scooted off into the

house. The hunt caused a lot of laughter. Julia joined Erica. "Do we really have to do these silly games?"

"Yes, we do. Isn't that a must at these parties? Thankfully, Gloria had them on her datapad. All her content was copied from her iPad. The next one is fun. Just wait."

Julia scrunched up her face. "Many of the games are so lame. I've always hated them at showers."

"You need another drink." Erica filled Julia's glass with chairi wine. "Watch that stuff. It's potent."

"Hey, the last thing I need tomorrow is to be hungover on my wedding day!"

After a little while, the women came back. Cylena had found forty-three charms. "And another winner." Erica fetched another bag of cookies.

"This next game the bride-to-be is in charge of." Erica handed her a pile of little cards. "We all need eldalas spirit for this one. Please take a glass off the trays on the table."

Julia turned over the first card. "Drink if you're the tallest in the room."

"Stand up, everyone. Donna, you win. Bottoms up."

Julia got to the bottom of the pile, and she was glad because the party was getting rowdy. Even Cylena was able to join in the fun because she'd pumped milk for the twins to last until the next evening.

Loud banging on the door interrupted the laughter and chatter. Erica jumped up. "Wonder who that could be."

Her wink at Laura did not escape Julia. Now what was she up to?

The loud base tones of *Nine Inch Nails' Closer* vibrated around them. Isabella had her datapad in her hands and had turned up the volume really loud. *I want to fuck you like an animal... I want to feel you from the inside...* Julia cringed and looked at the queen. Cylena appeared puzzled.

Erica returned, followed by two men, Anthony and Samuel. Samuel was dressed as a cowboy, and Anthony a cop. Julia could hardly believe Olivia had managed to make almost authentic-looking costumes. Where had she found the time?

"Make room, please!" Erica shouted and ushered everyone to the back and sides to form a circle.

The men began to dance. "Oh my God!" Julia felt heat rise to her cheeks as they began to strip and dance seductively. She glanced at Cylena again. The expression on the queen's face was priceless. Her jaw went slack, her eyes were as round as saucers, and her cheeks flushed bright pink.

Samuel ripped his shirt off and threw it. Cylena gasped, covering her mouth with her hand. "Your Earth traditions are quite strange."

Ciara and Liana didn't seem to be phased at all by the striptease. But the dragons had a different outlook on the human body, and nudity did not embarrass them. It came as no surprise to Julia. The dragons' wedding ceremony involved naked body painting. It had shocked the hell out of Julia the first time she witnessed their traditional joining.

The two men flung their clothes around as their hips swayed seductively to the music, tossing each item into the group of women. After they were down to nothing but a G-string, their gleaming, oiled bodies twisted, turned, and pivoted. Each took turns sitting on women's laps, even the queen's.

When Anthony landed on her lap, she felt mortified. Hell, he was a looker with his bronze skin, shoulder-length, dark brown hair, black eyes, and muscular body... But he wasn't Bernie. He kissed her fully on the lips, winked, then got up to continue assaulting other women, swinging his booty in front of their faces.

The men finally finished dancing. They picked up their discarded clothing and only put on what was necessary.

"We're going to the bachelor party now," Samuel said while quickly snatching some goodies off the table. "They're having a ball on the beach."

"You dance for the men, too?" Cylena asked.

Everyone laughed.

"No, Your Majesty. This is just a treat for the bride, her bridesmaids, and guests," Anthony told her and bowed. "The men get their own treat."

"Treat?" Cylena asked.

"It means a surprise. I suspect there will be female dancers for the men," Julia explained.

The two strippers left, and Isabella had changed her music to some mellow tunes. The women talked about the wedding and reception for a while, but they all seemed to be restless.

"Hey, everyone. I have a great idea," Catrice yelled.

"Yeah?"

"Our party is kinda dead. Let's go to the beach and surprise the men and liven things up!"

CHAPTER TWENTY-FOUR

A huge bonfire lit up the beach. To Bernie's surprise, one of their people had made beer, and it tasted pretty damn good. It was the first time he'd learned that Carter had been experimenting with wine and beer. Carter had kept it secret until he was successful, then wanted to surprise Bernie that evening. And that he had. On Earth, Bernie had loved a cold beer on warm summer days, even as fake and watered down as it was.

The king and the team were there for his bachelor party, and many of his Earth friends, but as the night went on, quite a few others joined them. This was supposed to be small?

He'd had quite a few comments about his Earth clothes from the Ierilians. Hell, he hadn't seen why he had to wear them, but at Erica's insistence that this was a wedding that was partially Earth-style, he had given in. He wondered vaguely how Julia was faring at her party when a horn sounded, and music echoed over the beach. Sexy music.

He almost choked on his beer at the little parade coming down the path. *No! How the hell did they manage that?* Two huge cakes on platforms, pushed by several men, headed his way. They were probably fake cakes, but whoever put them together had done a marvelous job. Three high tiers in mauve, the bottom one about four feet in diameter, were decorated with white flowers and white piping. They almost looked like real wedding cakes. The men stopped on each side of the fire, then stepped away from the cakes.

Everyone became quiet. The Ierilians had no clue what was going on. He saw them whispering to each other. The tops of the cakes burst open, and a woman rose from each one, both dressed in Ierilian dresses. They were Jenny and Talia. The women climbed out of the cake towers and down to the sand to begin their seductive dance. They slowly took off their sandals, their outer dresses, the underskirts and blouses, until they were wearing nothing but a G-string and nipple pasties with little gold tassels hanging from them. "Oh my God! Really?"

Biryn sidled up to him. "Bernie, these women are now mostly naked."

"Yes. It is custom on Earth to do this." Hell, he didn't know what to tell the king, or how to explain strippers. What was worse, Jenny danced up to him and rubbed her breasts against his chest. Then she swayed seductively, turned around and bent over, rotating her shapely bottom to the music. He had to admit she was a looker and he knew she'd been a stripper on Earth to earn extra money for college.

Talia was the other daredevil. She danced around the fire seductively, swinging her fairly large breasts around, making the tassels rotate in a circle. It was as if she were a fire goddess with her black hair flying and the flames reflecting on her olive-colored, oiled skin.

Brenn, Laro, Tanoth, and Ivran joined them. "This is a tradition on Earth, Bernie?" Brenn asked.

Bernie wiped the beer foam from his mouth. "At a bachelor party, yes. I'm sorry if it embarrasses you. Should I stop it?"

"It is rather interesting," Brenn said. "Very different from our customs."

Whistles from the group almost overpowered the music. The girls began dancing among the men flirtatiously, then slowly danced their way off the beach.

They had barely disappeared when a large group of women came running down the path. "Hey, you guys, we were told it's more fun on the beach. We've come to join you!" Julia shouted. "Hey, baby." She sidled up to Bernie and flung her arms around his neck.

"Damn, I feel like picking you up and rushing home with you," he said near her ear. "You just missed the strippers."

"Strippers? You, too? Who?"

"Jenny and Talia. Oh, look, they're back, but they've got clothes on now."

"They were at my party. I didn't even see them leave. They must have scooted off when Samuel and Anthony did their little strip performance. You should have seen them, hon. A cop and a cowboy. Damn, this is one hell of a party. I think all our people from Earth came and then some," Julia said while scanning the crowd, then gazed at the ocean. "I wouldn't mind going for a dip. Are you game?"

"Did you bring a bathing suit?"

"Hell no. Who needs that?" She promptly took off her jeans, pulled her t-shirt over her head, and in her bra and panties began running to the where the waves babbled onto the beach.

Bernie scratched his head, then stripped off his shirt, kicked off his sandals, and took his jeans off. In his boxers, he ran after Julia.

Other people had noticed, and within minutes, a lot of people joined them to frolic in the balmy water, some women in bra and panties, some only in panties, the guys in their underwear and some of them naked. The water sobered him up enough to wonder what the Ierilians were going to think of their behavior.

He didn't have to wonder for long. Brenn and Ciara were in the water. Of course. The dragons had no problem with nudity. But even the king and queen had joined them. Biryn had stripped down to Ierilian style underwear that hung nearly to his knees, and Cylena was virtually naked since Ierilian women didn't wear a bra.

Julia pressed her body against his and flung her arms around his neck. "I almost feel like canceling the whole official thing tomorrow. Let's elope, babe."

He burst out laughing. "Where to? Vegas?"

"Aren't we right now having the time of our life? Tomorrow is going to be all official with speeches and all that boring stuff."

"You'll think differently in the morning." He kissed the tip of her nose. "Hey, did you know that Carter Kennedy made beer? It's really good."

"I had no idea. I never had the chance to try a beer on Earth."

"The beer at the bars was all watered down and didn't have much of a taste. I guess what he made is real beer and I like it."

"Wonder how he made it? Does it taste like mead?"

"No, mead is much stronger. I don't know how he did it, but it will make a great addition to our taverns and future restaurants. That's of course if he wants to start mass producing it." He brushed his fingers through her wet hair. "Let's get out and go back to the fire."

"I need to leave soon. Seeing you after midnight is bad luck, remember?"

Not bothering to put their clothes back on, they slow

danced to the music. Julia had her arms tight around Bernie's neck, her face close to his ear. "I want nothing more than to be in your arms in a bed right now. Well...I wouldn't mind the warm sand, but too many spectators..."

"Tomorrow night, sugar. After the reception. And we'll have a whole week to do all that if that's what we feel like."

"Have you mapped out where we're going?"

"Yes. I asked Tanoth for advice where we should go. He gave me some great tips. We'll finally get to see more of this planet."

Erica tapped Julia on the back. "Hey, lady, it's getting close to midnight. Kiss the man goodnight."

They kissed—a long, lingering kiss. "See you at the altar tomorrow morning," Bernie whispered near her ear.

CHAPTER TWENTY-FIVE

"**W**ake up, sleepyhead. It's your big day," Erica prodded Julia gently.

Julia rubbed her eyes, frowned, and gave Erica a disgusted look. "Why are you here so early?"

Erica yanked the covers from Julia. "Laura sent me to wake you. Time to get up."

She threw a pillow at Erica. "Go away. Feels like fucking six in the morning."

Erica dodged the pillow and laughed. "Told you not to drink too much of that wine, and then you drank eldalas spirit, too? Go have a bath. You'll feel better. The hairdresser is waiting downstairs, as is Olivia to help you dress."

Julia gave Erica a frantic look. "Shit! I'm getting married today!"

"No shit you are. C'mon, girl. Get with it!" Erica pushed a cup of hot tea toward Julia. "Here, drink this. It will help with the headache."

"Is everyone else up?" Julia took a sip of the tea and sighed. It tasted wonderful. After a couple of quick swallows, she could feel her headache draining away.

"Mostly. I've been hustling them all out of bed per Laura's

instructions."

"How come you're so bright and chirpy?"

"I watched how much I drank, and I had that wonderful concoction." She gestured to the cup of tea. "Laro introduced me to it after Brenn and Ciara's joining celebration. Do you remember last night?"

"Hell, yeah. It was great. Thank you so much, Erica. But what are the royals thinking today, and the other Ierilians?"

Erica giggled. "That Earth people are a crazy lot. Now get your ass into that bathroom before I drag you there."

"Hey, what if Bernie gets cold feet like Ryan did to Laura?" That thought had suddenly occurred. The memory of what had happened to Laura at her wedding on Earth was still vivid. Laura had been so deeply hurt by it, she had sworn she'd never get serious with another man again.

"Stop being ridiculous. Look at Laura now. She and Taylith are happy as can be. Remember what they teach us here. Everything is written in the book of knowledge and must happen as written. I guess what happened to Laura was meant to be. Otherwise, she never would have joined with her lifemate."

"Do you think the big god, I Am, is the same as the God we were raised to believe in? Does I Am rule over all the worlds? Otherwise, how could it all be written in that mysterious book? Like us arriving here and finding lifemates."

"Your questions are too deep for me to ponder on right now. Go!" Erica pulled Julia by the arm to get her up.

Julia stuck her tongue out at Erica and sauntered to the bathroom, slipped off her nightgown, and stepped into the shower. The hot water invigorated her. After quickly washing and rinsing, she stepped out, grabbed a towel, vigorously dried, then slipped into some clothes.

She raced down the stairs to the kitchen, the last thing she wanted was to be late at her own wedding.

"Morning." She sat at the table beside Laura and grabbed the cup of coffee Erica pushed in front of her. "Where are the guys?" She popped a strawberry into her mouth.

"Getting ready to leave for Bernie's. Eat quickly. Your hair needs to be styled, and we will have to sneak you into the temple. I'm almost tempted to have Olivia help you dress there. I don't want that gorgeous dress to get ruined." Laura tapped her fingers on the table impatiently.

"The men look very distinguished, but I do not think my brother likes the suit at all." Liana entered, Ciara beside her. Both held small packages in their hands.

Ciara giggled. "I would have to agree. Brenn was scowling. He said something about looking feminine with all that lace around his neck."

"She can see them later. Right now, she needs to get ready." Erica motioned to Julia. "Get that ass moving, girl."

"One moment first." Liana placed her package in front of Julia. "Laura told us part of your tradition is that the bride has to have several different items from the women of her family for good luck. I have brought something new."

Julia gasped when she opened the package. A dainty silver tiara sat on a bed of soft cloth. Small mauve crystals encrusted the filigree design. It would match her gown perfectly. "Liana... I don't know what to say. It is so beautiful! Thank you."

Ciara set her package on the table. "I have brought something old, but it is also something borrowed. It used to belong to my grandmother."

Julia carefully opened the ornate box. If it had belonged to Ciara's grandmother, it had to be ancient. Inside, resting on a bed of silk lay a silver necklace and matching earrings. Several mauve crystals set in silver filigree sparkled in the light. The crystals were connected by four stands of perfect pearls, intermingled with the same mauve stones.

"Oh my God, Ciara, I can't wear this! It must be worth a fortune. What if it breaks!"

Ciara smiled and patted Julia's hand. "It will look beautiful on you."

"But I—"

"No, I insist. You will not damage it."

Julia sighed. "I will return it right after the wedding."

"And I have something blue. You gave it to me before I was supposed to get married on Earth." Laura handed Julia a small box that contained the blue satin garter she had given her younger sister. "It was never meant for me."

Tears welled in Julia's eyes. She had made it for Laura using material from one of their mother's dresses. The lace edging had been handmade by their great-grandmother for her own wedding gown.

"I don't know how to thank you all."

"No tears, Jules. This is a happy day! Come on. It's time to get ready." Laura pulled her from the chair.

Julia followed the women to the room Zaneke, the hairdresser, had set up to use as a temporary salon. It didn't take long to style her hair. Zaneke arranged her blonde hair in a loose, interwoven braid. Delicate flowers in white and pink were threaded throughout, and the silver tiara graced the top of her head. Julia loved the simple yet elegant style after she saw the results in the mirror.

"You look amazing, Jules." Laura hugged her.

"And you guys look incredible!"

Laura, and her bridesmaids, Ciara, Erica, Isabella, and Liana, were dressed in soft mauve confections that were a delightful mix of medieval and modern. The top was formfitting with off-the-shoulder cap sleeves. The sheer overskirts flared out from the waist and draped all the way to the floor. Delicate white-and-silver embroidered flowers decorated the sleeves, bodice, and waist and along the base of the bell style skirts. Silver sandals peeked from beneath the pouf of skirts.

"Is she ready?" Olivia poked her head around the door.

"Yes!" they all said at once.

Olivia entered the room and closed the door behind her. "Okay. Let's get her trussed up."

Julia felt like all hell had broken loose. She had removed her clothing and let the professional get to work. And she did feel like she was getting trussed up like a Christmas goose. A hand here, a pinch there. Lord, there was so much material. Somehow, she thought she had made it through without messing her hair up… She hoped. She had her eyes closed and was afraid to look. The flurry of activity stopped, and she felt someone turn her around.

"Go ahead, Jules. Open your eyes. Because hot damn! Bernie's going to flip," Laura said.

Julia slowly opened her eyes and stared at her reflection. *Unbelievable.* Though her dress was a mix of Ierilian and Earth styles, she looked like a medieval princess with the tiara nestled in her hair and the jewels Ciara had loaned her draped around her neck. And the gown was a work of art. The satiny cloth was white, but it glittered softly in the light. Olivia had painstakingly threaded the material with tiny silver pearls, from the off-shoulder sleeves, down the fitted bodice and throughout the organza skirts and train. Delicate flowers in an array of mauves, pinks, and silver adorned the edges of the long train, traveling up the sheer skirts and interspersed throughout the ornate beadwork. The back was laced in a crisscross pattern, the ties decorated with the same flowers and beads as the rest of the dress.

"Olivia, the dress is just incredible." Julia fingered the beadwork at the V of the bodice.

Olivia stepped behind her, fiddled with the back of the dress, and removed the train. "I made it removable, that way you don't have to worry about it dragging the ground before you get to the temple." She folded the train carefully and placed it in a garment bag.

"Are you ready, big sis?" Laura grinned at Julia.

Julia turned to face her friends. "I have never been so ready and at the same time so nervous in my life!"

Bernie pulled at the lace tied around his neck. A cravat. Of all the things Julia could have requested him to wear, a tuxedo and a lacy cravat was not his idea of comfort. He, his best man, Jonathan, and his groomsmen, Jim, Tanoth, Brenn, and Taylith all wore burgundy tuxedos. Their shirts were white silk with lace cravats and lace ruffles at the wrists poking out from the jacket sleeves. The outfits were a mix of Earth and Ierilian. Their vests were burgundy, embroidered with silver thread. Bernie's jacket was more ornate than the others. A wide band of silver embroidery graced each side at the front and at the edge of the sleeves. He tugged at the cravat again. Damn, his outfit was decidedly uncomfortable. He almost wished for a Las Vegas they could have eloped to. He glanced over the sea of faces. The temple held a lot of people. All the Earth people were there, and many Ierilians. The king and queen sat in the front row, the little prince and princess on their laps.

The temple looked like a flower garden. Garlands of flowers had been strung from one side to the other, crisscrossing each other. Two huge gold vases filled with fragrant lily-like flowers stood on the altar. All down the aisle, beside each row of chairs, stood vases containing very tall pink flowers and palm-like leaves. Just in front of the altar was an arch of fine ferns, tiny white flowers, larger mauve blooms resembling lilacs, and some kind of sheer material draped through it all. Bernie stood one step below it, his entourage beside him, Jonathan holding a little white cushion with their rings he'd had made. Julia's matched her engagement ring with tiny white diamonds set in two interlaced hearts engraved in the gold. His was just plain gold.

James, the minister, took his place just in front of the altar and behind the floral arch. Next to him was Astiana. Bernie and Julia had decided their vows would be a mix of Earth and Ierilian.

Hundreds of candles flickered everywhere. When the first notes of *A Thousand Years,* then Christina Perri's voice, echoed through the temple, Bernie's heart sped up, and he looked eagerly at the entrance. The matron of honor first, followed by the bridesmaids, each holding a candle, walked slowly toward them, then took their places on the other side of the arch.

The song began over. Julia appeared in the entrance. She, too, held a candle in both hands. He could hardly breathe. The woman who approached slowly, her gaze never leaving his, could not be his Julia. This was a mythical apparition straight out of a fairy tale.

Julia finally stood before him and held out her candle. He placed his hand above hers, and they stood before the minister and Astiana and waited until the last words, *loved you for a thousand years,* and the last musical notes of the song they had chosen faded. James opened his Bible and looked at the guests.

"Friends and family, we thank you for being here on this important day, the joining in marriage of Bernie Henderson and Julia Butler. We have gathered today to witness the joining of two hearts united in love and the bonding of two souls destined to be one. From this day forth, Bernie and Julia, you will stand as one, united to face life and the world, together. May you go forth with strength and courage and each waking morning deepen your love and commitment to each other. If anyone objects to this joining in marriage, speak now or forever hold your peace."

James waited for a moment as was customary, but who would be there who could possibly object to their marriage, Bernie thought.

"Let us pray. Dear God, today and every day, let laughter echo in the halls of their hearts and home; let joy fill every room, and let Your radiance shine on them. Bless them and give them a gracious peace that passes all understanding. Light a fire of passion that prompts them to love one another with all their heart, soul, and strength, and one that engulfs their union as man and wife in purity and oneness. Help them to bear each other's burdens, even as they cast their cares on Your shoulders. May they always choose to see the best in each other, even in the worst of times. Amen. Bernie and Julia have written their own vows. Bernie, you may now speak."

Bernie cleared his throat and turned to Julia. Still holding the candle with her, he began the vows he'd memorized. "Julia, saying a vow is only words—to say love, honor, compassion, can be false, but our love is in our deeds. As we solidify our union with a kiss, a ring, and a blessing, with the traditions of our families and our new world, I promise in front of all our friends and newfound family, I will give action to my words. I will love you, honor you, and cherish you above all others for all of our life."

"Julia, you may now speak," James said.

Julia began her vows. "Bernie, I am not promising it will be easy. Nothing worthwhile ever is. It will not be perfect, as perfection is a fantasy and we are but real and fragile humans. I will be with you always, by your side, supporting you, and trust that if I falter, I can rely on you to catch me. Let us love each other deeply and forever."

"The rings?" James looked at Jonathan.

Jonathan handed Bernie Julia's ring and gave Julia Bernie's ring.

Bernie slipped the ring on Julia's finger. A knot formed in his stomach when he gazed into her shiny eyes, tears threatening to spill. "Julia, I give you this ring as a symbol of my love. Its unbroken circle symbolizes that my love for you has no end and will never cease."

Julia put Bernie's ring on his finger. "Bernie, with this ring I pledge you my love, now and forever."

James read a scripture from his Bible. "God tells us in First Corinthians, verses four to eight. Love is patient; love is kind. It does not envy; it does not boast; it is not proud. It does not dishonor others; it is not self-seeking; it is not easily angered; it keeps no record of wrongs. Love does not delight in evil but rejoices with the truth. It always protects, always trusts, always hopes, always perseveres. Love never fails." He closed his Bible and smiled at the congregation. "What God has joined together, let no one separate. Please kneel."

Bernie and Julia kneeled. James raised his hands. "May the blessing of the Almighty surround you. I now pronounce you husband and wife. Bernie, you may kiss the bride."

Loud clapping began as Bernie kissed Julia.

James held up his hands to quieten the noise. "And now Astiana wishes to speak."

Astiana took a step forward. "Bernie and Julia, your god and our gods and goddesses bless this union. May your life together and your love grow day by day, and your vows be the cornerstone of your future. May life grant you patience, tolerance, and understanding. May I Am, the god of all gods and goddesses, and of all creation, watch over you as you walk through life. The bond you have created today is one that may never be broken. Your souls are now fused, and you will be as one." Reaching behind her, she produced a floral garland that she wound around Bernie and Julia's wrists. "Go now, children, and may your fountain be forever flowing, and your lives richly blessed."

James stepped forward to stand next to Astiana. He raised his arms.

"Blessings to all. Go in peace. I present to you Mr. and Mrs. Henderson, also known as Lord and Lady Henderson."

Together they blew out the candle, handed it to James, and turned to leave the temple. When they had finally reached the doors, Bernie looked down at his bride. "Are you real?"

Julia laughed. "I think so. But I wonder, too, is any of this real?"

CHAPTER TWENTY-SIX

Hovercrafts stood ready to transport many of the guests to Brenn and Ciara's estate. Laura quickly unclasped Julia's train, so she could make her way to the flyer where Jonathan, Taylith, and Liana waited.

Bernie couldn't help but grin. What a crazy, mixed-up family they were. His stepson was a demigod and his brother-in-law a dragon. He had no idea what Laura had become.

"Let me hug you quickly before I don't get a chance anymore," Laura said.

"Don't get me crying. Our makeup will smear."

"Brat. As if we're wearing that much. Can't buy the stuff here anyway. Now, there's an idea. Maybe we can open a little beauty shop and sell makeup and other girlie things. I'm sure there's information how to make lipstick, blush, perfume, and other stuff, in the books from Earth I have on my datapad." Laura let go of Julia and turned to Bernie. "You take care of her now, hear me?"

Jonathan embraced Julia. "You look amazing, Mom." He kissed her cheek and looked at Bernie, then embraced him. "I know you will keep her safe."

Bernie grinned. "Don't you worry. If the unmentionables

dare anything else — "

"Shut up, husband. Don't you dare mention those names today," Julia admonished him.

On the way to Brenn's estate, Bernie said, "Wasn't this the wedding of all weddings?"

"And now the reception. Can't we just skip out and fly off on our honeymoon?" Julia gave him a hot look.

God, she was beautiful. And if she kept gazing at him like that, he would happily bypass the celebration. He slipped his arm around her shoulder. "Tonight, baby. Patience. I can't believe how breathtaking you look today, like a princess from a fairytale."

Julia poked him. "Meaning other days, I'm just ordinary?"

"You know better. We're here. Now come the speeches and fun stuff."

"And food. You won't believe how hungry I suddenly am."

"Didn't you have breakfast?"

Julia shook her head. "As if I could eat this morning. My stomach was tied up in knots."

Laura helped Julia off the flyer, with Bernie lifting the dress from behind. He looked at all the hovercrafts and flyers already there. "Wow. There'll be a ton of guests."

Ciara greeted them at the door. After hugging and congratulating them both, she pointed them to the study. "You need to wait in there until everyone has arrived and is seated."

The study door closed behind them. Bernie took Julia into his arms and hugged her.

"Careful. You'll mess me up," she whispered near his ear.

"Damn, woman. All I want to do is get you out of this dress that's as big as a house."

"You said it's beautiful."

"It is. But will be hellish to take off you."

Julia giggled. "Silly, I have another dress to wear after the dinner. Imagine dancing in this?"

A knock on the door. Laura came into the study. "Everyone is here. Let me attach your train. Then give me a moment to get to my chair, and you can make your grand entrance into the ballroom."

After Laura attached the train, Bernie helped her spread it out behind Julia's dress. Laura quickly kissed her sister's cheek, then left the study. They waited a few moments before he and Julia followed.

Julia gasped audibly when arm in arm they entered the ballroom. "How on Earth? Look at it, Bernie."

Everyone stood, clapped, and cheered loudly as they made their way to the bridal table. Bernie had to agree with Julia. The ballroom was a picture of floral garlands, bouquets, and candles. A mauve silk tablecloth with garlands of flowers draped in scallops around it adorned the bridal table. Vases filled with flowers stood on it and all the other tables.

Bernie and Julia took their seats. The guests all sat, and waiters and waitresses began to bring in trays laden with food.

"I feel sick suddenly," Julia said softly.

"Sick? How? What's wrong?" Bernie asked. "Catrice is here. Want me to get her?"

"No. I think it'll pass once I eat something."

"Don't drink any alcohol until you've got something in your stomach," he warned.

Bernie kept an eye on her. He noticed she didn't eat that much, even though she'd claimed to be starving hungry earlier. He put it down to the nerves of the day.

The tapping of forks and spoons began on plates. "Oh, no. Not that again," Julia said.

"What? You don't want to kiss me? C'mon, girl. Let's give them something." He pulled her up and kissed her long and hard. "Are you okay now, baby?" he whispered near her ear.

"Yes, I'm fine now that I've eaten something. It was a sudden wave of nausea. I drank last night, so it was probably still from a hangover."

"Good. You had me worried for a bit."

The speeches began. The king spoke first. "Bernie and Julia, you are not the first of the Earth people to join, but you are the first couple where both are from Earth. The joining ceremony was a learning experience for us Ierilians, but one the queen and I thought was beautiful. For you to have merged Earth traditions with Ierilia's showed us how you have accepted life on this planet. The queen and I wish you a great future. You have become part of our extended family, and we have come to value you dearly. A toast to Bernie and Julia!" He raised his glass.

Laura was next. "Julia, in the absence of a father or mother, I will speak. Our life on Earth was a difficult one for many years. Then we embarked on a path to another planet, never dreaming we would crash here, on a world with people that have welcomed us with open arms. I would like to thank our extended family and our friends for all the hard work that made this wedding possible. Thank you, Brenn and Ciara, for opening your home and hosting this wonderful reception. Thank you all for attending and your many wonderful gifts. I know my big sister hates speeches, so mine will be short and the last. Bernie and Julia, I love you both and wish you many years of happiness!"

Bernie was glad he didn't have to speak and do the thank you to everyone. He reminded himself to thank Laura. They'd had their dessert, a medley of Ierilian sweets mixed with Earth delicacies. He noticed Julia dove into the strawberries and whipping cream and smiled. After dessert, they had to go and admire their gifts displayed on tables set up in the large entrance hall. There were so many. He wondered where they were going to put everything.

"Bernie, look," Julia exclaimed.

He followed her gaze and pointing finger. There was an intricately carved bassinette with bedding and frills. "Holy cow. Someone is ahead of the game."

"It's beautiful. I wonder who made it. Actually, none of the gifts have cards. I wonder who gifted this…"

Behind them, in the ballroom, servants were busy clearing the tables and removing them and the chairs until there was an open dance floor. "I guess it's time for the first dance." He led her into a waltz, her train draped over one arm.

After one round of the dance, Biryn cut in and whirled Julia around the floor while Bernie was confiscated by Cylena. Then all the other guests joined them on the floor.

"How are the babies?" Bernie twirled Cylena in the waltz.

Her face lit up. "They are content and sleeping soundly, though I think they have wrapped Tura around their fingers the moment she laid eyes on them."

The king and queen, as well as Cewrick, Hirsuta, and Astiana had been taking turns peeking in on little Aylie and Eliya. Taylith had enlisted the help of Tura, one of the jewel dragons, to help care for the infants while the royals enjoyed the reception.

Biryn and Julia joined Bernie and Cylena after making a circuit around the dance floor.

"I really need to get out of this dress, Bernie," Julia told him after Biryn relinquished her.

"Why don't you go and change, and I'll mingle with the guests."

It wasn't too long before Julia returned. The dress she now

wore was pretty and looked a lot more manageable to dance in. It was styled much like her wedding gown, with its off-shoulder sleeves and fitted bodice. Instead of white, the gauzy material was mauve, and the skirt flared down to the floor. Silver flowers and beads embellished the hem of the skirt and the front of the bodice. "You still look dreamingly gorgeous." He kissed her cheek. He had been chatting with Jonathan and Liana. Then Cidus, Tabeka, Evior, and Iridia joined them.

"Julia, your dress was so beautiful," Iridia told her. "I hope, when I join with my lifemate, I can have a dress like it."

Tabeka patted Iridia's shoulder. "I will make sure you do, daughter."

Bernie noticed Evior taking Iridia's hand and pulling her arm through his. Those two were in love. He could see it in their eyes, the way they interacted with each other, and their mannerisms.

Julia slipped her hand in his. "Tabeka, have you found a home yet, or are you still staying with Brenn and Ciara?"

"We are —"

The lights went out, and the candles snuffed, pitching the ballroom into semi-darkness. After a second or two, the lights came back on and so, mysteriously, did the candles flicker again.

Julia frowned. "Okay… That was weird."

"Where are Iridia and Evior?" Tabeka asked, looking around.

"They were here a few seconds ago," Bernie said. "They couldn't disappear that fast."

Tabeka's eyes went blank, and her head lolled backward. Before anyone had a chance to react, she seemed to snap out of it.

"It has happened. My premonition of doom had to do with Evior and Iridia. Someone or something has taken them." Her face had drained of color, and a distraught look clouded her features.

Bernie cleared his throat. "Tabeka, they must have scooted off for some privacy when it was dark."

Her eyes glistened with tears. "No. There was hardly time. If you look for them, you will not find them."

"Stay here." Bernie left their little group, in search of Brenn. He finally found him and Ciara on the dance floor. "Brenn, Iridia and Evior have disappeared. Tabeka is frantic."

"They are in love and probably seeking some privacy." Brenn chuckled.

Ciara shook her head, then looked vacant for a moment. "No. Tabeka is right. They have been taken. Come, we must find some privacy." She led them to a quiet corner of the ballroom.

"By who?"

"It has to be Zohmes. Who else could it be? And what does Zohmes want with them?" Bernie asked.

"Rania told me. It was not Zohmes. This time it is Odoxon," Ciara stated.

"Doxie baby?" Julia questioned. "Why would he take them? It doesn't any make sense."

Bernie scratched his chin. "Ciara, any idea where he has taken them?"

"No. That is all I can tell you for now. Let us go to the study and talk. We do not want to alarm the guests."

"I will discreetly notify the team to search the estate and the grounds for any sign of Iridia and Evior or any clues to where Odoxon could have taken them." Brenn pulled his communicator from his pocket. "Biryn, Cylena, and the infants must also return to the palace. We cannot chance their safety."

Ciara scanned the dance floor. "I have already notified

Liana and Taylith. Liana is with Tabeka. Taylith will inform the others."

Brenn opened the communicator. "Dunmore. There has been a security breach. Contact Tura to ready the twins, then escort them to the king's flyer. The king and queen are already on their way." He closed the communicator. "Ciara, take Tabeka and Cidus to my study. I will meet you there after I ensure the royals are safely on the flyer." He disappeared into the crowd of dancers.

Bernie and Julia led Ciara to where Tabeka was still frantically looking for Evior and Iridia with Cidus, Jonathan, and Liana helping.

"Tabeka, you and Cidus must come with us," Bernie urged, taking her arm.

"What is wrong? Where are they?" Tabeka was almost in tears.

Bernie's heart broke for the woman. He knew what it was like to lose a child. He could only hope that Iridia and Evior were safe from harm, but he had seen the horrible conditions where the two crazies had kept their other prisoners.

Once they were in the study, Ciara told Tabeka what she knew, which wasn't much.

Brenn entered the room, a grim look on his face. He shook his head. "They have found no trace of Iridia and Evior."

Tabeka clung to Cidus' arm. "What does that old sorcerer want with my girl? With Evior?"

"Tabeka, I do not know. Rania has shown me nothing else right now. Brenn and the king's team will get to the bottom of it, believe me." Ciara swiped a hand over her forehead.

"Odoxon is centuries old. He was once the most powerful sorcerer on Ierilia, and the evilest," Tabeka said, tears soaking her cheeks.

Cidus held Tabeka a moment. "We will find them, my

heart."

Brenn crossed his arms over his chest. "I have arranged a meeting with the team at the palace in the morning. For now, we must return to the celebration. Several of the Earth people are starting to ask questions."

Tabeka looked as though she would argue, then clamped her mouth shut and nodded. Bernie understood. If they were his children, he would move Heaven and Earth to find them.

"Bernie, Julia, would you mind terribly if Cidus and I excuse ourselves early? Celebrating is the last thing on my mind now."

Bernie patted her on the back. "Of course, Tabeka. Julia and I understand."

"I wish you both eternal happiness. Thank you again for inviting us."

Bernie's heart was troubled. The king and the team would find the missing young ones, he was sure of that, but it was a blemish on their special day and coming honeymoon.

"Come, before the guests begin to wonder," Brenn urged.

"Yes. There is nothing we can do at this moment. Let us go back to the celebration. If Rania shows me anything else, I will tell you right away. Bernie, Julia, you need to mingle with your guests," Ciara said, then turned to Brenn.

Bernie took Julia's hand in his and led her back to the ballroom. "Never a dull moment, is there, love?"

She squeezed his fingers and sighed. "Of course not. Because we can't have a wedding without the two crazies doing something to fuck it up."

Next:

TABEKA'S REVENGE
BOOK 8

A heart betrayed… A soul crushed… Plotting revenge never felt so sickly sweet…

Ignoring her mother's warnings, Tabeka forms a relationship with Lord Cidus Milhella, the man chosen for her by the gods as shown her by the goddess Rania. However, her vision does not prepare her for the terrible price she must pay.

Betrayed by Cidus, disowned by her father and abandoned, Tabeka forges a life alone in the forests of Wildevein.

Years later, Cidus seeks Tabeka's healing assistance to help his mate birth him a healthy heir. His request plants the seed for a plan of vengeance in Tabeka's heart—one that will destroy Cidus and his goal for Wildevein.

EXCERPT

It was almost dawn when Tabeka hurried home, carrying her precious bundle in a cloth bag. Ivia had delivered that night, but nothing Tabeka did, or the herbs and potions she had fed the woman, had stopped the bleeding. Ivia had passed on to the realm of dreams shortly after the birth of the feeble girl child. The infant had cried. Not a lusty wail as it should have been, but a soft mewling sound. Nevertheless, Tabeka had given her a few drops of sleep elixir. She could not chance Cidus hearing the child.

Earlier that night, she had brought the boy that Vilore had delivered a few days before, to the manor the same way — wrapped up well and hidden in the cloth bag, sleeping soundly from the elixir. He was a beautiful infant, healthy, and had a lusty cry.

Vilore had come to Tabeka's shack three days before to deliver him there to avoid questions from her older children and others and had left, happy with her bag of gold. She had told Tabeka she would tell neighbors and friends the infant had died at birth. And she was taking her children the next day and moving to another realm to start a new life.

For three days Tabeka had cared for the boy, in between visits to the manor, until a servant came banging on her door in the middle of the night to tell her that Ivia's time to deliver had come.

Cidus had not seemed to care that his mate was gone. He was only interested in the boy child and charged a servant to find a wet-nurse in the village. "I will call him Evior," he had told Tabeka. "I am in your debt, and if you will weave your magick to make sure the boy reaches maturity, you will receive a bag of gold every year from this day forth until he has seen twenty-five summers." He had handed her a large bag of gold.

Once inside her shack, Tabeka threw the bag of gold on the table and took the tiny girl out of the bag. She still slept but breathed normally. "Your name will be Iridia," she whispered as she held the infant against her. "I will give you a good life, little one."

Unwrapping the old blanket, she carefully washed the baby, then dressed her in the clothing she had bought over the last months and swaddled her in a new, soft, blanket. She was so tiny, it worried Tabeka. Now that she had a daughter to care for, she would use Cidus' gold to buy land and have the local carpenter build a cottage not too far from the village, and she would raise her properly. No one would ask questions. The type of clothing she wore could have hidden a swelling belly easily. And the villagers liked her services so would not question her.

She sang softly and rocked the infant, gazing into her now open eyes and stroking her downy black hair. She promised to be a pretty little girl. Then again, Ivia was a beautiful woman with her long black hair, brown eyes and heart-shaped face.

"You are my daughter." Tabeka rested her cheek against the tuft of hair. Her vengeance was almost complete, but it would take quite a few years for her revenge to come to its final conclusion.

Books in this series:

In Search of Pride – Book 1

The Dragon's Lion – Book 2

Sword of Betrayal – Book 3

Sword of Judgement – Book 4

Testing the Crown – Book 5

Shard in the Mirror – Book 6

Initiation Genesis – Book 7

Tabeka's Revenge – Book 8

Infinite Fury – Book 9 – Coming Soon

Related to this series:

The Lion's Stowaway
The Frozen Portal

EXCERPT:

Heading back on the familiar trail, that she could almost walk blindfolded now, she hummed a tune. That was something she missed. Music.

When she was close to her tree, a sound startled her. It was too loud to be made by one of the little furry creatures she so often saw darting around among the flowers. She stopped. Her heart sped up. She'd seen no other human in the forest since she'd lived there. Not once. The sound came from the direction of the crate.

Standing very still, she held her breath and waited. A crack, then another. Suddenly a huge lion faced her. She dropped her basket, her purchases spilling to the forest floor, screamed, and ran to the nearest tree.

She peeked at the lion from behind the trunk and started hitching up her skirts to tie them in a knot above her knees. "Go away, kitty!"

She hoisted herself onto a branch and started climbing. When she was halfway up the tree, she dared to look down. She couldn't remember. Did lions climb?

"Nice kitty, kitty, kitty." She climbed a couple more limbs but dared not go any higher. The branches were starting to get thin and might break beneath her weight. She leaned forward and peered down at the lion.

"Holy shit! You are one big cat!"

He was the biggest lion she'd ever seen. Their parents had taken them to a zoo when she and Hannah were still little. The lions had awed her and had seemed gigantic. But this one was huge. Of course, he had to be. It was an alien lion.

What in the hell was she going to do? Was it hungry? Was it looking at her for its next meal? She grabbed the piece of smoked meat she had in her pocket, pulled a chunk off it with her teeth and held her hand out. "Look, kitty. Mmm, it's good, see?"

She threw the piece of meat. It landed on the ground a distance from the tree. "Go get it, boy!"

The lion just stood looking up at her. He did not attempt to climb or approach the tree...nor did he go after the food. To her consternation, he suddenly growled. Then it appeared as if his bones were popping through his skin.

"Oh, fuck, no!"

It freaked her the hell out. It was like the movie *Thing*. An alien made itself look like a dog, but when it showed its true form, it was a grotesque monster.

She couldn't take her eyes away. It was all so crazy. It wasn't a hideous creature he was mutating into. When the transformation was complete, he had become the most gorgeous hunk of male flesh she'd ever seen. She rubbed her eyes and looked again. Was she going insane? *Okay... I'm dreaming. There is no way this is real.* She pinched herself. *Wake up, Izzy.*

ANTIQUE TROVE

TARYN JAMESON   GABRIELLA BRADLEY

Antique Trove, a best-selling stand-alone story available at eXtasy Books and all online retailers.

EXCERPT:

It felt like hours had passed when the pounding of her heart finally simmered to a steady beat. She dared to open her eyes again and screamed. Directly in front of her stood an enormous reptile with wings. With a snap of its jaws, it lowered its head and glared at her. *What the hell? Is that a dragon? This is not happening.*

Dazed, she began to climb out of the chest. If she stepped clear, she would be back in her grandmother's shop, right?

"This is a dream. It is not real," Azilia muttered.

"This is no dream," the dragon said.

She must have lost her damn mind. Even though she was out of the chest, the hallucination was still there. She held her hands, palms out, in front of her body and took a careful step back. The last thing she wanted was to be this creature's lunch. "Okay. Now I know for sure I am dreaming or going crazy. Talking dragons?"

"You have finally come home," the dragon spoke again.

"Home?" *Oh, my God. I am actually answering the beast.*

She calmed down a bit. The dragon did not seem as if he wanted to gobble her up. It was actually quite beautiful with its shiny blue, purple, and red scales. But in all honesty? A talking dragon? And where in the gods' names was she? *This is just another one of my stupid nightmares.*

"No nightmare. I assure you I am very real."

Her eyes widened, and her jaw went slack. *Seriously? The damn creature is answering what I am thinking?* She felt kind of silly as she made a V with two fingers. "Peace..." Her voice came out like a squeaky little mouse.

ABOUT THE AUTHORS

Taryn Jameson

Taryn Jameson is a mother, artist, and avid reader who lives in an enchanted forest that sparks her imagination to create. Her latest outlet is the written word. She is the alter ego of cover artist Angela Waters.

Gabriella Bradley

Gabriella Bradley has been a writer and artist all her life. Her hobbies include art, gardening, swimming, sewing, embroidery. Favorite movies are old timers like Gone with the Wind, Spartacus, etc. Favorite music is Abba. All-time favorite series is Fringe.